Our Way Back to Always

Our Way Back to Always

NINA MORENO

POPPY
LITTLE, BROWN AND COMPANY
New York Boston

Copyright © 2021 by Nina Moreno

Cover art copyright © 2021 by Erick Davila. Cover design by Karina Granda. Cover copyright © 2021 by Hachette Book Group, Inc.

Poppy
Hachette Book Group
1290 Avenue of the Americas, New York, NY 10104
Visit us at LBYR.com

First Edition: October 2021

Poppy is an imprint of Little, Brown and Company. The Poppy name and logo are trademarks of Hachette Book Group, Inc.

The publisher is not responsible for websites (or their content) that are not owned by the publisher.

Library of Congress Cataloging-in-Publication Data
Names: Moreno, Nina (Young adult fiction writer), author.
Title: Our way back to always / Nina Moreno.
Description: First edition. | New York : Little, Brown and Company, 2021. | Audience: Ages 14 & up. | Summary: Told in two voices, Lou Patterson reconnects with her neighbor and ex–best friend Sam Alvarez, now seniors in high school, after they rediscover their childhood bucket list.
Identifiers: LCCN 2020047224 | ISBN 9780759557475 (hardcover) | ISBN 9780759557611 (ebook)
Subjects: CYAC: Best friends—Fiction. | Friendship—Fiction. | High schools—Fiction. | Schools—Fiction. | Family life—Florida—Fiction. | Dating (Social customs)—Fiction. | Florida—Fiction.
Classification: LCC PZ7.1.M66953 Our 2021 | DDC [Fic]—dc23
LC record available at https://lccn.loc.gov/2020047224

ISBNs: 978-0-7595-5747-5 (hardcover), 978-0-7595-5761-1 (ebook)

Printed in the United States of America

LSC-C

Printing 1, 2021

To us,

before, now, tomorrow,
and every timeline in between

A joy it will be one day,
perhaps, to remember even this.

—VIRGIL, *THE AENEID*

LOU AND SAM'S TO-DO LIST
BEFORE WE GRADUATE:

GO TO BEACH DAY

help all the stray neighborhood cats

go to Disney World

join a club

pull off the most epic prank of all time

win the town Halloween costume contest

apply to the same colleges

work on our Spanish

Lou will hold her breath longer than
Sam underwater

go to an actual party

get super good at kissing

kiss someone at midnight on New Year's Eve
(after getting super good at it)

be serenaded (à la 10 things I hate about you)

beat the viejitos at dominos

bury a time capsule

write a letter to our future selves

SAM'S ADDITIONS:

MASTER "TOM SAWYER" BY RUSH ON DRUMS
(AND SOME CUBAN JAZZ FOR DAD)

DRIVE THE BARRACUDA

ALWAYS HOLD MY BREATH LONGER THAN
LOU UNDERWATER

GET A DOG (I'M ALLERGIC TO CATS,
YOU KNOW THIS)

AUGUST

I AM STILL waiting for the perfect summer my twelfth one promised me. That was the year Papá El sold mangonada Popsicles in the town square, Sam and I started a YouTube channel, and my parents let my curfew stretch past dusk. That miracle was only because everyone in Port Coral reported our whereabouts anyway, but the freedom was intoxicating. And it was that summer when two preteens—high on spicy, sweet mango—discovered the Port Coral High tradition known as Beach Day.

On the first Saturday of every August, incoming seniors take over our local beach with all their drama, excitement, and bass-heavy speakers. Sam and I spied on them from the harbor like they were starring in a music video. Which made sense, since watching them made me feel the way Janelle Monáe songs did: bold, carefree, and flushed with new feelings. They were so alive, with their broad shoulders and filled-out bikinis. Sam sat beside me, just as enraptured. We couldn't *wait* for high school, and that spicy mango excitement went into penning our bucket list of all the things our thriving future high school selves would do.

But Popsicles melt, summers end, and Sam Alvarez turned thirteen and into an idiot.

And now after almost five years, I found that cursed list in a notebook after digging through my closet last week. *"Clean your room,"* Mom said. *"You have to become more organized!"* But now look at me: cursed. Because by reading that little slip of paper, I opened a tomb. This was breaking-a-mirror bad. I've earned myself seven years doomed luck, because it turns out that I've barely accomplished anything Seventh-Grade Lou dreamed up for herself. And while I'm used to being an underwhelming disappointment to everyone else, letting my bright-eyed former self down is brutal.

So it's time to remedy that.

From my perch at the edge of the bathtub, I shout, "Mom! I need shaving cream!"

The door whips open and my heart jumps. My mother never enters spaces quietly. "What? Why are you in your bathing suit?"

"I'm going to the beach." I gesture to my stubbly legs. "But I ran out of my coconut stuff." The shaving cream is so fancy, it calls itself butter. I stole it from Elena when she moved out, and I was stretching it out by saving it for special occasions.

Mom searches the cabinet, then tosses me a metal can. I catch it, disappointed. "This one is Dad's."

"So? The other one was your sister's."

Dad's smells like mint and medicine and does nothing in the way of helping me feel bold and carefree. I lather one leg. "I smell like an old man now."

"You and your picky nose. I think it smells nice."

"You would. I'm attracting all the wrong energy."

"I get enough of the energy talk from your sister." She checks her watch. "Hurry up, Elena should be here in ten minutes. A towel, sunglasses. ¡Vamos, niña!"

She leaves but doesn't get far, as I hear her call down the hallway, "And your brother will be late for tutoring if he doesn't get up now! You get one more warning!"

I finish in five and smooth (also stolen) lotion over my legs before slipping into denim shorts (not stolen—my hips sailed past Elena's last year). My suit is a dark blue one-piece with sunflowers all over it. And while I'm confident I could fill out a two-piece just fine these days, I like the coverage and retro appeal.

I turn one way, then the other in front of the mirror. Nerves twist my stomach, and I press a hand against my fluttery middle. I try to call back the taste of spicy mango and bright-eyed moxie, but I am now so far from the person I thought I'd be back then. I'd imagined parties, great kisses, and midnight adventures, and I cast it all in a washed-out filter that made high school look like an indie teen movie. But where Sam became a golden social butterfly, for me, school hours mean acquaintances whose tables and circles I move through like a stray cat. It's fine, because I save all my quests for home, where my throne is a gaming chair and my computer lets me disappear into another hyper fixation with like-minded souls in servers and online RPGs.

And maybe I don't have a lot of friends because my abuela is right, and all that screen time really has melted my brain along with forcing me to need these reading glasses. I slip them off my nose. To my uneasy reflection, I murmur, "We're really in it now, Janelle."

Back in my bedroom, I find Jupiter in my beach bag. My orange tabby cat is too big for it, but she doesn't care. I snap a picture for her account. Hers, not mine. After documenting the many feral cats and kittens I fostered last year, a post about Jupiter—my feline assistant—went viral. She now has over a hundred thousand followers.

My personal account is private and has twelve followers, two of which are my older sister and younger brother.

Jupiter curls deeper into my bag before closing her eyes. I wonder if I can bring my cat to the beach just as my bedroom door swings open and the knob bounces against the wall behind it.

My hand flies to my chest and I yank on my cover-up. "Mami, please."

She moves through the room, picking up discarded clothes along the way. My mother is a hurricane of order. "Which sunscreen do you want?" She holds up two bright blue bottles, shakes both, then makes a face. "This one is empty." She slips the other in my bag beside Jupiter. "You know you can't take her, right?"

"I know that," I lie.

"Your new friend is going to meet you there, right?"

"Please stop making me sound like I'm five. But yes, Rocky is coming."

Veronica Chen moved to Port Coral last year. I met her over the summer at the animal shelter where we both volunteer. She's there for mysterious community-service reasons but has recently given me permission to use her nickname, Rocky. Feeling like this is a pretty significant step for us, I told her about her new school's Beach Day tradition. Her reply was a long-suffering sigh and quick shrug, so I'm hopeful she'll actually meet me there.

Mom finally stops tidying my room to knock on Max's door again. "Last! Call!" She heads downstairs, confident in her threat.

With Mom gone, I check the bucket list, tacked on the bulletin board, behind all my *other* checklists that haunt me with their various scholarship and application dead-lines. This board has recently invaded my room and head-space because two things happened in May:

- I started researching impressive colleges that weren't ten miles away.
- Elena, the perfect older daughter and my super smart nineteen-year-old sister, informed us she was pregnant and *not* taking Princeton up on its offer.

It's been a real busy summer in the Patterson household.

Jupiter gets up. "Ooh, big stretch," I croon before she nimbly hops out of the beach bag. "I guess you don't have to come with me." I shove a purple towel into the spot she vacated.

On my way downstairs, Max growls as he walks past me to the bathroom. He's taken to puberty as happily as I have to planning for college.

I grab a Pop-Tart and glass of orange juice, and watch Mom do five things at once. My mother is a professor at Port Coral Community College and also a published author who's written a lot of short stories, important papers, and poems. They're successes to be proud of, but Mom continues to struggle in academic spaces that want nothing to do with her or her politics. Mom's parents were both immigrants from Colombia, who worked hard in a foreign land, and it's the sort of feel-good story of sacrifice and success that most people love about people like us. But now my sister is five months pregnant and on her way to becoming a teen mom like her grandmother before her, which means the huge pressure of writing the next chapter of my family's American Dream is all on me.

Lazy Lou and her digital kingdom of video-game fanfiction.

I try not to choke on my juice.

Max takes a seat at the other side of the table and tries to brush his cowlick down without opening his eyes. Mom pours his cereal and checks the time. "She's late."

I glance at my phone. No new texts. My sister *is* technically late, but she also knows how big a deal it is for me to want to do anything involving other people. She remembers her own senior Beach Day, and I'm sure that—

My phone buzzes.

> **Hey, listen, soooooo sorry but I can't drive you. I'm stuck on the bathroom floor. I swear morning sickness is a never-ending hangover.**

Disappointment strangles me as I discreetly set my phone aside. I was meant to share the Honda with Elena, but because I failed the driver's test twice, everyone collectively decided Elena needed the car more.

"She's not picking you up, is she?" Mom asks, the bloodhound.

9

"Elena said—"

Before I can even get the words out, Mom is grabbing her purse and keys. "Come on, I'll take you."

Max finally wakes up. "No tutoring?"

"Yes tutoring," she says without missing a beat. "Finish your cereal."

My anxiety kicks into overdrive. First, I have to smell like an old man, and now this? Janelle Monáe would *never*. I grab my beach bag and sunglasses and race after her. "I'm not going to be dropped off at the beach...in front of everyone...by my *mother*."

Mom stops on the front porch and turns to face me. "Then how are you going to get there?"

Across the street, the front door opens. Sam Alvarez steps outside wearing a white shirt and short, faded blue swim trunks. He heads toward his black truck. Because if anyone is attending Beach Day, it's Golden Boy Sam.

For the first time in five years, I shout his name.

"Sam!"

Sam

HALFWAY TO MY truck, I stop. A girl calls my name again, louder this time. I stare across the street, dumbfounded. Luisa Patterson is calling my name. The very same girl who hasn't spoken to me in years.

I spin my keys around one finger and walk closer, my curiosity piqued. "What's up, Luisa?"

She visibly flinches before slipping on a pair of heart-shaped sunglasses.

"Sam?" Mrs. Patterson asks Luisa, sounding shocked.

I'm shocked, too, I think while holding on to my pleasant smile.

"Yes, Sam," Luisa insists. "Sam can drive me."

My mind is registering the delightful rasp in her voice. I cock my head, confused but willing enough to play along.

"Nice to see you both." Neither says anything. It's a real weird vibe I've stepped into. "Warm out already, huh?"

Mrs. Patterson hikes her purse onto her shoulder, and something in her gaze softens toward me. "How's everyone?"

I spin the keys around my finger again and hold back a sigh. So many months later, and I still hate the question. "Abuela moved in and took over half the house, and Mom's working too much." Didn't mean to say that. With a smile, I aim for levity. "Cora's starting third grade this year and has decided that means she deserves a dog."

"Better than Luisa with all her cats," Mrs. Patterson teases, jerking a thumb back at an increasingly annoyed Lou.

Oh yeah. This is *Lou*. I can't help but smile at the little electric zing that hits me as my mind slips right back into the habit of using her nickname.

"Can we go?" Lou says, marching past us with her huge bag. A purple towel sticks halfway out.

"Go where?"

"The beach," she impatiently shoots back. "I need a ride."

"Oh, are you—?" Before I can even get the rest of the question out, she points her death ray gaze at me. Or so I guess, since I can't see past the hearts, but the threat is implied. Beach days are a dime a dozen when you live on the coast, but this is a senior-year tradition and our turn.

And yet, I'm surprised Lou is going. She isn't someone you ever see at rah-rah events like this. No one would ever mistake her for the school-spirit type. "Yeah, sure. All right, then. Take it easy, Mrs. Patterson."

"Sunscreen, Luisa!" she calls before climbing into their minivan with Max.

"How old's your brother now?" I ask Lou on the way to my truck.

"Listen, we don't have to do this."

"Wait, so you don't really need a ride?" I ask, but she continues to my truck and tries to open the locked door. When it doesn't, she quickly yanks on the handle twice.

I lift the key fob.

"Yes, I need a ride," she says in a near growl. "But we don't have to do the awkward small talk."

"I only asked how old Max is, but awkward silence is fine with me." I hit unlock and we both get in.

She curls her legs beneath her in the seat next to me and holds her bag tightly in her lap. Two seconds into sitting and she already has her feet up off the floor. Funny how I remember that about her.

Or...is it because of the mess on the floor? I'd meant to clean the truck earlier in the week, but between work and getting ready for band camp, it's one more thing I forgot to do. I lean forward to grab the shoes and drumsticks beside her feet and toss them all into the back seat. I crank the truck, and the AC hits us with a blast of cold air. With a hand behind her headrest, I turn to check behind us as I back out of the driveway.

She settles deeper into the seat, looking the definition of grumpy. "I'll rate you five stars if you stay quiet."

I hit the brakes a little too hard for the stop sign at the end of our road. "You have a real weird way of asking for a favor."

"You're right. My bad. Elena bailed on me, so I appreciate it." And then quieter, to herself, "I got this."

Lou may think she's got this, but I'm not so sure I do.

I'm a good driver. Cautious and never one to speed or text. But having Lou sit beside me is a distraction. Especially as I feel her attention skip from me to the back seat. The receipts in the cup holders, my aux cable. I can't help but wonder what new picture of me she's drawing in her mind. As I feel her gaze on my legs, goose bumps spread across the exposed skin of my thighs.

I sigh. "Abuela put my swim trunks in the dryer. They're not supposed to be this short."

Ever since she moved in with us, if my grandmother sees clothes anywhere in the house, they're fair game. And she's a new convert to the power of a dryer.

I wait for Lou to ask me what it's like having Abuela move in. Is she getting along with my very Midwestern white mother? Speaking of, how is it watching Mom become a widow who lives with her mother-in law? Two islands, no bridge, dead dad. The tension is *great*, and my clothes are all shrinking, thanks for asking.

I wait, but instead Lou says, "My brother is twelve."

I blink, taken aback. I remember him starting kindergarten, chasing us, always mad that Lou never let him hang out with us in their treehouse whenever we were up there. "Twelve, wow." I slide her a quick glance. "A great year."

She laughs a little, the sound rough. I really don't remember this rasp to her voice. I glance over again and see her gaze is focused out the window. The moment feels heavy with nostalgia and memory, two things I avoid at all costs lately. But instead of thinking about Dad, I'm wondering why—despite being neighbors—we never made amends.

"It's cool to see you again," I say. "I mean, it's not like I haven't seen you, but you know what I mean."

Her expression is wary. The Lou I remember is not quick to trust.

"I'm glad we got over the middle school shit, you know?"

Lou doesn't acknowledge this for a full minute. When she finally responds to my easy offer of peace, it's in a full growl. *"Middle school shit?"*

If my first mistake was referring to our final fight in such a way, my next is to act like it's all an old joke. "Yeah, come on," I say after a short, surprised laugh. "You can't still be mad."

"Of course not, because it wasn't my fault."

It definitely sounds like she's still mad. My laugh strangles into a cough. "You're kidding, right?" It was *totally* her fault.

"This is so far beyond small talk."

"How on earth would it be my fault?" I continue. "I asked you to a dance and you flipped out on me about it."

"A drummer should never bring a guitar to a grand gesture."

Promposals were really big back in middle school, and some viral video on the internet gave me the idea to stage my own after I lost my mind and found myself half in love with my best friend. And it's not like seventh grade wasn't terrible enough already. "Again, I'm so sorry for trying to be creative."

"And *again*, you caught me by surprise in front of everyone." She says this like I broke some huge unspoken rule between us. "I didn't know what to say."

"So you walked away without answering," I add.

"And not ten minutes after your overwhelming production, you had another date lined up."

"It was not ten minutes," I argue. It was a couple of hours at least. "I thought you were rejecting me!" My mind flashes to Lou showing up at my door in that purple dress. Her arms crossed and lips pursed. Lou, who had never worn a dress in her life.

The limo with my date and some band friends pulled up before either of us could get a word out.

"And then you ran away to South America." Lou Patterson, slow to trust and lightning fast to take off.

"I did not *run away*. I visited my abuelos in Colombia."

I turn into a gas station and pull up to a pump. I cut a frustrated glance at Lou. "I need to get gas. Will this affect my five stars?"

"The fact that we have not yet reached the ocean is the only reason I'm not slitting your tires right now."

While Lou sulks, I get out to fill the tank, and do some not-fun budgeting math in my head. I also try to chill out. It doesn't matter that she thinks our fight was my fault. We don't have to talk ever again after this. We've been great at that for the entirety of high school so far. That I want to yank open my door and get close enough to finish this fight is probably just due to low blood sugar. Or these increasingly uncomfortable swim trunks.

Back in the truck I'm met with a wall of silence. Fine. Perfect, even. She doesn't break it until I slow in front of the bodega.

"What are we—?" She pauses as Benny and Tasha come into view. "Isn't that your girlfriend?"

"Yup," I lie through my gritted teeth. I have no idea why I say it. Tasha is a good friend. We used to hook up on band trips, but it's been a while. Friends with expired benefits.

"And you're picking her up right now?" Lou demands.

"Obviously."

"You fool!" In one swift move, Lou unbuckles her seat belt, throws her bag behind her, and dives after it into the back seat.

"What are you—ow!" I curse as her knee catches me in the head. "What the hell, Lou?"

"—*isa*," she corrects, breathless in that new, older voice of hers. "It's *Luisa*."

It's the slamming of a door.

Lou

SAM GETS OUT of the truck to help his girlfriend and Benny Peña load a cooler and beach gear into the back. I deeply wish I could start this whole terrible day over. This time I'd let my mom drive me. And bring my cat.

I hunch down in my seat, kicking aside the shoes and drumsticks. Surprise, surprise, Sam is still a slob. It's comforting to know that some things stay the same even as *everything* else changes. Sam used to be all arms and legs—everything too big on his angular face—but puberty caught all the way up to him and was really nice about it. Where I got zits, bigger but ultimately uncomfortable boobs, and darker hair that seems to sprout from everywhere like weeds, he became broader and taller, and his wide nose and big, dark brows settled into sharper angles. His hair is still a floppy mess, though.

He leans down to kiss Natasha, laying it on thick. Showy Sam with the full lips. The viejitos around the ventanita all clap. So does the server inside the open window. When Sam lets her up for air, she laughs and playfully slaps his arm.

They're so attractive—both brown, moisturized, tall— and together they look the picture I envisioned after witnessing that first Beach Day. But instead of smiling beside them in a poster for summer, I'm hovering in a back seat, smelling like old man soap, and can't stop anxiously touching the stubbly spot on my knee that I missed.

I regret every choice in my life that has brought me to this point.

The inside of the truck is silent, because Sam is a robot who didn't turn on his radio, so I put my phone up to my ear just as the back door swings open. Benny's smile turns into one of surprised delight. "Luisa! And here I thought Sam's booty shorts would be the biggest surprise of the day. What are you doing hiding back here?"

Benny Peña is a fellow senior whose family owns El Mercado. Afro-Cuban, wildly charming, and quick with a joke, he knows everyone.

"Beach Day, baby," I say dryly.

"Nice! Listen, there's, like, thirty Cuban sandwiches in that cooler. Feel free to call dibs on one."

The front doors open as Sam and Natasha get into the truck. She brings the smell of warm vanilla perfume and sunscreen. Her long dark hair cascades over her shoulder in a soft mermaid braid. All I know about Natasha is that she's a trumpet player in the school band with Sam and that she's South Asian. My stomach twists into a nervous knot when she spots me. She looks surprised but friendly. "Hey, Luisa."

I sink deeper into the back seat and squeak out, "Hey."

"You okay like that?" Benny asks me.

I am not. I'm grumpy and hungry, a stressed-out anxious thing whose neck is starting to cramp from the weird, hunched angle.

"Did y'all ride here like this?" Benny looks between Sam and me. "Is this like a ride-share situation?" He grins at me. "We pooling it?"

"No, she just dove back there," Sam grunts.

"Aw, you wanted to sit with me?" Benny asks, grinning.

"I didn't want to take her seat." I check Natasha, who laughs and slaps Sam's arm again. In a smaller voice, I say, "Girlfriend privileges and whatnot."

"*Girlfriend?* Oh, no." Natasha aims her teasing smirk at Sam. "He's very stingy with that label. Sam's not the boyfriend type." To me she offers, "You didn't have to vacate for me."

Sam stays silent. I feel all of ten years old.

Benny sits forward and rocks the back of Sam's seat. "Let's *go*, the ocean awaits."

Sam sets off, still silent. Natasha turns around in her seat to face Benny. "To finish our earlier conversation, what did you narrow your list down to?"

"Ah, well, the usual suspects. Florida. UCF. Miami Dade."

Oh no. They're talking about college. Between summer classes, volunteering at the animal shelter, and promising to build an app for Port Coral's new tourism board, all I've thought about lately has been colleges—and nothing about my summer has been cool or carefree. That's probably why I was bamboozled by an ancient bucket list into believing today could be fun.

"Nice," Natasha says to Benny. She looks at me. "What about you, Luisa?"

What if I open this truck door and pull a Lady Bird? I consider the need for my left arm. "Uh, well, Georgia Tech—"

Before I can finish, her eyes light up. "Nice! What's your intended major?"

Sam's neutral gaze meets mine in the rearview mirror as I say, "Computer science." His brows twitch before he jerks his attention back to driving.

"Love that for you! My dream school is USC. The Spirit of Troy is a killer band, but we'll see." Natasha casts Sam an aggrieved but affectionate look. "This guy isn't applying there anymore, though."

California? I don't know why the distance between

coasts hits me like a sucker punch. Where is he applying now? There's so much I immediately want to know, but it isn't my place. Because we aren't friends.

Natasha turns around as she and Sam start to discuss band camp. Benny goes on about some murder podcast as we ride past the busy marina. Dad is down there working with his college students. They've been running tests on the water all summer and will soon start their big aquaculture project.

This year's Spring Fest back in March saved our harbor from developers who would've chopped it up into condos and gentrified the fishing folks right out of here. The festival raised enough money to bring in the university's biology nerds like Dad to establish an extension program after the waters around our town were certified as a conservation area for clams and oyster reefs. To help bring in tourists and more donations—as well as impress colleges—I'm developing an app for next year's festival. It will have an interactive map of the town that local businesses can use to bring visitors into their shops and down to the marina to gawk over all the science.

When we finally reach the public parking lot, I'm the first one out of the truck as Benny and Sam start unloading their stuff. I nervously check the busy beach, and when I spot Rocky getting dropped off, I nearly sing out in relief. Beach Day is saved. Sun. Sand. Sea. *Not Sam*.

"Thanks for the ride," I tell Sam. And his frown softens until I add, "Zero stars. I will not be requesting another."

Benny and Natasha laugh. Sam does not.

I welcome the roar of the ocean as I hurry toward Rocky, who's wearing a purple one-piece, blue soccer shorts, and a huge hat. "You saved my life," I tell her.

"Yeah, yeah, I'm slathered in sunscreen and up before noon on a Saturday." Rocky lost her scholarship to a pricey Miami prep school last year. We talk a lot at the animal shelter, where it's just us and way too many feral cats. Our conversations have mostly been about big stuff like her recently divorced parents and what it's like to watch my knocked-up sister's life change so much in only a few short months. She tells me about how an old hobby of jewelry-making has turned her on to 3D printing, and I fill her in on all the fanfic I stayed up all night reading. But why Rocky has to do community service is still pretty much a mystery.

We find a spot on the sand and set out our towels. Rocky offers me a family-sized bag of pickle chips. We eat and watch the crowd.

"Why'd you text so desperately if you came with friends?" she asks.

I shade my eyes to follow her gaze toward Sam. "They're not my friends."

Rocky raises her brows.

"Not in a snobby way but, like, literally. I've never really talked to Tasha, and Benny is friends with everyone, so that doesn't count." As if to prove my point, Benny moves through different crowds, smiling and laughing at several jokes at once.

"And the other guy?"

Sam is currently in a staring contest with the ocean. He's taken off his shirt and waded into the water. His shoulders are so much broader than I remember. Probably thanks to hauling those drums around in band and cleaning pools all summer. "That's Sam. Old friend. Like seventh-grade old. We haven't hung out in years." It's not totally true. There was one terrible, vulnerable night after his dad's funeral. But we didn't talk that night, either.

"His dad died in December. Cancer," I explain as both of us watch Sam alone in the ocean. Mr. Alvarez was first diagnosed when Sam and I were kids. I remember watching his face and body change and how scared we all were. That was when Sam became obsessed with documenting everything, so his parents bought him a nice camera and we started our YouTube channel. We hoarded memories and the best stories. When Mr. Alvarez won his fight, we all celebrated. It was affirming to see the hero win the terrible battle.

But cancer doesn't care about story rules or heroes, and it doesn't care if you beat it once.

"Oof, that sucks," Rocky says. "And I thought I was having a bad year."

I slide her a curious glance. "Are you going to finally tell me all the dirty details?"

She lays back with a gusty sigh and covers her face with the hat. "It's too pretty a day to talk about terrible things."

She's right; it's an exceptionally pretty big-blue-sky day. I stretch out beside her, wiggle my toes, and sigh, content. The day doesn't look like the picture I kept in my memories. The friend beside me is different, the other one no longer mine, but the day is warm, real, and here and now.

~~GO TO BEACH DAY~~

First bucket list item down.

Sam

BEFORE SUNSET, AS others contemplate a bonfire, Benny and I grab our stuff and head back to the truck. We have an early morning of pool scrubbing ahead of us. In need of extra money and a way out of his family's store, Benny took a job with Tío Emilio's landscaping and pool company. Emilio's not really my uncle, but nothing outlives us like nicknames in Cuban families.

"Now that I get the front seat, does that mean *I* have girlfriend privileges?" Benny asks as we toss everything into the back.

"If you play your cards right," I say.

Benny laughs. "You're too much of a flirt. I don't want someone who will outcharm me."

We climb into the truck. "Your loss."

The lampposts around the square are all lit as I drive through downtown Port Coral toward the bodega. Dad always wondered why everyone here called El Mercado a bodega. Benny explained that his parents lived in Brooklyn for a while before coming to Port Coral and buying the corner store. After everyone got hooked on Mr. Peña's sandwiches, the place expanded. Now there's a deli, window service, and even an outdoor dining area. It's where one can usually find the four neighborhood viejitos playing another round of dominos or drinking their cafecitos, sentinels who watch over the town.

They sit there now as I pull up to the curb to drop off Benny.

Mr. Alvarez—no relation—shakes his head. "¡Oye, mira! Estos dos muchachos pasan todo el día en la playa."

Benny sidles closer to them as I grab his cooler. "You could've gone to the beach, too." He glances back at me with a laugh. "Give new meaning to senior day."

"We have to work," Mr. Gomez says importantly.

Benny scoffs. "What work do y'all have to do?"

Mr. Gomez puffs out his chest as he holds up his phone. "We update the blog."

"The blog, Benny," I offer, smiling. I'm ready to get out of there, but I like checking in with the viejitos for the quick hit of serotonin I get from the smell of cigar smoke, coffee, and rough, raspy laughter in Spanish.

"Right, the blog," Benny agrees. "How could anyone

in Port Coral forget about the town blog fueled by chisme and dead links."

"¡Descarado!" Mr. Saavedra accuses. "We have a new website now. ¡Es buenisimo!"

Benny shakes his head. "How y'all keep tricking people into helping you understand the internet is beyond me."

Ignoring Benny, they look at me. "¿Y tú, Papito? Cómo andas?"

At some point after Dad died, I became Papito to everyone, not just Abuela. They're looking out for us because, by virtue of losing Dad, I'm somehow young and vulnerable and also the man of the Alvarez house. So, where Benny gets jokes and teasing, I get solemn nods and sincere questions. It's a weird line to walk, and probably why I can handle only small doses of that serotonin.

With all four of them looking at me, I desperately wish my mouth would open and a stream of Spanish would roll smoothly out. Something quick and funny that would assure them I have it together. The house, my family, all these bills. But my Spanish is something else I'm losing.

"Good," I told them.

"Bueno," they chorus back.

Good. Bueno. Right.

When I finally get home, my skin feels tight from so much sun and salt water. My pool equipment is in the garage, but

I'll deal with switching it out for the leftover beach stuff in the morning. On my way to the door, I glance across the street at Lou's house. It's such a familiar sight, but it makes me stop tonight as my gaze skips to her bedroom window, which is dark except for the flicker of a computer screen.

The day went off the rails the moment she called my name. She dug her way under my skin so much that I still can't believe I called Tasha my girlfriend, like an idiot. I look at her treehouse and can't help but remember the winter Dad helped her parents build it. My stomach turns over, and heartburn sizzles up my chest. I rub the spot and head inside.

Our house used to have a "formal dining room" that we only ever used as a den with Dad's big TV, but it's now Abuela's bedroom.

"I'm home!" I call out, and the curtains I hung as some kind of door for her whip aside.

"¡Papito! ¿Tienes hambre?" Without waiting for a reply, she goes past me into the kitchen.

"No, Abuela, just coffee, please."

"¡Yo sé que tu no comiste hoy!" she calls.

"I did eat today," I insist. "I had, like, six sandwiches."

"Un sándwich no es comida."

Sandwiches from the bodega are a full-course meal, but I'm not getting into what is and isn't considered food with her again. The front door opens behind me as I'm kicking off my shoes. Mom steps inside, wearing her barista uniform, her name—Josie Alvarez—pinned to her chest.

"Hey, you," she chirps, then points at my swim trunks. "Are those mine?"

I huff a laugh and explain, "Dryer."

Mom sighs. "I had to stop her from putting my purse in it the other day."

We head into the kitchen, where we find Cora at the table, her slime-making supplies all around her. After a summer of finding the sticky goo everywhere, Abuela now makes sure to keep the table covered in newspaper. I gently tug on my little sister's ponytail, and Mom drops a kiss on her head. Abuela hands Mom and me each a small cup of Cuban coffee, and despite having spent her entire day around the stuff, Mom gulps hers down in one shot. My mother, a tiny white girl from Ohio, now swears by Bustelo. She hands the cup back. Neither says a word.

It's not that Mom and Abuela don't get along, but we're all bound by this terribly sad thing now. The ecosystem of the house is out of whack because Dad died. Mom has to work so much more now, which meant needing extra support, so Abuela sold her small condo in Miami and moved into the den. The two matriarchs now orbit each other, constantly testing boundaries and roles. And on days when everyone is too tired to grieve right, the line between English and Spanish feels like a stubborn fight that's been left up to me to translate.

The absence of Dad takes up so much space.

"How was the beach?" Mom asks me. She lets out a heavy sigh as she settles into a chair beside Cora, boosting one leg on the chair beside her. She starts digging into the slime supplies, to my baby sister's delight.

"Sandy. Sunny. The usual." Abuela offers me and Mom plates of food. Rice, shredded chicken, and sliced cucumbers that are dressed with salt, garlic, and vinegar. Despite all the sandwiches I'd consumed, my stomach grumbles and I dig in.

"He took a girl," Cora says.

"What girl?" Mom asks between bites.

My mouth is full, so I hold up a finger, signaling for her to wait.

"The one across the street," Cora says.

"Lou?" Mom asks, sounding surprised but delighted. "You two are hanging out again?"

"No, I am not hanging out with Luisa." See? Not using her nickname. I'm not thinking about her or her sunflower bathing suit at all. "I drove her to the beach. Her sister bailed on her."

"Ay, esa pobre niña," Abuela says, and sighs.

I frown, mad that she's taking her side. "Luisa?"

Abuela shakes her head. "No, la hermana."

Mom rolls her eyes. "Elena is having a baby with her boyfriend. Not the end of the world or her life."

I leap at the opportunity. "Because not going to college isn't that big of a deal, right?"

Mom's gaze shutters and flicks away as she digs into her rice. She and I have to rely on each other in new ways. There are bills and appointments, schedules, and so much debt, and while she won't argue with me about my changing plans for next year, I know she's not happy about the idea of me not going to school, either. I'd take a fight over her stark silence.

"It would be nice to have a baby," Cora says.

I choke a little, and Mom sighs as she rubs her brow.

Abuela moves to replace the caps on all of Cora's glue bottles. "You cannot have a baby."

My seven-year-old sister looks affronted. And disappointed.

"You got work in the morning?" Mom rushes to ask me before Cora can start to wonder where else she might find a baby. My little sister is on a kick of trying to add to our family, be it a pet or an elderly man she saw at the grocery store—she's not picky.

"Yeah, a couple of vacation houses," I say. "You?"

"A Sunday double." We finish our dinner in strained silence.

Mom moved to Florida to play college soccer as a forward. "*Watching her run was like tracking a shooting star,*" Dad used to say. She started playing professionally after graduation and had Olympic aspirations until another player kicked her shin and her fibula snapped. Afterward, she began working for the physical therapist who helped her through the injury. She started taking night classes in exercise science two years ago to finally become a physical therapist herself. But without Dad, she stopped school and picked up a second job at a coffee shop by the college. She's always on her feet, and more and more, I watch her body shut down. And more and more, I panic that I will somehow lose her, too.

But it's no use telling her to work less. She's stubbornly determined to put everything back into my college savings. I had handed it over while sitting in a funeral home, facing the cost of Dad's last arrangements. We can't fix what losing Dad cost us by putting everything back to where it was before. *Before* is gone. It went with him.

After a quick shower, I sit at my desk and open my laptop to check my email, then glance out the window in front of me instead. The light still flickers in Lou's bedroom. Is she on her computer? We used to play so much *Mass Effect 3* together, but I lost interest in video games after we stopped being friends.

And in addition to games, there'd been our videos.

My gaze leaves the flickering light of her window and

returns to the empty search bar on my screen. The silly impulse is undeniable as I go to YouTube and search for our old account. I know she probably deleted it, but it's been an overly sentimental day for me.

Our tiny faces pop up.

"Holy—" I sit back and clutch my head.

I click on the first video, and a tiny Lou appears on-screen. Her braces are pink and teal, and her curly bangs sharply uneven. Sixth-Grade Lou jumps right into a story about a stray cat she saw stealing from the bodega. She followed it all the way to the woods outside our middle school. *"There's a huge tree with crooked branches, and it has a face."*

I'm behind the camera, filming her, and my awkward, prepuberty voice is full of disbelief. But still, I follow like always. *"Yeah, right."*

"It was big and dark gray, with a white spot on its nose."

"The tree?"

Lou shoots a scowl over her shoulder. "No, the cat!"

The YouTube channel was my idea after my parents bought me the camera that is now buried in my closet. Our first videos were just shaky recordings of us talking, but they evolved into taste tests, challenges, scripts—all complete with clumsy edits. We were our own biggest fans, and my only goal that summer was to make Lou laugh.

That burning feeling in my chest returns. I tell myself

to stop watching and go beg an antacid off Abuela. But I can't drag myself away.

"The tree is over this hill. Watch those rocks." Lou marches through the woods, narrating everything, smiling at me like she used to: big, bright, and unguarded. We reach a clearing, and in the middle is a huge ancient oak tree with an expressive metal face. My seventeen-year-old brain tells me, *It's just garden decor,* but I still remember how it felt like finding a piece of story magic in the real world.

Lou walks closer to it and, with a look of reverence, tells me, "We should bury the time capsule here."

"Definitely."

"Promise?" she asks. And a second later, she smiles brightly at whatever I did from behind the camera. And then taps two knuckles against her collarbone.

I hit Pause, a sudden chill running down my spine. That was the way we'd once promised each other everything. A solemn, most serious of oaths.

But we never did bury our time capsule.

I sit back, knowing I ought to stop. If I go to bed now, I might actually get some sleep. Instead I rub my face hard, then reach over and grab my headphones. When I hit Play, the world disappears except for her voice right in my ear.

And I'm gone—lost to my first act of remembrance in so long.

Lou

I FINISH MY second pineapple soda while hiding from Mom in my old treehouse. School starts Monday, and now that it's August, she's dead set on finalizing her ultimate spreadsheet with each of my prospective colleges' deadlines, essay requirements, and available scholarships detailed. Desperate to distract her so I can have one last summer weekend, I gave her free reign to clean (or snoop through) my room. The prospect of throwing away my crap sparked so much joy in her, she dropped the spreadsheet in her rush to find a trash bag. I snatch the bucket list from the bulletin board on my way out.

A lawnmower sparks to life next door, and the noon-day sun warms my bare toes that poke beyond the ledge of the treehouse deck. I'm a bit bigger than the last time I climbed this ancient live oak.

I try to study the next items on the list, but my mind conjures up the memory of sitting beside Sam in his truck. I press my hands against my closed eyes and let out a tiny scream. New Sam and his stupid shoulders and easy smile. The list practically screams his name, but that was Middle School Sam. Not the guy who suddenly has abs and kisses girls full on the mouth in front of everyone in Port Coral. This list and me have a new life together. Like fanfiction, canon has no place here.

Focus, Lou. Okay, so Disney World means money. I don't have any, but I can buddy up with someone who has family that works there. And going to a party should be easy enough. I don't even need to be officially invited. I'll just show up and then leave. A prank will take serious thought, though. I can't let any of this chaotic good stuff mess up my college plans.

My attention snags on be serenaded. The one where it all went wrong.

I'd been so high on Heath Ledger after watching *10 Things I Hate About You* way too many times with Mom. I wrote it here only because I wanted to experience the *feeling* of that moment, but not in the same, public way. That was torture.

Kissing is still on the list, though. I click my pen and

add a quick note before dropping the list to my side. I readjust my stretchy bra and pucker my lips before blowing a kiss to the ceiling. I could flirt. If I really wanted to. I know my tropes, and some of my most popular *Dragon Age* and *Fire Emblem* fics are *real* NSFW.

"Lou!" Dad calls out.

I sit up, feeling caught. Elena and Dad are on the back porch. He has his hand on her rounder stomach as he laughs. "Lou, you gotta feel this! The baby's kicking!" Dad is a big, burly white guy from Norwegian stock who met Mom in college. A science geek with a Savannah accent, he loves fishing, puzzles, and daring us to do silly stuff for a dollar. Martin Patterson was born ready to become a doting grandfather.

Elena looks up at me, shading her eyes from the sun. "What are you doing up there?"

"Avoiding Mom." I glance at Dad. "Don't tell her I said that."

"I heard nothing," he assures me, but Dad can't keep a secret to save his life.

Elena leaves the porch and stops in front of the tree. "Drop the ladder and let me up."

"Are you sure?" Dad and I ask at the same time.

Elena rolls her eyes. "If pregnant people can rock climb, I can shimmy up ten feet into a treehouse."

I drop the rope ladder, and after a bit of wobbling, she

manages to climb inside. I scoot over to make room and hide my list between the pages of the notebook I found it in.

Elena exhales like she's run a mile. "I don't remember it being this cramped in here."

"When were you ever in this treehouse?" I spent my childhood playing outside with Sam, and Max spent a few years up here with his friends, but Elena wanted nothing more than to get out of the house. She raced to leave our nest and be with her friends away from the rest of us as soon as she could.

"I used to make out with an ex up here."

I cringe. "Gross. Is this where you got pregnant?"

"No, you pervert. And don't look at me like that. You used to be up here with Sam all the time."

"Never to do that." Yesterday, I watched Sam's smile become all cowboy lazy before he slowly ducked his head to kiss a girl who is his not-really-girlfriend. So mature and beyond me. He'd even done the whole head tilt thing, and it didn't look as if he were trying to eat her face. Sam may not be the boyfriend type, but he commits to a kiss.

Watching it, though? Terrible. Awful. So bad it gave me a stomachache. And no, I do not plan on analyzing my strong reaction. It's never smart to look too deeply into stomachaches.

Later, just before dinner, the doorbell rings and Elena flies out of the kitchen. "I got it!"

Dad follows her but stops beside the table. "Weird that he rang the doorbell." In search of an accomplice, he looks at me. "Right? It's weird."

"Would you rather he kick the door open and barge in?"

Max laughs. "That would be sick."

"If he doesn't greet everyone, you better give him as much crap as your mother's family gave me," Dad whispers, conspiring with us.

I lean into the table and match his tone. "If someone doesn't feed me soon, I assure you that will not be a problem."

Mom pushes her office chair into the room. "Sweetheart," she says patiently to Dad, "you walked into a Colombian household and didn't say hello."

Dad gapes. "I said hello—I just didn't repeat it to every single person in the room."

"Yikes," I say.

She just laughs. It doesn't make a whole lot of sense that Mom—who is always arguing with Elena—is the parent actually making things easier for my sister's boyfriend, but as far as I'm concerned, family is a D&D party of dysfunction.

Elena returns with Nick beside her. He's in his uniform from the marina. "Hey, everyone." He greets the room at large. Dad scowls. Nick is a Puerto Rican guy who has been dating my sister since the end of their junior year. He's a nice guy, and I don't doubt he'll be a good dad, but he's a real sensitive Pisces.

Plates are passed around as Mom's big rice pot is finally settled in the middle of the table. Tonight's meal is one of our weekday regulars: arroz con pollo with Tater Tots on the side. (*Both of our cultures,* Dad likes to say, to my embarrassment.) Tonight, we also get avocados from our tree.

"How's the app, Lou?" Elena asks. "It's all Liliana can talk about at work." Liliana Santos owns Mimi's, the botanica where Elena works. Yes, that's right, my once bound-for-Princeton sister now works at a spiritual shop selling herbs and candles. "She was showing everyone the map you drew of the town. It's so cute and bright, it looks like a game."

"It's not a game," Mom insists, and it's not hard to see she would love to stop talking about the botanica. "It's a lot more than that."

"You're brilliant, baby." Dad beams at me.

"Thanks, Dad. But I didn't really draw the map. I bought an asset set—"

"What's that?" Nick asks, but Mom is on a roll now.

"And the app is for a scholarship from the state tourism board. The mayor is writing her a letter of recommendation from the whole town."

"You're getting paid in *exposure*?" Elena demands.

"Well, I need the recommendation letter, and I'll need scholarship money," I say. "'Cause the test scores ain't there." I laugh because what else am I going to do? And raise a hand for a high five. Dad would jump over the table before leaving me to hang, so I'm not surprised that he slaps his palm against mine even as he insists, "Your test scores are perfect."

"Yeah, but you do need money," Elena says. "College is not cheap."

And to get those scholarships, I need to show colleges something *unique and interesting* about myself. But trying to define "Luisa" within the context of academia has been a *really* fun anxiety spiral for my ADHD. Needing something bigger than me, I picked the obvious answer of Port Coral.

"Can I have more rice?" Max asks, the lucky jerk who gets to be twelve, Mom's baby boy, and not deal with any of this yet.

Mom pushes the pot closer to him, but her attention is still unfortunately zeroed in on me as she says to Elena, "She's applying for plenty of other scholarships, too. Don't stress her out."

"We have some candles and herbs that could help," Elena says.

"At the botanica?" Mom asks, sounding way too pleasant now.

"Yes, at the *botanica*, Mom."

"That herbal soap you brought to the marina was a huge hit," Dad says. "Gets the fish smell off everything."

"That's one of my favorites, too," Nick agrees.

"Of course it is," Dad says, not sounding pleasant at all.

Family dinner proves that this party of adventurers would never make it out of a dungeon.

Elena pushes her plate away, and Nick immediately turns to her. "Feeling okay?"

"Yeah, just full." Elena looks at me. "Do you have your list of schools narrowed down?"

Mom smiles at me, pride shining in her eyes, and it tears me in half that I want to bask in the glow of that attention and simultaneously run from all the expectations that come along with it. I rattle off my list, "Miami, University of Florida—"

"Go, Gators," Dad cuts in, never missing the opportunity.

"—Georgia Tech, Duke—"

Elena interrupts. "You're applying out of state?"

"You got into Princeton," I shoot back, feeling little-sister defensive. It stings knowing she doesn't believe I can get into a school outside of Florida.

But I immediately regret the outburst and tension that falls over the entire table.

"You're right, I did," Elena says, quieter.

Unlike me, Elena was good at school. High test scores, plenty of clubs, extracurricular activities for days, which made sense since our mother drilled in us the need to become Educated Latinas and Do Big Things. But now my popular, genius sister has gone all earthy, teen mom, leaving just me to Do Big Things. Once I figure out what that means, maybe everything will settle into place.

After dinner, I escape upstairs. Despite the stress, one good thing about all this new work is that I now have *responsible* reasons to duck out of social situations. There is coding to learn and essays to write. College applications are due at the end of December, but the big presentation for the app isn't until March. Preparing to get into college wasn't terrible…at first. But I *hate* multitasking, and now all these different tasks are starting to pile up and the urge to jump ship is growing with every deadline.

Which is why I'm grateful for that cursed bucket list. Because it reminds me that here in the warm sunshine of summer, I'm still safe. There are treehouses and childhood quests about cats, songs, and costumes. I dig past all the spreadsheets and printouts on the bulletin board of doom, looking for the crinkled piece of paper. And then I check through them again as my breath catches.

It isn't here.

That old slip of paper isn't on the board. Did Mom throw it away? I'm sure I brought it back inside after I looked at it in the treehouse. I spin around and search the clutter of my desk, then tear through all the pillows on my bed. I shake out the duvet, much to Jupiter's annoyance. I dive down to the floor and dig around under the bed, and even heave my dresser aside to look behind it.

"Luisa, are you okay?" Mom calls upstairs after all the noise I've made.

"I'm fine!" I return breathlessly, but I'm not.

I lost the list.

Sam

I'M DEAD ON my feet when I get home from a morning of band camp and late afternoon of scrubbing pools. I have new blisters on my hands and, because I forgot to reapply sunscreen, the back of my neck is screaming. But I have an extra hundred bucks in my pocket.

Inside, Abuela is in the living room with her evening telenovela's dramatic intro music blasting. Mom recently upgraded the TV package to one that includes all the extra Spanish channels. Cora, meanwhile, is in the kitchen with her markers and paper. My sister is always making something. She glances from me to the clock. I know her ears are tuned to the front door as she waits for Mom.

"What are you drawing?" I ask her.

"A picture of Moose."

"Who's Moose?" I fill a cup with water and take a long drink.

"My dog."

I immediately choke.

Cora rolls her eyes as I catch my breath. "My *future* dog."

"¿Quieres comida?" Abuela asks, and Cora casts me a stubborn look. I know she wants to wait to eat until Mom gets home so we can all sit together and Mom doesn't feel left out.

I check the time. Mom ought to be home in an hour. Cora and Abuela watch me, both waiting for me to make the call.

"Tomorrow's trash day," I announce instead. "Gotta take it out."

Abuela stirs the rice, worrying out loud that it's going to get cold despite the steam that rises when she lifts the lid. Cora says nothing but continues to color with a mulish set to her mouth.

I escape outside and am met with the wall of heat I only just escaped. I toss the trash in the bin and roll it down to the curb. I need Mom to come home. And I need sleep. I'm unraveling from waking up every single night at three on the freaking dot, chilled, anxious, and a total mess.

Closing my heavy eyelids, I try the breathing exercises that I learned in therapy to steady myself. Six weeks was all I got without insurance.

When I open my eyes, I'm looking right at Lou's window, and the instinct pulls a small, tired laugh from me. It wasn't a lie that she and I hadn't spoken since our fight. But it's not the whole truth, either.

Dad's funeral was on a bitterly cold January day that feels a million miles away from this suffocating heat. I was drowning in a fog of shaking hands, accepting condolences and other people's tears, when I saw Lou, in another dress, standing on my doorstep.

I ignored her. Nothing in my broken spirit could bear to hear her tell me she was sorry for my loss. But late that night, when the house was empty of guests, and Mom and Cora finally slept, I took off that awful suit jacket and escaped outside, where I kept walking until I reached the familiar branch of the avocado tree next to Lou's window. *Muscle memory*, I told myself as I climbed. And even though it was January, her window was open.

I climbed inside and found her wrapped in a blanket on her bed, wide-awake. Neither of us said a word as she sat up, the only sound the hum of her computer's fan. But she didn't look surprised to see me in my rumpled state. She simply pulled the quilt back, and the relief almost brought me to my knees. I fell into her arms, and I finally let go of everything long enough to break.

Sometimes that night feels like a dream. Something else lost to the fog.

Tonight, Lou's treehouse is lit up, and despite my reluctance to walk down memory lane, the idea that Lou is up there again propels me forward. When I reach the oak tree, I test the ladder. "Lou?" I call out but am met with silence. I climb, then pull myself inside—and immediately smack my head against the ceiling.

I curse and knock my knee against the wall as I try to sit. "Lot smaller than I remember." There's no sign of Lou.

The only things up here are two empty cans of Jupiña soda and a notebook. It's bright yellow and covered in stickers. Some of them look familiar. I pick it up and a piece of paper slips out.

"Lou and Sam's to-do list before we graduate," I read out loud as a feeling of recognition dawns.

A noise sounds behind me, and the next thing I know, a flying, irate Lou is slamming into my back. "Give it!" she shouts in my ear.

"Get off!" I try to shake her off, but she drives an elbow into my side, and air rushes out of me in a grunt. I grab her ankle and try to yank her off me. She knocks the lantern, and the light swings above us, and I can barely see in the dizzying flashes of light and shadow. Lou rolls away until we're sitting on opposite sides of the treehouse. We're both breathing hard as the lantern finally stills.

"What are you doing in my treehouse?" she demands as we size each other up. I'm bigger, but I worry she's still faster. "And why are you so sweaty?" She makes a face and wipes her hands on her jeans.

I roll my eyes. "It's a million degrees outside. And what are *you* doing in your treehouse?" I shake the list between us, and she leaps forward to snatch it, like I guessed she would. I pull it back quickly. She scowls as she retreats back into her corner.

"It's *my* treehouse," she points out. "And that's *my* list."

"Technically, it's *our* list." I straighten one leg to hold her back and finally let myself get a good look at the slip of paper, my mind still trying to catch up with what I've found.

"It's funny," she says with fake cheeriness. "I found it today while cleaning my room. My mom's on a real Kon-Mari kick." She brushes her hair back and laughs, the sound too animated, not at all like her real cackling laugh. "I read it for old times' sake, but no worries—I'm throwing it out."

"There are new notes on here," I point out.

Her smile slips. "Those aren't new."

My gaze skips down to the list. Lou lunges again, but I hold her back with my leg and stretch away in time. I hold the paper out the window beside me. "*Get super good at kissing* is from our original list, but the addendum of *hang out on second base* is very new." My eyes flick down to her shirt and stay a beat too long. "I would have remembered adding something like that."

She growls, but I also see the calculating gleam in her eyes. She wants to kick me.

"This is why you went to the beach," I say as I put it all together. "You're finishing our list."

"If you say *our list* one more time, I'm going to throw you out the window."

I'm too shocked to worry about the threat. "I can't believe you found *our* bucket list and didn't tell me."

Lou launches herself at me, but instead of going for the list like I expect, she dives for my ribs. Still ticklish as hell, I choke on a harsh laugh and move to block her. She pushes away from me and scans the floor around us with wide, desperate eyes.

"Where is it?" she demands.

The list is safely hidden behind my back now.

She looks down at my right hand, which is spread across her stomach because I'm trying to hold her back. I slowly let go and point at her. "Stop tickling me," I say as I try to catch my breath. "And listen to me for a minute. The list is—" The murder in her eyes is warning enough this time. I hold it up and point halfway down the list. "Be serenaded is still on here."

She's studying me carefully, and it feels like we're finally getting somewhere real.

"Well, one doesn't get over Heath Ledger," she admits through gritted teeth.

"*I* serenaded you," I point out.

"You *ambushed* me," she says darkly. "But go ahead and mark it off if that makes you feel better."

Without dropping my gaze from hers, I lean up and dig into my pocket. I pull out a pen that reads *Tío Emilio's Pool and Landscaping*, bite the cap, and then spit it out before drawing two very decisive swipes: ~~be serenaded~~.

Lou scowls at my work. "See, you still don't get it!" she argues. "It wasn't about putting on some big show for other people."

"Are we finally having this fight?" I ask, ridiculously happy about that.

"Of course not, because it's just 'middle school shit'!"

The porch light flares to life, and I hear the back door squeak open. Lou's dad's deep voice calls out, "Lou? You out here?"

Lou jerks forward and shoves me aside so I'm out of his sight. I fall onto my elbow as she sticks her head out the window. "I'll be inside in a minute, Dad."

"Look at you up there again. What is this, a senior-year crisis of childhood?" He laughs at his own joke. "Don't let the mosquitos get you."

She turns and catches me looking at her, both of us closer now. I sit up enough to lean back against the wall as I drink in her familiar face. I don't want to reminisce, but the sight of this list—and if I'm honest, being with Lou again—has done something to me. Something I clearly haven't figured out yet as I rush to explain, "I used to want a dog, Lou. Cora wants one now, but I can't give her one. I can't do anything about Mom's schedule or cold rice or not going to college, but I can do *this*."

She frowns like she's not following me. "You're not going to college?" I shake my head, and her brows fly up. "Like *at all*?" When I shake my head again, she stumbles back to sitting. "But you were the one who...you were always..." She's spiraling with this new information, and I hate it. It's so much worse than when I told Mom my plan, because telling Lou—my first and oldest friend—is like going back in time and telling the person I used to be. Even if I feel good about this decision now, I'm not sure he would. But that kid's dad was still alive.

"You were the one who came up with apply to the same colleges," Lou says.

"I know, but things change." I hold the list up between us and take a picture of it with my phone. "We should finish the rest of it together."

She still looks unsure when I return the list to her for safekeeping. I climb back down the ladder and wait for her. The yard is dark except for porch lights and stars. It feels like I've returned from somewhere else, like walking out of a theater at night after a really great movie. Lou switches off the lantern, and when she's halfway down the ladder, I abruptly say, "You left your window open for me that night."

Lou stops her descent. I don't know why I said it, except

the night feels liminal—and I want to believe, despite the past four years, that maybe we never really stopped being friends. "I was a mess," I continue. "And never thanked you."

She climbs down the rest of the way but stops a few feet away from me. She kicks at the dirt and looks thrown by my vulnerability. Finally, she admits, "I locked and unlocked my window at least ten times."

I can't help but smile at the image of her going back and forth in her room, pacing the carpet. I push my hands into my pockets. "I guess we were both running on old instincts." I tilt my chin toward the list in her hand. "Which one should we do first?"

She looks away with a half shrug.

"Promise me we'll finish it together." I want to make sure she won't shut me out again.

She lets out a heavy sigh and concedes with a grumbled, "You already scribbled on it."

"Lou—"

"Fine, I promise!" Impatient, she taps her collarbone with two knuckles, and we both freeze. She looks shocked, unprepared for the rediscovery of another lost artifact even as heat rushes across my skin.

"You remembered," I say with wonder, and I don't know if I'm saying it to her or me.

She's still and staring at her hand with a frown.

I tap her collarbone, and she looks up at me with uncertain, dark eyes. I tap mine, returning the promise— and then with a small grin, I walk away backward, never breaking eye contact.

"Deal's off if you trip," she calls out.

"I won't." I confidently keep walking backward across the street. I just spent my whole day marching every which way with a whole set of drums strapped to my chest. "Drumline," I explain to her, knowing I want to charm her.

When Mom gets home, she's exhausted but happy to sit and talk about our days over the late dinner, and Cora can't wait to tell her everything. Abuela is pleased when we all ask for seconds. And when I wake up at three in the morning, panicked by all the terrible things that overwhelm me at this terrible hour, I calm my racing heart by reaching for my phone and reading the list again. My eyes skip down to the bottom of it, lines scribbled in my middle school handwriting:

MASTER "TOM SAWYER" BY RUSH ON DRUMS
(AND SOME CUBAN JAZZ FOR DAD)

DRIVE THE BARRACUDA

ALWAYS HOLD MY BREATH LONGER THAN
LOU UNDERWATER

GET A DOG (I'M ALLERGIC TO CATS,
YOU KNOW THIS)

My eyes flick farther up the list.

apply to the same colleges

Lou's right. That one was my idea. And while I don't want to move away to college, I do miss the version of me who did.

Lou

ON THE FIRST day of school, I find Rocky during lunch. Or she finds me. It's hard to say, as we spy each other from across the cafeteria. Rocky raises her brows in a question, and I gesture to the double doors that lead outside, where there are several picnic tables. I hate eating inside because of all the various food smells and noisy conversations. Rocky follows me out to an empty table. We're a couple of stray cats breaking bread together.

"So, how are you liking Port Coral High?" I ask as I pop the top off a container of last night's leftovers. Inside is rice, beans, and the bit of chicharrón that I fought Max for this morning. The grassy area outside the cafeteria is busy around us, everyone looking new-school-year sharp and excited as they map out their new tables and groups.

"It's fine," Rocky says on a sigh, opening her own container. Her lunch smells like a rich, spicy meat but looks like tofu. Starving, I dig into my rice. "Many of your classmates seem to remember me working at the ice-cream shop last spring so that's fun," she says, not sounding happy about it at all.

I swallow a bite. "When did you work at the ice-cream shop?" I'd been under the impression that Rocky had arrived in Port Coral this past summer. This girl is an enigma.

She gives me a dry look and repeats, "Last spring." She takes a bite of her food.

"Why didn't you start school then?"

"I had enough credits for this school's junior-year requirements. One shining spot in a crap year, because who wants to start a new school in the middle of the semester? Cool nightmare, no thanks."

I pop open my soda. "But access to all that ice cream? You were living the dream, huh?"

"It wasn't terrible, but I only worked there for a few weeks since it was getting in the way of my community service hours."

"Ah, yes," I say. "The mysterious community service

requirement, for which I am grateful, as otherwise it would just be me and all those cats."

Rocky looks at me sideways. "Don't act like that's not *your* dream."

I like that she knows this about me, and that we have achieved this level of banter. And I am so relieved that our friendship has carried over from the forced proximity of the animal shelter to school. First day back, and I don't hate it? I instead have a new friend who also brings home-cooked food steeped in her family's culture for lunch? Maybe this year won't be terrible after all.

"How's SAT prep going?" Rocky asks.

Ah, there it is. All the reasons school is the worst. I lower my head to the table with a groan.

"That great, huh?" Rocky continues to eat.

I've already taken the SAT twice. Last year with everyone else, and then again this summer. And twice my scores have been abysmal (I refuse to even think of the numbers) because I hate timed tests with the burning fire of a thousand suns. But I've got one more shot next Saturday, and I *literally* cannot afford to screw up again.

Rocky chuckles. "You can have my study guides."

I lift my head. "Thank you," I say, grateful for the gesture, even knowing they won't help. The doors to the cafeteria open, and I watch Sam walk outside with his friends. My stomach sinks. I woke up this morning filled with regret, the kind that always swamps me whenever I leave my comfort zone and say *way* too much to new people. But this wasn't some mood swing that resulted in a confident urge to be social, and this wasn't some new person I'd never see again. This was Sam, breaking into my treehouse and stirring up old promises. I believed the guy in my treehouse, but I don't know the one surrounded by shiny cool friends in the cafeteria. That guy probably doesn't toss and turn in bed each night, agonizing over everything he said that day.

"It won't be that bad," Rocky says, and I'm confused for a moment until I remember the SAT *again*. "Or it will be, but it won't be as big of a deal as you think it will be."

Sam and his friends walk past—without even noticing us—and head toward the band room. When the doors open, I can hear the clattering of instruments.

"Were you ever in band?" I ask Rocky.

She shoots me a doubtful look, then glances over her shoulder and simply says, "Ah."

Defensiveness strings me tight. "Ah what?"

"The boy who's not really your friend anymore. Band kid, huh? Ouch."

I don't argue the first point, distracted by the second. "Why is that an ouch?"

"Because crushes on band kids are difficult," she explains in a world-weary tone.

"Now hold on a minute." I try to laugh, but even to my ears the shrill squeak sounds nervous. "I don't have a crush on him."

She digs back into her lunch. "Sure, sure."

I lean in closer. "But what's wrong with band kids?"

Rocky gestures toward the band room. "They get very territorial over interlopers."

I don't have a crush, and I am *not* an interloper. I asked him for a ride to the beach out of desperation, but Sam broke into my treehouse. Climbed through my window. It's unnerving to feel so unsure about someone I'd once known so well.

"Are you going to eat that?" Rocky asks, and points at my chicharrón. I'm stressed by these new questions and doubts, but I'm not foolish. I split the fried pork in half.

By the following Friday, I've chalked the night of treehouse confessions up to another momentary fluke driven by nostalgia. Perhaps when Sam is feeling emotional, he finds comfort in seeking out the girl next door. Well, bully for him—that girl's busy. Tomorrow morning is my last chance for a decent SAT score.

At my locker before the last period of the day, I return the study guides Rocky loaned me. She lets out a winded exhale when I push them into her arms.

"Did you do the practice tests?" she asks.

"Yes, Mom," I reply. "And I intend on getting a full night's sleep and eating a balanced meal in the morning." I switch my AP Computer Science textbook for my Intro to Calculus one. Both classes are already so beyond me, and it's only the first week. RIP me.

"Hey, Lou."

I whip around and am surprised to see Sam. Confused, it takes me a moment to respond. We've never talked at school. "Hi." I shut my locker and lean back against it, then slide a quick glance at Rocky, who's smirking. "What's up?"

Sam is wearing a light blue T-shirt I've seen on a lot of other people today. He notices my attention and explains, "Friday," with a shrug. *Oh, right. Go, Port Coral High.* I again check Rocky, who mouths *band kids* before leaving to unload the guides before seventh period. Sam, on the other hand, is still standing in front of me. "I was wondering if you want to get started on some stuff." He leans a little closer and lowers his voice like he has a secret. "Off the list."

It's been two weeks without a word from him about the list or anything else. But he sounds as sincere as he did in my treehouse, and that's as disarming as it is perplexing.

"You haven't told anyone about it, right?" I ask.

He shakes his head, confused. "Why would I?"

"Because what happens in the band room stays in the

band room?" I ask ominously, and he rolls his eyes. "I don't want this 'middle school shit'—"

"Oh my god, I said that *one* time."

"—to become some punchline when you and your friends get bored blowing each other's horns."

Sam's laugh is so abrupt, it takes him a whole minute to settle down enough to look serious again. When he does get ahold of himself, he taps his collarbone twice.

I offer him a jerky nod because, as earnest as he sounds, it's still a big exposed vulnerability for anyone to know I take this silly, childish thing so seriously. But Sam did write the list with me. "Well, if you have any thoughts for an epic prank or theme park tickets, let me know." I move to pass him, but he steps up to walk alongside me.

"I figure they're not all going to apply to each of us," he says. "The cats and joining a club are all you. I'm already in band and, as we said, allergic to cats. But I was thinking we could work on our letters to our future selves. And then we could swap and hold on to them for each other to open later, like at graduation or something."

I stop and look at him, surprised. "You put a lot of thought into this."

"Well, yeah." He continues like it's no big deal. "I know we'll have to brainstorm the prank and stuff, but we still have time as far as everything else, I think."

"Sam!" someone shouts, and I notice a bunch of guys with matching light blue shirts, but Sam stays focused on me, waiting for something. Assurance? Another promise? I try to compartmentalize all this new information under the Sam column in my brain: He isn't going to college, and he's very serious about finishing this bucket list together.

And I *might* have a crush on him?

No, impossible. It's only a week into senior year, and everyone is already nostalgic over everything. This is just a weird mix of sentimentality and guarded hope over us becoming friends again.

Sam

Dear Future Sam—

"Doing homework on a Friday, Alvarez?"

I look up from my phone as the band director, Mr. Covington, stops in front of my chair. It's the first football game of the season, and the band room is buzzing with game-day energy.

"Uh, sort of," I hedge. "It's more of a personal project."

"Sam said no to homework this year, and I think that's brave." Orlando, a fellow tenor player, laughs from the other side of the room.

I say nothing as I kick back in my chair and rest my hands behind my head, the picture of ease. I'm one of the only seniors in marching band with no plans to go to college. It wouldn't be that big of a deal except for the fact that before Dad died, I was *that* drummer. The always tapping, never-without-my-practice-pad drummer with DCI dreams.

"I can't believe you're willfully going to miss out on college football games," Carter, a white kid who plays snare and recently moved from Jacksonville, laments. "Saturday nights in Tallahassee, dude."

Jeers ring out around the room. "No one here is trying to get lost in Tallanasty," I shoot back, holding on to my smile.

The drumline rumbles with jokes until Rosie, our center snare and drum captain, moves to the front of the room. "Ten minutes until last bell! Let's actually start the pep rally on time this year, people."

The drumline gets up to follow Rosie like always. We've got one freshman this year, on cymbals. Jordan is Black and quiet and has big shoes to fill as Rosie's cousin. He's one of the few ninth graders who killed it at camp, so everyone in drumline hasn't stopped bragging.

"Excuse me," I say as I move out and toward the front, doing my best to slide past everyone with my tenors strapped to my chest. The room is loud with the sharp, chaotic sounds of cases being slammed shut and warm-ups.

Vicky, a flutist, rolls her eyes. "Drummers think they're hot shit 'cause you get to actually play on the way to the pep rally. Never met anyone cockier than a drummer."

"And for good reason," Orlando crows.

The marching in the halls is my favorite band ritual. Drumline leads the other senior band members through the maze of school hallways before ending up in the gym to start the pep rally. At the sound of us marching past, teachers will release their eager students. Our presence means Friday. Game night. We set and hold the beat for the entire school.

Okay, maybe we *are* a little cocky.

I twirl my sticks. "Let's go, Rosie."

She looks back at us, her gaze serious as she makes sure she's got all her drummers up front. She glances at her watch. "The bell, Alvarez."

"You and this bell, Rosie. It's a little obsessive," I say.

"Our year will be the year I get these jokers synced perfectly."

The hallway reverberates with the clatter and I glance from the clock to Rosie. She looks at her watch again, whistles sharply, then nods for me to count us off. I tap my sticks and start just as the bell rings.

Rosie laughs. "I'm amazing."

And away we go.

Students slip out of classrooms as we march down the main passageway. We play our fight song on a loop, and my hands fly in front of me. Here, I'm powerful and in control of something again. I slide sideways to fit my drums through the open door at the end of the hall. Port

Coral High is an older Florida school, with concrete buildings connected by breezeways, so our route requires going in and out of the heat. It's so painfully humid, it feels like walking into a muggy shower. But my hands don't stop. I love this feeling too much.

As we turn the corner to head into Hall A, I spot Lou at the edge of the sidewalk, talking to the new girl. Lou meets my gaze and raises her brows with an impressed grin.

I am a drum god.

Until we reach the gym, and the packed room erupts over the introduction of the football team.

This is the point of every pep rally when the band is forgotten by everyone except the players. Those dudes love to dance over to us and beat on our drums as part of their call to get the room hyped. One of these days, I'm going to risk it and "accidentally" pop the quarterback's hand with my stick.

Coach Mendez grabs the mic and shouts, *"Port Coral, let me hear you!"*

Beside me, Orlando groans as the room explodes.

"Just think, you're a junior," I tell him. "You got a whole other year of this."

"Band would be so much cooler if it wasn't about football." The team's kicker runs forward and does a running flip.

The crowd screams, and the cheerleaders shake their pom-poms in response to another chant.

Anthony, a wide receiver, heads our way with a gleam in his eyes.

"I swear to god, I'm gonna hit him," Orlando growls.

Fortunately for Anthony, he goes for the bass drum instead.

Later that night, we line up on the track before half-time. Once the players clear the field, we march into our first positions. They announce the title of our show—Reflections of Earth—over the loudspeaker. Our band director has annual passes to Disney World and is so obsessed with the place that he's still in mourning over the end of the beloved Epcot fireworks show. As a kid who never got to go to the parks, I'd anticipated something whimsical and campy.

But this song starts like thunder.

Laura, our drum major, calls us to attention. Silence settles over us before a deep, booming call rolls out from our drums. The sound swells into a fever pitch before crashing into a screech. I love that suspended moment of uncertainty just before the show comes alive with the rest of the band.

I glance into the crowd and catch sight of my abuela and little sister. Cora waves both arms, and Abuela looks delighted with the spectacle—and while I'm happy to see them, neither of them is my parent.

Because Mom is at work. And Dad is dead.

My stick hits the rim. I hear it. Orlando next to me hears it. One missed beat, and I'm playing catch up with a sinking feeling in my stomach. For the first time, my parents aren't in the audience like they have been since I first picked up a drumstick at four and smacked it against the bucket in the garage with a look of awe. At least, that's how Dad tells the story.

Told. Another smack against the rim. My pulse beats too fast in my ears.

"You're dragging!" Orlando calls out beside me.

During a lull in the show, we're toward the back, and Orlando doesn't bother asking me if I'm okay but instead reminds me, "Whatever is up with you, don't lock your knees." Everyone still remembers the time Matt passed out two years ago.

"I'm fine," I insist. But I'm not. Because as we move forward into the center of the field—before a drum feature—I do the inconceivable and drop a stick. My hands and face are dripping sweat, but ice crawls up my neck. My breaths are becoming too fast and choppy as I dig into the narrow pouch hanging off the side of my drum.

It's empty. I don't have a spare stick.

For a second or entire year, I'm stuck. Frozen to the spot, and I'm either going to pass out, puke, or quit. The wave is cresting—I can feel the shadow of it looming over me, and everything it stirs up is rising inside me, needing release. But I can't fall apart here. In a two-beat pause, Orlando tosses me a spare stick, and by some miracle, I catch it and find my way back into the song.

"Saved your life," he says.

I can't speak. Once the song and show end, I'm ripping my instrument and hat off, ignoring the call of my name, my eyes burning as I stumble away.

I'm not even safe here, doing this thing I loved.

Behind the concession stand, I find a storage closet and throw myself inside. I kick aside boxes and close the door, holding it shut with both hands. My head drops and my chest cracks, and I try to let out this choked sob as quietly as I can.

But it builds and pulls from too deep. I try the steadying breathing exercises, but my next inhale is a big, gaping sob as the wave of grief breaks over me and all I can do is choke, sink, and drown.

Until the door shakes.

"Simon?" someone calls out. "I thought you said this was unlocked?"

I jump back and shove the boxes aside. The door flies open.

"Oh, there's someone in here! I'm so sorry!" the man says, and I realize it's Mr. Taylor, Orlando's dad. He volunteers at the concession stand with some of the other football and band parents. "Sam? Are you okay?"

"Yup," I say, and quickly drag a hand across my face.

If this year has taught me anything, it's that there's never enough time to grieve.

He hesitates, like he needs to say something. He knows that I lost my dad, and I'm obviously a mess. But I just need to get past him and out of here.

He grabs the popcorn. "Hey, if you need to talk, son—"

It's the word *son* that gets me. The way it's meant to reassure, but it just unravels me further. "I'm fine, thanks," I say, and school my expression as I squeeze past him and head back out into the night.

Lou

AS I'M SETTLING into bed Friday night, I find myself torn between my two selves: Lou and Luisa. Luisa is a good egg. She's so organized she's *ahead* of schedule. That level of responsibility means she's guilt free as she slides between soft sheets at a reasonable hour before heading straight to dream town. No detours. Luisa remembers to wash her face, floss, grab her retainer, and wrap her hair up before bed so it doesn't frizz. Luisa downloads meditation apps and audio books because social media is a no-go before bed. And she always remembers her meds in the morning.

Lou, though? She doesn't believe in rules.

Lou doom scrolls and gets mad about stuff on Twitter before burning off all that anxiety by looking for a new webtoon or fanfic. She reasons that it will help her have something good to think about as she tries to fall asleep. A short fic maybe, an itty-bitty one-shot about our latest favorite comic or couple. It's the night before the SAT, and Responsible Luisa is ready. But unfortunately, Lou finds a prolific writer who updates regularly.

It's seven AM on a Saturday, and I can't figure out why I'm awake. I blink and search around for my phone, but it's not on the charger. It's dead on the floor. I plug it in and wait for it to power up. More sleep is what I need. But a parade of notifications sounds off from my phone.

"Oh my god, *what*?" I snarl and snatch it up.

There are several texts from my sister.

> **Hey, what time?**
> **Do you still need a ride?**
> **Lou???**
> **I thought you wanted to get there early?**
> **I told you I have a dr. appt**

The last one is from Mom.

> **Don't forget to eat! And not a Pop-Tart! I left**
> **you an egg sandwich in the microwave.**
> **Did Elena pick you up yet?**

Oh *no*.

Panic hits like an ice bath, and I stumble out of bed.

Testing starts in one hour. I try to think around the day's usual schedule. Dad's at work. Mom is at the tutoring center with Max. If I call her, she will drive that minivan way too fast to come get me, cursing me the whole way. And then it will be a long ride for the two of us because today's testing is at a high school in a different county.

Outside my window, I see Sam loading the back of his truck with pool-cleaning supplies. Running on pure desperate panic, I open my window, stick my head out, and shout, "*Wait!*"

Startled, Sam drops a bucket.

"Sorry! Please wait!" I pull on a pair of baggy jeans over the soft shorts I'd worn to bed, and a sports bra under the shirt I slept in. Teeth, toilet, wash hands, grab hair tie and egg sandwich, pop my meds, slip on shoes, and I'm out the door.

Sam waits by his truck, looking sleepy and rumpled. A dusty blue baseball cap is pulled low over his eyes.

"I know what you're thinking. I sure do need a lot of rides lately, but I come by it honestly. I woke up late. So late." My voice is a hoarse mess. I pray he doesn't make any Lazy Lou jokes. "I say we add *drive Lou where she needs to go* as an amendment to the list," I joke.

His dark brows inch up his forehead. "What happened to zero stars, never again?"

His moodiness throws me. All the lightness from yesterday afternoon is gone.

But he still asks, his voice sounding as rough as mine, "Where do you need to go?" Above us, the morning sky is already darkening with clouds.

"I'm retaking the SAT in half an hour. At Nova Creek High." I cringe in fear that the small backwoods town of citrus groves and natural springs is out of the way for him. When he glances at his watch, the rejection is clear. "You know what, forget it." I turn to march back home.

He slams the tailgate shut. "Sorry," he says. "I'm a bear on zero sleep. But I can drive you." He twirls his keys, and I wonder if he also has two selves—Sam and Samuel—that he has to deal with every night. I nod and tell him thanks before getting in the truck.

Sam says nothing more as he drives off. His mouth is set in a hard line, and like that day he drove us to the beach, he doesn't turn on the radio as he drives. The silence is as oppressive and somber as his mood. He changes gears as the truck speeds up on the empty county road.

The feeling of imposing on him makes me want to crawl out of my skin.

I lean toward the window and watch as the ominous clouds give way to rain that pours over the windshield in heavy drops. Late-summer storms are brash reminders that we're at the height of hurricane season. Hunkering down into the din of thundering rain, I let myself sneak a look at Sam. He's pushed the hat back, revealing shadows beneath his eyes. I want the liberty to lean closer and ask him if he's okay.

"You said *retaking*." Sam finally breaks the silence and I jerk back, feeling caught. "Why are you taking the SAT again?"

I clear my throat. "I need a better score. Because I'm trying to get into a good school now."

"*Now?*"

"Elena got into Princeton," I tell him.

His brows shoot up. "Really? Wow."

"Yeah, but then she got pregnant."

He glances at me. "So now you have to go to Princeton?" he asks with obvious confusion.

"God no. I'd never get in. But I have to go somewhere good. Somewhere ambitious."

He shakes his head a little, and I want to explain, but my reasoning and motivations sound like childish ramblings whenever I try to make sense of my sudden determination to get into a college that makes people gasp the way they did when they heard about Elena's acceptance. And Sam already knows about the bucket list. That's enough vulnerability for this week.

Three mind-numbing hours later, I am ready to burn standardized testing to the ground. I grab my phone to call Elena for a ride because that's her comeuppance for passing *her* driver's test. Once outside, I find a blue sky. And Sam's truck waiting for me.

My phone falls to my side as I suck in a breath, speech-less. I check around us and then try to ignore the fluttery rush of anticipation as I head toward him.

Sam is fast asleep.

I tap the window, and he jumps so abruptly his elbow hits the horn. He looks at me like I make as much sense to him as my dead phone made to me this morning. He pinches the bridge of his nose, then leans over to open the door.

I climb inside. "You didn't have to wait for me."

He rubs his eyes. "How'd it go?"

I'm still so shocked to see him here that I just raise one thumb but then, registering his question, I lower it before adjusting to somewhere in the middle with a shrug. His warm, callused hand takes my fist and turns it so my thumb is up again. Chills spread over my skin and I nervously laugh them off.

Crush, the voice in my head hisses, sounding suspiciously like Rocky's.

"I have one more pool I have to do on my way back. You mind tagging along?"

With nowhere else to be, I wave him onward. "Wouldn't want you driving all over Florida because of me. Do I get a cut of this money?"

Something about that makes him smile, and I'm relieved to see the shadows under his eyes are mostly gone.

We drive past vibrant green rows of orange trees that

give way to dirt roads and lead nowhere we can see. Sand-hill cranes find lunch in ponds that have formed from the rain. Cattle lounge in whatever shade they can find. We aren't that far from Port Coral, but it's a whole different world from our sleepy beach town. But as we drive, the wild swamp is built over with vacation developments where whole neighborhoods are packed with matching houses and screened-in pools. They all sit so closely together I bet you could splash your neighbor.

Sam's GPS alerts him that we've reached our destination as he parks alongside the curb.

I study the house but don't see any cars in the driveway. "Is this another breaking-and-entering situation?" I ask as we unbuckle our seat belts and climb out of the truck.

Sam grabs some of the huge poles and a jug out of the back. "It's a vacation house. A family is arriving in the morning." He heads toward the screen door and I follow. Something about going into a house that isn't mine feels sneaky. Bold and carefree.

"We should have put pool hopping on the list," I say.

He laughs. "That's all I do these days."

The pool area is empty of any personality. It's a blank canvas for a vacationing family to paint with all their crap for a sunburnt week. The water is bright blue as Sam skims the pool. I never got to finish charging my phone, so it's dead in his truck, leaving me to my own devices—and bright, horny eyes.

His body is so different now.

I watch his broad shoulders and follow the tension in his arms as he works. My pulse speeds up like it did yesterday when I watched him easily carry his drums before the pep rally.

I understand attraction. The way my stomach bottoms out and chest tightens when I'm reading great romances or writing fanfiction about a couple I can't stop thinking about. But this is something else. Our history combined with my new, complicated feelings for Sam makes that familiar heat burn hotter. Because it's no longer an imagined situation with beloved characters I'm thinking about. It's one that stars me. And him.

"Lou."

My guilty gaze jumps to his face. "What?"

"You can dunk your feet," he says. "I can see you thirsting over the water."

Yeah, right. The water. That's exactly what I'm thirsting over.

I kick off my flip-flops, roll up the cuffs of my jeans, and sit on the edge of the pool. I slip my legs into the cool water, and my whole body sighs, it feels so good. I need to catch my breath and relax. Hanging out with Sam is supposed to be about nostalgia, not new feelings. "We really should've put it on the list."

He laughs. "Even if it was, you wouldn't do it."

My head shoots up. "Excuse me?"

"Breaking into other people's pools? Come on, now."
He continues to slowly walk along the other edge of the
pool. "That's not something Luisa would do."

Sam doesn't think I'm spontaneous, bold, or carefree
enough. My heartbeat pounds everywhere, and the cool
water against my heated skin is nearly too much. *"Lou will
hold her breath longer than Sam underwater,"* I recall out
loud, my pulse racing.

He continues to sweep. "Yeah, but—" The rest of his
argument cuts off as I peel away my shirt.

Sam

Wearing only a neon-green sports bra, Lou unzips and shimmies out of her jeans in a clumsy dance, revealing the shorts she has on underneath. Technically, except for the show of midriff, it's the same amount of clothes she wore at the beach...but the impact is very different watching her *undress*.

Without another glance in my direction, she cannonballs her way into the pool.

I still haven't moved. Seconds pass as Lou stays underwater. Holding her breath.

She's beating me.

I drop the pool brush, yank off my shirt, kick off my shoes, and jump in. Underwater, her eyes flip open wide in a look of surprise that quickly shifts into a competitive frown. Our bodies sink into sitting positions along the pool floor. Down here yesterday disappears. Last night's panic attack. Messing up on the field. Coming home to a quiet house. And waking up at three again this morning.

Lou tilts her head, and her loose hair floats around her. Her face becomes pinched, but there's laughter in her eyes, and it's a revelation: I'm playing with Lou again.

My lungs screaming, I shoot up out of the water and Lou swims up right behind me. "I did it!" she cheers, gasping for breath. "I beat you!"

I cough. "Barely."

"I jumped in first! Oh my god, I can't believe I did it." She sounds wondrous as she spins in place, taking in the entirety of the space. Still a little breathless, she says, "Our parents should have gotten us a real pool."

She plucks another memory from Before, and it doesn't hurt. I can't help but laugh as I remember Lou and I presenting our savings to our parents in a bid for one of them to build us a pool. "It's a shame our thirty dollars wasn't enough."

She purses her lips and I look too long at her mouth. "I threw in a whole twenty, so technically the pool would have been two-thirds mine."

"That's fast math."

She clucks. "I have taken the SAT three times."

We tread water into the deep end, and I want to tell her more things. The afternoon is warm and hazy and we're alone.

"Sorry about earlier," I say again. "I didn't get any sleep last night."

"So the bear told me this morning," she says with a hint of a smile.

It's a playful and easy acceptance, but I want to tell her more even though exposing myself further makes no sense. I rub my hands over my face. "Ever since my dad died, I wake up every night at three in the morning, and it's like some internal anxiety alarm has gone off in my body." I exhale sharply. "I don't know how to explain it."

Her smile disappears, and I turn away but still feel the intense scrutiny of her gaze.

"Brains are weird," she offers. "And I'm terrible at sleep, too."

I can't help but laugh, relieved that she doesn't try to reassure me about my insomnia. "Maybe we should find our old flashlights and try to learn Morse code again."

She barks a laugh. "I have enough coding in my life right now." At my look, her brow crinkles and she explains, "I'm learning to code to make an app."

"Wow, really?" I ask, impressed. Lou was always really good with tech stuff.

She sweeps her arms out to swim backward, putting distance between us. "It's for a state scholarship that's awarding a nice chunk of change to students who find inventive ways to support their local small-town businesses."

"What does your app do?"

"Nothing yet," she says with a frustrated laugh. "The plan is for it to be an interactive map for Spring Fest. Some light promo with some functional geolocation." She's saying all this with such a blasé air, but all I can think of is how whenever we used to play fantasy RPGs, Lou's favorite parts were always the big, sprawling maps. "And even if I don't win the scholarship," she goes on matter-of-factly, "it'll add something real to my otherwise very unimpressive applications."

"I'm sure they're not that bad."

"Oh, they're boring. I didn't do any clubs or honors classes before this year."

Curious who she became in high school, I ask, "Why not?"

It takes her a moment to answer, as she studies the empty house past my shoulder. "Somewhere around the end of freshman year, school got hard for me. When teachers started discussing repeating ninth grade with my parents, I got tested and we all learned some things about ADHD."

We're circling each other through the water, and I'm starved for more information. I want to know everything, connect all the dots I missed.

"It's not that I'm not smart—I know that. But school is the worst. I'm not fast and I forget stuff on the spot." She leans back, and her body stretches out as she floats. "I get fixated on the wrong stuff, and somewhere in a new intense infatuation, sure, I'll learn some coding or watch eight hundred TED Talks about productivity—but then I get over it. And that's just not sustainable."

I trail her floating form, her brown skin drinking up the sun. Her hair floats around her, the neon-green bra bright in the afternoon sun. I'm studying her like a watercolor when a selfish thought strikes me: *Maybe we could both stay in Port Coral.*

Surprised at myself, I sink into the water. When I swim back up again, I push my wet hair out of my eyes and ask, "If you hate school, why the last-minute Hail Mary to get into a good college?"

She hums in thought, her eyes closed against the sun. "Because I came upon a fork in the road, and on one side was my sister, who's gone all spiritual teen mom. And on the other is my mother's tenure track with college degrees, health insurance, and an impressive, tangible definition of success meant to heal all the intergenerational trauma we carry as Latinas."

I think of the viejitos and their solemn looks and wonder what will heal mine. "So you picked your mom's road."

"It's not like I can run away to a circus in Albuquerque."

A small laugh escapes me. "Is that the third hidden road?"

She smiles with her eyes closed. "I'd need someone to drive me." Her smile disappears on a long exhale. "I will become exceptional because, left to my own devices,

I would float in this pool forever." She drifts around me, lost in thought. When she is close enough that one smooth leg slips past my stomach, I hold my breath. She abruptly raises her arms and lets herself sink. When she pops back up, she looks at me, her chin just above the waterline. "Why aren't *you* going to college anymore?"

Lou is getting to know me again, and I am afraid of this version disappointing her. "The easy answer is that I don't have any money."

"But what about scholarships and grants? You're in marching band, a very noble extracurricular."

"We're choked by debt, Lou." I don't want to talk about the gritty details of money, but it's also a relief to say it plainly.

"If that's the easy answer, what's the hard one?"

I push my wet hair back again. "I'm tired of friends and teachers acting like me wanting to help my family is some huge step backward. Every time I imagine saying goodbye to Mom, Abuela, and Cora, I shut down. I can't do it. Not yet, and not like this. But I need money and a decent job." Lou and I are so close now, she could reach out and touch me. It's dizzying to wish she would. "Growing up sucks," I admit quietly. "I guess that's the hard answer."

"You don't know what your other road looks like yet," she says thoughtfully, drawing me even closer. "You just have to find your circus." Her grin turns impish before she splashes me in the face. I move to retaliate but miss as she dives beneath the water. I reach out and grab her arm to pull her back up, but she spits a mouthful of water at me.

"Gross!" I shout.

Her huge, delighted smile sinks past all the shadows and pulls a matching one from me. Trust means everything to Lou, and I remember what it meant to receive hers. And whatever else, I want to be this version of me— the one who shares secrets with Lou, knowing she'll keep them all safe.

The screen door slides open with a loud squeak, and a family of five steps outside.

There's a long moment of confusion as we all take in the unexpected sight of the other.

"Excuse me," the adult woman says in a heavy Jersey accent, breaking the stalemate. "We rented this place for the week!"

"You're right," Lou says. "You're totally right." She looks at me with wide eyes before we both lunge for the edge of the pool.

"Of course!" I call as I climb out. "We were getting the pool ready for you."

"She's in her underwear!" one of the kids shouts.

"Are you kidding me?" the woman asks, not sounding like she believes us. "Florida people are something else." The way she says it sounds like *Flah-rida*, and I know Lou is trying not to laugh as she hops back into her jeans. I pull my shirt on and grab the equipment I'd dropped.

"Have a great vacation!" Lou calls. "Enjoy the pool—the water's great!"

Back in the truck, we both crack up and shake the water from our hair. The windows are down as we take off, and the warm air is welcome. Lou is more relaxed now as she snoops around the console. That's where she finds my camera.

"Hey, you still have it," she says happily.

I had charged the camera and brought it as far as the truck but have yet to take a picture. Lou turns it on and aims it at me. I do my best to smile. At a red light, I return the favor—and with Lou in my lens, she smiles, slow and unguarded. I snap two, to be sure.

We hit the stretch of county road that will lead us home, and I change gears, wishing I didn't have to focus on driving right now. Yesterday was a disaster, but thanks to Lou and the list, today has been the best. I slide her a quick look, and I'm filled with rightness at the sight of her beside me.

"What if growing up doesn't mean abandoning all the stuff that makes us happy?" she asks. Lou is leaning back against the door, the open window making the curls around her face dance in the wind. A bright smile blooms on her face, and when she offers it to me, all I can think is, *Found you.*

"Let's do more stuff off the list," she says, like she's only now committing to the idea.

I laugh. "That's the plan."

"We've already checked off me holding my breath longer than you. And we could retroactively add breaking into a pool. I love adding something that's already done to a checklist. And, *oh*! I know another easy one we can do right now!" she sings out over the wind rushing into the truck. "Let's work on our Spanish!"

Ice water drowns out all my warmth. "Lou, listen. My Spanish sucks."

She tut-tuts me. My mind spins with the smell of coconut as she shakes out her drying curls. "Ya dejó de llover," she says.

Warmer air hits us, and I think of the sun on her skin. The morning's rain is gone, the day now bright with sunshine.

"Y salió el sol," I return, and Lou smiles, proving my point.

Lou

"IN SOME PERSONAL news, turns out I'm a dog person."

I laugh at Rocky from the other side of the cat room. "You're only saying that because we've been cleaning litter boxes for the past thirty minutes." I love the cat room and all the mama cats and wild kittens, but it's a *lot* of smells. My sensitive nose always goes a little haywire in here.

"Dogs go outside. Sure, you gotta bag it, but who does their business in a box and leaves it there? Serial killers and cats." Rocky gags.

"They teach themselves to use that box—*we* don't even do that. You know what? We're not getting into this again." Cleaning the cat room will probably take another half hour since the cats are overpopulated as usual and the shelter just took in another colony from a nearby farm. "Let's get some air."

We go outside, where there are cages and traps to hose down.

Rocky grabs the hose and lets it rip on one of the cages. "How'd it go yesterday?"

I move away to avoid the spray. "Yesterday was great." Yesterday was a *lot*. Swimming with Sam felt like before but *more*. So much more. It was everything I'd once wished Beach Day would be, but with just Sam and me, which made it perfect. So much skin stretched across his new muscles—and up close, I saw all the freckles that still dot his shoulders. I'd felt bold enough to be open and honest with him, but this morning I realized I need to be careful. Nothing is more dangerous to my productivity than redis-covering an old favorite interest.

"I told you the SAT can't be that bad the third time."

"Oh, you mean the test!" I say, and Rocky looks at me. "*That* was terrible."

"What did you think I meant?"

I wonder how much to tell her. I want to be friends with Rocky—and to have someone to share IRL stuff with who isn't Elena. Or Mom. But I don't know how to talk about Sam to someone who doesn't know him. "I went swimming," I say cautiously.

Rocky turns the spray on the next cage, and I move the first into the sun to dry. "I used to be on swim team and hang out at the pool a lot," she says, then glances over at me. "I still like to do it."

"Swim?" I ask.

She sighs, sounding frustrated. Like I'm not picking up what she's putting down.

"Do you...want to go swimming?" I say hesitantly.

Rocky marches to the next crate. "*Yes*, only friend," she bursts out. "I would like to go swimming again. But not at the beach. The ocean is gross."

I freeze, surprised but reassured by the vulnerable bout of honesty. "I'm your only friend?"

"Also, gross, no—of course not." Rocky doesn't look at me. "It was a joke." She raises the hose toward me threateningly.

I wave my hands to placate her. "You're my only friend, too." I feel like a toddler, pointing at my chest, asking, "Friend? *Friend!*" But I really want to officially confirm that I, Luisa Patterson, am capable of making a new friend, no nostalgia necessary.

She lowers the hose again. "What about the boy at the beach?"

"I told you, Sam is—well, we're sort of friends again. But it's a new thing. A new old thing." I make a face. "It's hard to explain, but we're doing a thing."

Rocky marches away to turn off the hose. "I understand what things are, Lou. And people who are doing things with hot boys don't get to commiserate with me about my current abandoned hermit status. Because let me tell you, I used to have plenty of friends. I had a best friend, and then she ruined my life—so I'm trying not to deal with all that trouble right now."

I'm acutely aware that what Rocky is saying does not match the tone in which she is saying it. She showed me her underbelly and will bolt at the first sign of me not respecting her boundaries. I have to be careful here. "How did she ruin your life?"

Rocky rolls her eyes at the sky, then shrugs. It's a long moment before she gives in with a sigh. "We stole a car."

I gasp. Rocky flinches. I quickly get my act together and nod coolly. "Go on."

"We were at a fundraiser, and she'd been acting weird for a while. Started hanging out with some obnoxious rich twats. Me, the scholarship kid with a gift for tools—pun intended—tried to prove myself and got caught in a stick shift I didn't even know how to drive. Terrible getaway." She pastes on a fake smile. "I lost my scholarship, my parents got divorced, and now I'm starting at a new school my senior year while trying to get my very strict Chinese-American mother to trust me again. But in the meantime,

I'm surrounded by cat shit." She crosses her arms. "Tell me about your and Sam's thing."

Her honesty deserves the same in return. "We have a list."

"What kind of list?"

"A bucket list. We wrote it in seventh grade but lost it. I found it this summer and got super bummed about how much of it I never did. And then Sam broke into my treehouse."

"Is that a weird metaphor?"

"No, I have an actual treehouse." My eyes widen with a sudden realization. "And technically, this is on the list."

"What is?" Rocky asks, sounding suspicious.

"*Help all the stray neighborhood cats,*" I say, smiling and excited to cross it off. Rocky's looking at me like I have two heads, so I hurry to say, "I have an old best friend who is finishing a bucket list with me—and I have you, my new friend. And I really think we should go swimming some-time," I finish in a rush, fisting my hands on my hips.

Rocky studies me. Her short black hair is matted to her head with sweat on one side; the other side is shaved, but the hair is growing out.

"I would really like that," she says in a small voice.

And just like that, I officially have a new friend.

"Also, it sounds like you're dealing with a lot of nega-tive energy," I say, channeling my sister.

She erupts in a quick, brash laugh. "No kidding."

"I know just the place."

Entering the botanica is like leaving Port Coral. Or finding the best part of it. Somehow, it's always breezy and smells like fresh herbs, lemons, and a little like the beach. There's a big window that looks out on the square, with a bench where you can usually find the owner, Liliana Santos, painting or reading tarot cards. As we walk past, I see Luna, the local bodega cat, lounging inside. The bell above the door sings out like wind chimes, and Elena looks up from the register. My big sister happily grins at me, like we're on a playdate. "Welcome to Mimi's. I'm Elena."

"Veronica," Rocky says, studying the store.

"My friend here is dealing with a lot of negative energy," I explain to Elena.

Elena moves around the counter. I'm still always a bit surprised to see her baby bump.

Rocky admits, "I've got some bad friends who maybe no longer wish me well." She moves to the shelf of crystals.

Elena moves beside her. "Let me show you some of our tourmaline and stuff to ward off bad vibes from others."

I leave them to it and head down the back aisle with all the tall glass candles. They come in every color, and some are decorated with pictures of various saints and prayers.

Even unlit, the space around them feels charged. Electric with potential magic I do not know. Mom has plain candles. Some are glass, one or two with a saint. But they are tucked away on shelves like bric-a-brac, and despite my own late-night online research about folk magic and spiritualism, they still feel like words my mother hasn't translated for us. I reach for a light blue one.

"Oh, I like that for you." Elena plucks it out of my hand as she walks past with Rocky, her arms loaded with crystals, bottles of perfume, and incense.

I follow them to the register. "You're getting all of that?"

"Your sister is a very good salesperson," Rocky says.

"Thank you!" Elena beams. The phone starts to ring. "I'll be right back."

We watch her race to the back of the store, and Rocky explains, "She's giving me the friendship discount. Big day all around." She uncaps one of the perfumes and sniffs it. Even from where I stand I catch the potent citrus scent. "So she's the smarty-pants sister whose shadow you're outrunning?"

"Yup. Thanks to her getting knocked up, I have to get into a fancy college."

Rocky rolls her eyes. "I still don't understand why you're hung up on out-of-state schools. They're harder to get into and more expensive for no good reason. Why make it harder on yourself?"

"I started my search by looking at the obvious,

big-name schools. The ones with a lot of merch and active fandoms."

"I think you mean *alumni*," Rocky says.

"But they're like the Marvel of colleges, and I can't get into those."

"Because you're not an Avenger."

"You should've seen my mom's face when Elena got into Princeton. If I could do something like that? All my underperforming years will be gone in one Thanos snap."

"I don't think we're meant to aspire to the snap, Lou."

I barrel on, barely keeping my tendency to ramble about this in check. "So, with those schools off the table, I looked into the smaller ones that still sounded very collegiate. No big sports teams, but instead old brick buildings and ancient libraries. But they're just as pricey and don't always provide the same scholarships."

"Big or small, they all want the same crap," Rocky argues. "Money, clubs, connections. I should know—I went to a feeder school that spit out *so* many wannabe Avengers."

"You're right." I lean against the counter with a thoughtful sigh. "We should join a club."

Rocky grumbles like I haven't heard a word she said. I glance at the counter filled with stuff she picked out. "How's your mom going to feel about all of this?"

"We'll see in a minute. I texted her earlier, and she's already outside in the car."

Rocky pays and Elena bags up all the stuff.

"Hey, by the way," I say as Rocky heads for the door. "About the divorce and your friend? I hope you know that neither was your fault. Sometimes stuff implodes around us, but it's not ours to fix. Your friend wasn't a very good friend to you, and I don't think there's ever a really great time to get divorced, but you're not to blame for it."

Rocky doesn't meet my very awkward gaze, but she smiles a little. "Thanks." I watch her steel her shoulders before heading out to meet her mother. I text Mom to pick me up from the botanica instead of the animal shelter.

What are you doing there?

Brujería

I get three dots for a minute before she sends me an eye roll and tells me she's putting in a dinner order at the bodega next door and to go pick it up.

While I wait for our food, I go to the table of viejitos. They're swirling the dominos around in the middle of the table, about to divvy them up. There are only three of the old-timers today, and Mr. Gomez spots me. "¡Siéntate, niña!" he commands, and I take the fourth seat.

"¡Bueno!" Mr. Saavedra claps his hands, and I see how many pieces they've picked out and count the same out for me. They all slide their dominos closer, face out toward each of them. They talk me through the rules but are very mindful to not let me see their stacks.

"How else am I supposed to learn?"

"No vas aprender aciendo trampa," Mr. Restrepo grunts.

I roll my eyes. "I'm not cheating!"

I'm also not winning. They beat me neatly. "No te preocupes," Mr. Gomez says. "You'll beat them one day."

I get up from the table. "Yeah, I know. It's on my list."

LOU AND SAM'S TO-DO LIST
BEFORE WE GRADUATE:

~~GO TO BEACH DAY~~

~~help all the stray neighborhood cats~~

go to Disney World

join a club

pull off the most epic prank of all time

win the town Halloween costume contest

~~apply to the same colleges~~

~~work on our Spanish~~

~~Lou will hold her breath longer than Sam underwater~~   ~~*break into someone's pool~~

go to an actual party

get super good at kissing
*hang out on second base

kiss someone at midnight on New Year's Eve
(after getting super good at it)

~~be serenaded (à la 10 things I hate about you)~~

~~beat the viejitos at dominos~~ (not gonna happen)

bury a time capsule

write a letter to our future selves

~~drive Lou where she needs to go~~

SAM'S ADDITIONS:

MASTER "TOM SAWYER" BY RUSH ON DRUMS
(AND SOME CUBAN JAZZ FOR DAD)

DRIVE THE BARRACUDA

~~ALWAYS HOLD MY BREATH LONGER THAN~~
~~LOU UNDERWATER~~ (LOST ON A TECHNICALITY!)

GET A DOG (I'M ALLERGIC TO CATS,
YOU KNOW THIS)

Sam

OCTOBER

"HOW MUCH LONGER?" I ask.

Ms. Francis doesn't even look at her clock. My school's guidance counselor sways one way and then another in her office chair, her laptop open on her desk with paperwork scattered around it. Bright handouts about colleges, self-care, mental health.

We've spent the past ten minutes in relative silence except for the tapping of her keyboard and my drumsticks against the edge of her desk. Not loud enough to annoy, but to work off some of the nerves that always build up when I sit here. The regular meetings started in

January after Dad died, and I figured I'd be done with them by now, but here we are in October, and I'm still in this chair. Ms. Francis says she makes mandatory appointments with every senior to make sure we're all "well-informed agents of our own destinies." Her words, not mine, and yet it never seems like we talk about the future.

"How are Flotsam and Jetsam?" I stop playing to point at the picture of her two Dobermans on the shelf behind her.

She sighs. "They're such snobs and hate every dog walker I get for them. The latest one is a perfectly nice lady, but they've decided to stage a coup."

I laugh. "My little sister wants a dog now."

"Needy beasts. Have you ever had one?"

"My parents had one—Lucky—but he died a couple of years ago."

"How did he die?" she asks, and the question makes me flinch.

"Old age. They adopted him when he was older."

I don't like the way she watches me now. It's that silent, measuring look I remember from last year. She still hasn't glanced at the clock. She never does until the very end, so I don't, either. She picks up one of the sheets on her desk. "If you were applying to college, you'd be finalizing letters of recommendation at this point."

I begin drumming again.

"But there are so many other avenues you can pursue instead of the traditional college or university route," she says.

My timing falters. Ms. Francis chuckles. "Sorry, it's not you," she says quickly. "I'm remembering one of my students from last year. She was so focused on college, college, college, and then ended up spending her entire summer on a boat at sea."

"Isn't it a breach of trust to tell me that?"

She taps her pen against her chin as she considers this. "I didn't tell you her name."

"The viejitos posted enough about her." Last spring is buried beneath that deep fog, but news about Rosa Santos was inescapable. "And as fun as that sounds, sailing isn't really an option for me."

"Why not?"

I try not to roll my eyes. "Come next summer, I'll be working full-time for Emilio again. Too busy cleaning pools to set sail. And I'll hopefully find another job so my Mom can quit the coffee shop and go back to school."

Ms. Francis makes that same thoughtful face she always does when I start talking about work. "It's a great time for you to explore hobbies and interests. Something new might lead to an undiscovered passion."

I need to get my family out of this awful spot, and I doubt I'll find purpose at the bottom of it. But Ms. Francis has been good to me, and I want to give her something hopeful. "I'm helping a friend who's developing an app."

Ms. Francis perks up.

"I'm taking some pictures around town for her." Lou asked me to help after seeing my camera, so when I'm not at work or marching band practice, I take pictures of the town square, marina, and boardwalk for her.

"You're a photographer?" Ms. Francis is desperate to find some kind of meaning for me.

"Just have a nice camera." They're the first pictures I've taken since the last ones of Dad. I saved those files to a folder I don't open. Dad coloring with Cora at the table. With his arm around Mom in the garage. Sitting alone on our porch, his face to the sun. The brutal honesty of those final moments is hard to look at in the face of remembering all our tireless optimism.

I spin a drumstick in my fingers. "I'm working less right now because pools are closing up and the summer storms have stopped. Instead, I'm playing drums, taking pictures, and hanging out with my best friend again."

It's not the kind of productive purpose found on any of those checklists scattered around her desk, but in some ways, our bucket list was my first five-year plan—and while I don't have the time or headspace for new dreams, maybe there's time to wrap up some old ones.

Ms. Francis smiles suddenly and then finally looks at the clock.

My entire body relaxes. She gave in first.

Outside, the main office has turned into chaos as classes let out. I spy Benny and Lou talking by the reception desk.

"Tell your Mom I'll give her plenty of warning before any photo shoots," Lou is saying as I reach them. When she sees me, she smiles, and it's both shy and familiar, a magnet that pulls me to her. "What are you doing here?" she asks me.

I point my thumb back at Ms. Francis, who is standing in the doorway of her office, watching us, and I bet she's put together that Lou is who I was talking about.

"What are you two up to?" I ask them.

"I am but a delivery boy turning in some forms to our lovely school receptionist," Benny says.

The receptionist, Miss Tina, cuts a look at Benny. "And you're free to go back to class now, Mr. Peña."

Lou smirks. "And I'm starting a club, which apparently means an obscene amount of paperwork," she says with a sigh. "Story of my life."

"You're *starting* a club?" I ask, because according to the list, she only had to join one.

She scrunches up her face. "I know, right? Me, of all people, but an idea hit me, and I saw a real need for a crochet club."

"Do you know how to crochet?" Benny asks.

"Of course I don't know how to crochet. The intention is for other people's grandmas to share the art of textiles with us wild adolescents. And after teaching the viejitos how to start a blog, it's time for them to help me learn how to hem my Halloween costume."

"Devilish," Benny says, impressed.

"Genius," I agree.

Lou rolls her eyes at both descriptions but looks pleased.

"How's the app coming along?" Ms. Francis asks Lou, proving she *definitely* knew who I was talking about the whole time.

"Más o menos," Lou returns, grinning at me over the Spanish. To Ms. Francis, she says, "You need to see the pictures Sam's taken for me."

Benny elbows me. "You a photographer now?"

I say, "Not really," at the same time that Lou says, "He's amazing. Tell your mom sometime next week, okay?" Lou offers us a quick wave goodbye, then heads over to Ms. Francis, pulling her laptop out of her bag.

Benny follows me, and once we're out of the office, he asks, "So, what's the plan?"

I slip my wallet out of my back pocket to get some change for the drink machine. "For what?"

"Your birthday tomorrow, my guy. The big eighteen."

I'm not avoiding it. I'm simply ducking my head and

barreling past it. We have to survive this year of firsts, and figuring out how to celebrate my birthday without Dad is more work than it's worth. "No plans, but feel free to shower me in gifts."

"Do I look like Santa Claus to you?" He shifts closer. "What's up with you and Lou?"

"We're friends again," I say automatically, and there's a bone-deep relief in saying this. In this year of losing, I got something back.

"Just friends?"

My mind trips over the *just* in a real awkward stumble of self-awareness. "Yeah, friends."

"Cool. 'Cause I was thinking of asking her out. She's funny and hot, and I think she thinks I'm the former, and I'm hoping for the latter."

Benny watches me, waiting. My response matters to him. He won't go for her if he thinks there's anything between us, but Lou is her own person who deserves to have the senior year of her dreams, and she still has a lot of things left to do on her list.

Get super good at kissing lights up in my mind like a marquee.

"Cool," I say, hopefully not sounding like a total robot.

"I can be quite charming, but since you two seem close, test the waters for me. She's tough to read, and I don't want to make it weird between us. Can you ask her what she thinks about me?"

I count the change in my hand. Lou and I are friends again. This is fine. Friends look out for each other. "Sure."

"I've heard I'm a good date," Benny assures me with that easy charm he offers everyone, then turns away.

I drop some coins into the vending machine and press the numbers for something with caffeine.

Lou

AFTER SCHOOL, I head home and am enveloped by the smell of nirvana.

"You're cooking, Mami?"

"No, the mailman is!" she calls back, then laughs at her own joke. At least my parents find themselves funny. "Had a short day at work, so I did some gardening."

Mom's happy place is her garden, so she must be flying high on organic vegetables and the hint of fall in the air. Even before I reach the kitchen, I know I'll find her sancocho simmering on the stove. Roasted chicken, garlic, potatoes, yucca, green plantains, corn—everything in her soup sprinkled with herbs and spices. The smell fills the room, and even better, a very familiar yellow bag of cornmeal sits on the counter. I almost whimper. "Arepas, too?" I ask.

She grins as she reads the letter in her hands.

Grilled, buttery arepas for us to eat alongside the soup, or if you're me, to dunk for a ticket straight to heaven. I toss my backpack onto a kitchen chair.

Mom glances up from the mail she's sorting. "How was your day?"

"Pretty good, actually. Ms. Francis complimented my app, my new club was approved, and I finally figured out what AP means."

Mom ignores the joke. "Your sewing club?" She smiles as she takes in my high-waisted jeans and striped top. "The nineties called, and they want their aesthetic back."

I mirror her smile as I grab my phone and reading glasses. "Well, tell them to text next time, because we don't answer cold calls like heathens. And it's a *crochet* club."

There's a knock at the door, and I open it to find Sam on the front porch.

"Hey," I say, confused but pleased to see him.

He starts to say something, then stops. He blinks. "You wear glasses now."

It's so abrupt and unexpected, I self-consciously touch them. I really only ever wear them at home. "They're blue light."

He takes a wobbly step forward like a puppet on a string, and I lean back a little, a nervous flutter in my stomach. He inhales deeply and, sounding dazed, says, "Your mom's soup." He lowers his gaze to mine, and drags a hand through his hair. "I need to talk to you about something."

"Okay," I say, unsure what to make of his nervous energy. He's all over the place, and Sam's usually way more easygoing than this. A total Libra. I remember what day it is. "Hey, happy almost birthday." It's been so long since I've been able to say that to him.

He smiles a little. "Can we go inside?"

"*S-u-re*," I drawl, and step aside. I'm still not sure if he's here for me or the soup. I assume we're headed up to my room until Mom stops us in front of the stairs.

"Sam, hey, good to see you. Where are you two headed?"

I give Mom a desperate look, but she doesn't care about subtlety. "Upstairs," I answer coolly.

"Wait a minute. You guys aren't eleven anymore."

This is new territory for us. *"Mom—"*

"Luisa."

"We're working on college essay stuff," I finally say.

This gets her. We stare each other down, and she at last relents. Barely. "Arepas will be ready in fifteen."

I salute her and signal Sam to follow me.

On the stairs, it hits me that I'm headed to my bedroom with Sam right on my heels. Not my boyish Sam, but a taller one who knows how to drive and has kissed other people. And has probably done even more than that. I stumble on the last step, and when his hand comes to my hip to steady me, I nearly leap out of my skin. When we reach my room, I blurt out, "I was thinking about the time capsule," just as he says, "Benny is going to ask you out."

I close the door behind us with a soft click. "Come again?"

For one breathless moment, I thought Sam said *he* was going to ask me out. But Benny? Too many questions bounce around in my head. Sam stares at me as I process this information.

"Okay," I finally manage, and walk past him to my gaming chair.

"Okay?" he asks. "Like okay, thank you for the information—or okay, I'll go out on a date with him?"

I grab a pen and do a spin in my chair. "Benny Peña. Popular. Charming, slightly roguish." I continue to spin as I lay out his stats. I bring the pen to my mouth. Sam leans down and stops my chair with his hand. In my best Katharine Hepburn impression that definitely sounds more John Mulaney, I ask, "I don't know, Sam, should I get myself a boyfriend?"

"Hold up," he says, sounding alarmed. "He's not asking you to be in a relationship, just out on a date."

"I can be quite charming."

His face falls. "He said the same thing."

"About me?" I ask, brightly.

"No, about himself." Sam turns away and paces before stopping to do a slow circle as he examines my room. The walls are still the soft purple of years ago, and many of the same geeky knickknacks clutter the shelves. But my desk is now a neon-lit gaming center.

Sam sits at the edge of my bed and slowly moves his hand closer to Jupiter, waiting for her approval. She gives him a sniff, and when he goes to scratch her head, she lets him. "Hey," he says, under his breath. "It's been a while."

It does something warm and terrible to my chest to see them together like they've missed each other. I throw my pen at Sam's chest. He looks at me but continues his gentle scratches.

"Should I tell him yes?" I ask, wanting his answer but not knowing what I want it to be.

"Do you *want* to tell him yes?"

A year ago, I would have said no to avoid the self-doubt and nervous stomachache. But now I want to know what it feels like to go on a date. To kiss a Level 10 Rogue and be good at it. I glance at my bulletin board. The corner of the list sticks out from behind *Howl's Moving Castle* fanart. Without looking at Sam, I admit, "I've never been on a date." Baby steps.

I slide him a quick glance from the corner of one eye. He shrugs like it's no big deal.

Navigating around the knot in my throat, I continue. "I haven't ever kissed..."

This obviously derails whatever he was about to say. He looks confused.

116

My nervous heart thunders as I cross my arms. "Anyone," I concede, embarrassed, but ready to fight.

"Okay," he says slowly.

I lower my arms with a roll of my eyes. "It's not that big of a deal."

"You're right." His eyes are wide and serious as he nods. "You're absolutely right."

Great, now he sounds like my dad trying to reassure me that I'm a great singer during karaoke. "I don't want my first kiss to be Benny Peña and then mess up. He's way too out of my league to do that." Benny isn't even here, and I'm starting to sweat. I get up and begin to pace. This is why I've always avoided even the concept of dating.

Sam looks affronted. "No, he's not. You are"—he gestures at my face—"very pretty."

I push my glasses up on my nose. "Don't do me any favors, but I'm not talking looks here. I'm talking combat levels. This is like running toward a dragon when you've still only got a wooden sword and no armor. My XP is too low."

"Who says you *have* to kiss him?"

"Always assume the most from dragons." At his look, I stop my anxious march around my room. "Besides, I might *want* to kiss him, and I'd like to be prepared for that."

We look at each other as a wild idea starts to form in my head. The idea is so absurd and embarrassing that even thinking it makes me want to hide. But I remember how great it was to be so honest with Sam in the pool. I cut another glance to where the list sticks out on my bulletin board and fear Sam can see the thought bubble that just popped up over my head:

get super good at kissing

"You could help me," I say in a quiet voice with every drop of nerve I have. But when Sam smiles brightly, my defenses kick in and I'm ready to laugh it all off as a joke.

"Of course I can," he says.

All the air leaves my lungs as I drop down into my chair. Shocked, I ask, "*Really?*"

"Absolutely," he says, reassuring me as he sits forward. "I'll take care of everything."

I know Sam has kissed other girls. I saw him kiss Tasha, after all. But his total ease with this throws me. "I guess it's not really that big of a deal for you." The comment comes out more like a question.

"Of course not." He sounds so confident, all his nervous tension gone. "Benny asked me to make sure you're into it. I'm here to help, Lou."

My mouth drops open.

"It won't be weird. He knows you and I are good friends."

I'm suddenly back in his truck on Beach Day, slowly dying as Tasha laughs over my misguided idea of anyone having girlfriend privileges when it comes to Sam.

They were so cool and casual. Perhaps helping your late-blooming friend learn how to kiss can be cool and casual, too. My skin feels too tight, like I'm watching Sam out by the pool again. We aren't those same kids racing our bikes anymore, but this is still the boy I once sat side by side with as we made out with our own hands for practice.

This is *Sam*. Bigger, taller, and more experienced, but offering to be my weird friend again. I look at his mouth. The memory of him ducking his head and smoothly kissing Tasha flashes in my mind again before morphing into the nightmare image of me slobbering all over Benny one day.

I swallow hard as I sit down next to Sam on the bed. I remind myself I'm learning to become bold and carefree. And being this close to Sam shows me how impatient I am to test these waters with someone I trust. To break down all the steps of kissing. I want that. And I am realizing how badly I want to do it with Sam.

I place my palm on Sam's chest, above his heart—and find it's racing. His eyes widen. We are friends again, and apparently friends help each other with stuff like this.

"Let's practice a kiss," I say.

Sam

EVERY WORD I know disappears in one swift rush.

Lou scoots closer, her words tumbling into one another. "Because you're right, of course, you're right," she says, almost to herself. "This isn't a big deal. *Get super good at kissing* is on the list, and we used to practice kissing our hands in front of each other like a couple of prepubescent perverts, so how is this different?"

I need to say something, but there's a roaring in my ears. Somewhere between Benny's request and seeing Lou's room again, I lost my freaking mind. I wanted to show her how good I could be at this friend thing again. I thought she wanted me to help her turn him down.

But instead she's got a fevered look as she bites her

lip and studies my face. She wants to practice a kiss. With me.

So she can kiss Benny.

My mind is racing to catch up, but that's hard to do when it's short-circuiting as Lou's hand slides up and down my chest.

"Let's say he's also into it, he might put his hand on my—" She grabs my fist from where it's clenched on my thigh and searches my face carefully as she brings my hand to her waist. I blow out an unsteady breath, and my fingers squeeze her a little before I can relax my hand. I'm about to kiss Lou for the first time and would sell my soul for a mint.

"Or would he go straight for my chest?" she wonders.

I drop my hand like a rock. "No. No, he would not."

She grasps my hand and puts it back on her waist. "I'm just asking. You have more experience."

"Not with this." A nervous laugh strangles me. "I've never *practiced* kissing."

Her brows pull together when she frowns. "We totally did." She makes a fist, then lowers her wrist. She looks at her hand like it's a puppet. "Look away, it's time to kiss a real boy," she says.

That very hand goes to my neck and pulls me all the way to her. And then she goes and does it. Lou kisses me. Mouth-to-mouth. Unfortunately, I'm holding myself so tightly that I've turned twelve again and am terrible at this.

She sits back with a frown. "You have to kiss me back."

I close my eyes, pained. "I know, I know."

She begins to pull away, already closing herself off. "If you don't want to do this—"

In a quick move, I close the space between us and cover her mouth with mine. For one breathless moment, we're still. A peck. Featherlight. We can stop here in this suspended moment with our eyes wide open. Tiptoe out of the dragon's cave to avoid crossing the line. My hand slips up to cup her face as she makes a soft, curious sound, and I slide my thumb against her jaw. Her soft lips part as her eyes close. So do mine as I follow her lead. We move in a lazy rhythm, slow enough to learn each other in this new way. Her lips curve against mine before she breaks away suddenly. My mouth chases hers. "This is good, right?" she asks, breathless.

This is everything. I nod quickly, my arm tight around her. "Super good." My voice sounds far away.

She's halfway in my lap and grinning like she's discovered a new game. "Oh my god. I might be good at this, Sam."

"Super good," I repeat, too light-headed to think. Bold as can be, she leans up on her knees and kisses me again.

"It's not all spit slobbery as I feared," she says. "It's fun and feels really good."

Thank god. I gently bite her bottom lip and she quietly gasps then does the same to me.

"What about tongues?" she wonders against my mouth.

Strangled, I ask, "What about them?"

"Let's practice that," she says, her voice excited and curious. This is Playful Lou. Peter Pan Lou. With every kiss, I'm trailing after her and the promise of another adventure again. Each kiss a bewitching whisper. *Let's stay here and never grow up, Sam. We can play this new game where we kiss until we melt.*

She deepens the kiss, and when her tongue touches mine—it's too much, and we fall back onto the bed. I sink into all her pillows, and she kisses my cheek, my jaw. Her lips find my throat as my hand discovers the warm, soft skin of her stomach.

Too much, too much.

My heart pounds in my ears, and Lou pulls away, her eyes wide. Did she hear it, too? I want to bring her back, but she flies backward, stumbling off the bed.

"What are you doing?" Max's voice calls from somewhere I can't see. Oh god. The door. Her little brother is on the other side of her closed door.

"Playing," she returns automatically, and her face screws up. *Playing.* Like when we were kids. No big deal.

This is just a game that completely wrecked me. She cautiously gets to her feet and looks down at me, still sprawled across her bed. Her glasses are askew, and she's wearing a victorious look of awe.

Kiss me again. My head swirls with her scent and touch. I'm memorizing and drowning.

The door whips open, and I bolt upright, sitting among the pillows. Lou's mom gives me a suspicious scowl. "I forgot to tell you to leave the door open."

"Oops," Lou says casually, leaning against her dresser.

Her mom looks between us for a long moment, and I consider jumping out the window and making a run for it when she finally says, "Arepas are ready."

Lou lets out a nervous laugh once her mom leaves. She lifts one hand for a high five. After a deep, steadying breath, I smack my hand against hers, and with the biggest, brightest smile, she says, "I'm a good kisser."

"Yeah," I manage, dazed. "Real good."

On my walk home, with extra soup and arepas for my family, I'm reminded of why I just had the best kiss of my life.

Benny: **Did you talk to her?**

I stop in the driveway to my house and hesitate before replying with a 👍.

And then I immediately wish I could take it all back. Everything but the kiss. *Practice* kiss.

Cool thanks, bro

I curse myself and go inside.

My phone wakes me the next morning. I changed my old notification sounds and ringtones, but I still flinch every time it goes off—lingering fear over getting terrible news. I roll over to check the latest text.

Benny:

Lou said yes to Benny. I throw my pillow over my face and smother a frustrated groan. Another text chimes.

and happy bday dude!

I drop my phone on the floor. I have no reason to feel this burn of jealousy. Lou and I are friends again, and I refuse to ruin it *again*. And yet, my mind slips back to her smile as she climbed into my lap. And then I slowly die as I imagine her turning that smile on someone else.

My bedroom door flies open. *"Happy Birthday!"*

I shoot up with a death grip on my blanket. Mom, Cora, and Abuela stand in my bedroom. Mom holds a cupcake with a lit candle in the middle. They launch right into the song.

"Make a wish!" Mom says, bringing the cupcake closer to my face.

"¡Feliz cumpleaños, Papito!"

"Do we get to spank him eighteen times now?" Cora asks. It was one of Dad's jokes.

Today is my birthday. I am eighteen. A new age, one my dad won't get to see. I meet Mom's sad gaze and then blow out the candle.

I wish for the day to hurry up and be over.

But of course it drags on, and I get plenty of out-of-tune singing from teachers and friends, an extra slice of pizza at lunch, and way too many jokes about getting to play the lottery now. What I don't get is to see Lou until I drive home after band practice and find her waiting on the front porch.

"Hey," I say, surprised but pleased.

She lifts the gift bag beside her. "Can't let another birthday pass without getting you something."

"Do you want to come inside?" I ask. "Abuela's making bistec empanizado." The fried breaded steak is my favorite.

Lou's eyes widen before she jumps to her feet, and she doesn't wait for me before going inside. Abuela's face lights up when she sees her.

"¡Hola, Doña Alvarez! It smells so good in here," Lou says to my abuela. They kiss cheeks, genuinely happy to see each other. Lou updates her on her family in Spanish that's way better than mine.

I take the opportunity to dash upstairs and make sure my room isn't a total disaster, but as I'm about to head back to the kitchen, Lou appears in my bedroom doorway.

"You got to snoop around my room *and* treehouse," she says with a small smile. She offers me the gift bag, then walks past me. "Turnabout is fair play."

I stumble back to sit on the edge of my bed as I watch her move through my space. While hesitant at first, she quickly warms up to the game as she curiously explores my room. I want to ask her about Benny and the details of their upcoming date, but I'm light-headed as I catch the warm, soft smell of her. My throat tightens when she slides her hand across corners and shelves. She picks up a pair of drumsticks and taps them against my dresser for a beat before moving onto my mug of pens. She uncaps one and scribbles her signature on the edge of a scrap piece of paper. I make a mental note to keep it.

I hold my hands in my lap so I don't reach for her.

"Open it," she says, and I remember the gift bag beside me. I reach inside and find a red scarf. It's soft and looks handmade.

"Did you make this?" I ask, awed.

She looks shy all of a sudden. "It was pretty simple once I got started, and then it just got away from me. New hobbies tend to go that way for me." She shrugs.

I slip it around my neck and can tell that pleases her. "You look like Mako." When I hesitate, she laughs. "From *Korra*! Come on, it used to be our favorite show."

"I remember," I counter. "I also remember you hating him."

"I did not. I struggled with him and the second season, but he was always hot." She picks up my camera and snaps a picture of me. She smiles down at it, and I feel myself crumbling because I'm desperate to know if she thinks that *I'm* hot. My head's a mess. She sets the camera aside, and her hand slides against my laptop, waking the screen.

Our old YouTube channel is on the screen.

"What is—" She drops down onto my desk chair with a gasp when she realizes what it is. "Holy crap, is that us?" She hits Play. It's one of our taste tests. Time folds in on itself as I listen to us as kids but watch delight dance across older Lou's face beside me.

"Help! The Candy Is on Fire!" Lou reads the title with a laugh and leans closer to the screen. "We were ridiculous."

In the clip, Lou and I are sitting on my bedroom floor with an array of candy in front of us. The camera must've been on a tripod.

"First up, we've got cinnamon hot." Middle School Lou picks up the bright red bag and waves it closer to the camera.

"Oh man," she says now. "I need to get more of that stuff."

Unlike Lou, I'm terrible with spicy stuff. As far as Cuban food, I've grown up around a lot of bananas, sweetened milk, and rice, while Lou's mom keeps a big jar of home-made hot sauce in the fridge. My gaze returns to the computer, where on the count of three, Lou and I pop the candy into our mouths. Almost immediately, the pain on my face is obvious, while Lou seems to consider the flavor notes.

"Hate it, hate it," I say, giving in and spitting it onto a napkin. I chug the glass of milk she has on standby.

"This is the first one!" She laughs and gestures to the pile of candy in front of us. "We haven't even gotten to any of the peppers yet."

On-screen, the door to my bedroom opens. With us sitting on the floor, the camera catches his feet.

Present-day Lou's face freezes as my heart sinks.

"What in the world are you two doing?" Dad asks us with laughter in his voice. He gets down on his haunches and smiles. "Ay, but your old man looks good, yeah?"

"I dare you to eat that one," I tell Dad, holding up the awful ghost pepper.

He considers the challenge. "What do I get if I do?"

"I'll mow the lawn."

He laughs and settles down beside me. "You're on."

Dad bites into the candy and chews it quickly. His eyes water but he gets it down, showing his empty mouth to us and the camera. The next clip is Dad standing on the front porch, the sound of a mower somewhere behind him. Lou turns the camera and zooms in on me as I push that mower across our front yard.

In the present and past, Lou and I both laugh. Dad looks good here. Healthy, strong, and happy.

He was diagnosed earlier that year.

My eyes flicker down reflexively. Regret fades the scene in front of me, but there's also relief that the memory is safe here. I pick up my camera and take a picture of Lou, sitting on my side of our windows, and it's all golden light and brown skin—and I find myself punch-drunk with relief to be beside her again.

"We should do another taste test," she says. "I could bring over my mom's hot sauce."

I laugh nervously even as I know I'll do it. I'll bear it without complaining, because I'm falling for my best friend. *Again*.

ON HALLOWEEN NIGHT, I let Mom drive me somewhere. The town square is closed to traffic for the festivi-
ties, so she parks a block away. "Give your sister this." She
hands me a tub of butter. The container has been repurposed and filled with soup. Work has been stressing her
out, so she's been nonstop simmering. Mom looks at my
costume again and smirks.

"First you dress like the nineties, now the eighties?"
she asks.

"You can't hold a time traveler like me down."

The lamps around the square are flickering tonight
in a very extra bid to appear spooky. In the middle of the
square are carnival games and food stalls. I can smell the
cinnamon sweetness from here. Pumpkins sit outside all

the shops, and kids race past me up to each one with their bags out. The botanica is busy, and I find Elena behind the counter. She's wearing a witch's hat and gauzy black dress that's tight around her baby bump. She's due in December. Just what our dungeon party needs, an impatient Sagittarius. Elena does a double take when she sees me in my costume.

"Who are you supposed to be?" she asks.

I lower my hands to my hips. "Can you really not tell?"

She studies me. "You look like an old white man." She shrugs and guesses, "A senator?"

"I'm never going to win the contest."

"Not if it's a fair one."

"Ugh, here's your soup." I leave it on the counter.

On my way out, I pass Liliana Santos, the store owner, sitting by the door, handing out candy. When she spots me, she grins. "Hey, Doc, where's Marty?"

"Thank you!" *Back to the Future* is a classic. And with that boost of confidence, I head back out into the busy night and get a few more comments about my costume—from chuffed parents—before I reach the middle of the square. I measure my Doc Brown against witches, scarecrows, goblins, pirates, and even a classic ghost with the cut-out eyes. There's a small stage with some speakers that are currently playing an old jazz song about rattlin' bones. Doubts over my chances grow worse when the viejitos stroll past, each dressed as a different member of the Avengers.

"Luisa! You look as old as us," Mr. Gomez cackles.

I laugh heartily, but once they're out of earshot mutter a curse.

"Hey." Benny stands in front of me, a dashing, retro vampire. He looks like Viago from the *What We Do in the Shadows* movie. Benny Peña. Level 10 Rogue, and me here with my base armor. Benny takes in my costume with an impressed look. "I could hardly tell it was you."

"Thanks," I say. "I'm glad you don't think I look like an old white man."

He laughs. "You look great. Hot scientist vibes." Compliments from Benny are sweet, but it's part of his hardware to make the people around him feel good. Still, though, I try not to sweat in my doctor's coat and scratchy wig.

"I'm here," someone calls out dryly.

We both turn as Mermista from the *She-Ra* cartoon walks up to us. All my bottled-up nerves burst into potent excitement at seeing Rocky decked out as the powerful princess.

"You look amazing!" I say breathlessly.

"Yeah, yeah," she says with a shrug. Everything about the aquamarine outfit—from the crop top to the trident—is spot-on. Mermista isn't a character someone could find off the rack, so Rocky definitely had to have already owned it or invested in some real express shipping. But something tells me it was already in her closet, a token from a past Halloween with old friends that she brought out for me.

Rocky and I are friendship official these days. We have our designated lunch table, we work on our college applications together, and I even introduced her to Jupiter.

"And our last caballero," Benny announces as Marty McFly strides over to us in a denim jacket, red puffy vest, and fitted jeans. The sunglasses on his head push his dark hair back.

Sam lifts his wrist and checks the clunky calculator watch he's wearing. "I'm not late."

I bark an abrupt, nervous laugh, and my heart flutters for entirely different reasons.

Benny's text about hanging out on Halloween arrived shortly after Sam left my house, meaning that while my head was still spinning from all my new discoveries, Sam was being a *good friend* and letting Benny know I'd be into a date.

But I wasn't. Not with Benny. Not when I couldn't stop thinking about the calluses on Sam's hands gently scratching my hip and cheek. Boy soap on his warm neck and the hint of chlorine always on his clothes. Being completely disarmed by his lips softening into a smile against mine.

When I texted Benny back, I knew my feelings were only platonic for him and becoming increasingly crush-like for Sam. So I mentioned hanging out as a group—with Sam and Rocky. Benny, being Benny, was into it. He makes friendship so easy.

"Oh, I get it now," Rocky says, glancing over my costume again. "I thought you were Bernie Sanders. Is this like a couple thing?" She points at Sam and me with her trident.

"No, it's a list thing," I tell her.

Benny looks between Sam and me. "What list?"

I've already told Rocky about it, so I motion for Sam to explain.

"Luisa and I made a bucket list many moons ago, and now we're finishing it. Winning the Halloween costume contest is on it." He points from his Marty to my Doc.

Benny's grinning like he's heard the best thing in the world. "Really? Listen, as a member of the team that discovered the infamous Golden Turtle last year"—we all groan, because Benny never misses an opportunity to tell people about this—"you know I love a good quest." The Golden Turtle is a lost treasure discovered off the coast forever ago. Some teenage yahoo found it, then used it in a treasure hunt that endured so many generations it became a local tradition. Until someone went too hard at hiding it and lost it for, like, twenty years. Benny and his friends found it last year, and now it sits across from us on the other side of the town square on a pedestal as a boring statue.

"Who turns a quest into a statue?" I ask him, disappointed.

"Trust me, it breaks my heart, too." Benny sighs deeply. "So, what else is on your bucket list?"

"Make sure Lou wins the costume contest, and I'll tell you." Sam checks his huge watch again.

"Or you," I concede, barely masking my competitiveness.

He smiles like he knows how little I mean that. "I'm here to make sure people know who you are, Doc."

There's a box by the stage with slips of paper for voting. We head over to it, and I shamelessly write down my own name.

Rocky thumps the ground with her trident. "I was promised snacks for my vote. Fried things covered in chocolate and sugar." Without waiting for us, she heads toward Papá El's cart, and Benny jumps to follow. Sam steps in front of me, and with a soft smile, he taps a knuckle against the goggles strapped to the top of my head.

"You make for a very cute mad scientist."

Compliments from Sam hit me like a whispered secret. Something just between us.

I swallow and try for an easy smile, but a hundred butterflies are battling for dominance in my chest. "Good luck for both of our sakes," I quote.

He smiles. "We'll be fine, Young Doc."

We all get a Popsicle, mine a creamy, sweet dulce de leche that makes me close my eyes on a happy groan. When I open them, Sam blinks and clears his throat. "Good?" he asks.

"Yeah," I tell him, and wonder if he still remembers the mangonada ones.

Benny bobs for apples, Rocky gets her tarot cards read, and Sam blows almost twenty bucks at a ring-toss game he swears is rigged. When I ask him what he's trying to win, he nudges me away and buys me another ice cream. I don't complain.

When we reach the Golden Turtle statue, Benny sighs. They've recently built a weather-protective case around it with intricate wiring for the lighting. It's a little ridiculous.

"Ah," Rocky says, and nods slowly. "The Rusted Turtle."

"*Golden*," Benny corrects her.

She squints and looks closer. "You sure about that?"

I turn to Sam. "If we'd found the turtle, it would never have gotten stuck up there."

"Wow, rude," Benny says. "Whatever, I don't care. I bet your list sucks anyway."

It's a taunt.

And I'm pathetic because I feel my hackles rise as Sam casts me a quick look.

"Our list is *super* cool," I insist indignantly.

A group of cackling, tiny witches dash away from one of the carnival games. They run between us with a huge, stuffed cat in their clutches. "We won!" one of them screams, and Sam mutters a curse under his breath. It was the game where he lost all his money.

"Tonight is even a double feature for our super cool list," I continue to Benny, who rolls his eyes, but I'm a very stubborn Taurus. "First is the costume contest, and later tonight we're going to bury a time capsule." The box is currently in Sam's truck.

Benny stops and clutches his chest. "That's the cutest thing I've ever heard. I want in."

"*In?* It's our list," Sam argues.

"Rocky and I are part of this now," Benny insists. "We're here for the contest."

"And the senior day at the beach," Rocky adds. "That was on the list."

I widen my eyes at Rocky, who shrugs, enjoying the game now.

"See?" Benny says, vindication ringing in his voice.

I glance up at Sam. He's standing so close that his arm is touching my shoulder. He doesn't move away and neither do I. My brain folds up this feeling and tucks it away for me to obsess over later. "What would you even put in it?" I ask them. "Neither of you are prepared."

"Oh, Luisa, I am always prepared." Benny digs into a pocket and pulls out a firecracker.

"Do you always carry those around?"

He shrugs. "It's Halloween." He looks at Rocky. "What about you?"

"I don't know how to package existential dread for the future to find, so I guess—" She digs into a pocket and pulls out a Popsicle stick. "I can put this in." She shrugs. "I'll write a joke on it or something."

Mayor Simon steps up to the microphone. Feedback rings out, and we hurry toward the stage.

"Welcome to Port Coral's spookiest night!" Mayor Simon calls out, dramatically drawing out *spookiest* to full effect by deepening his voice to sound like Dracula. "We're so happy you're all here, and grateful for the donations to the local food bank." His service dog, Commander Shephard, stands at his feet like always. "And I hope you'll all join us in March for next year's Spring Fest."

Sam elbows me, but I don't want to think about my app right now. I check my wig in the reflection of his sunglasses. We're so close to winning, I can almost taste it.

Simon continues. "Our town's biggest festival, sponsored by El Mercado, will feature a regatta, concert, silent auction, and this year, a tour of the new facilities at the marina. There will be a presentation on the oyster reefs—"

"Get to the winners already!" someone shouts.

Mayor Simon sighs. "All right, Gladys. We've tallied the votes, and the winner of tonight's costume contest is..." Simon unfolds the paper in his hand. Without thinking, I grab Sam's hand, and he squeezes back. "The ninja mermaid!"

I drop Sam's hand and look around. "Who?"

There's confusion throughout the square until one of

the Avenger viejitos points at Rocky. "Her. She's the ninja mermaid."

She looks affronted. "I'm *Mermista*."

"Rocky, you won!" I tell her, halfway laughing because it's so perfect.

"What?" she asks, still confused.

"You won the costume contest," Benny says, and gestures toward the stage, starting the applause. Everyone follows suit.

"Oh my god, I won," Rocky mutters to herself, then looks at me as it dawns on her. "I won!"

Sam and I not winning technically means this one item won't be completed as written, but it doesn't matter—because as I watch Rocky go up onstage and accept the award of a half-off coupon to the diner, I cheer like she's won the lottery.

Sam drives us to the middle school and parks in the empty lot later that night. After discovering our old videos, I watched them all. I turn to him now. "I wonder whatever happened to that stray cat that led us here?"

He grins as he grabs the box and a shovel. "Leading new kids on their own adventures."

Benny looks doubtful after hearing about our first trip out here. "Yeah, that cat's probably catching the lizards inside our store."

We follow the trail to the woods behind the school. We take careful steps lit only by the flashlights on our phones.

"Are you sure there's a path? I see nothing," Rocky says, unfamiliar with our old school.

"Where we're going, we don't need roads," I tell her.

We scream when Benny shoots off one of his firecrackers.

"Sorry!" he yelps, and puts his lighter away.

Sam stops just before the tree we've been looking for. He stabs the shovel into the dirt so it'll stay in place, then hands me the box before holding up his camera.

"It has a face," Rocky says, confused.

I smile as I walk up to it. "Because it's a very old, wise tree." I know those eyes, nose, and mouth are decorations anyone can buy at a gardening store, but out here in this clearing—and with us in our costumes beneath moonlight—it still feels like finding magic. I turn to Sam with a playful smile. "We made it."

Sam's face softens, and maybe he realizes all the ways I mean it.

"Don't people usually bury the time capsule as kids and dig it up their senior year?" Benny asks, frowning in thought.

"Well, we forgot, but we're here now," I say. "We'll come back in another ten years or something."

"Don't think I won't hold y'all to it," Benny says.

Sam turns off the camera, then grabs the shovel and

begins to dig. I glance through the contents: a pair of drumsticks, his ancient iPod we used to listen to, my old Nintendo 3DS with a copy of *Fire Emblem Fates*, a can of my favorite pineapple soda, and a picture of Jupiter. It's everything we agreed on years ago, but I spot two other pictures. One is of Sam and his family a couple of years ago. They're somewhere up north, all of them laughing in the snow.

"Tennessee," he says, and I glance up to see him studying the picture. The other one is of him and me, sitting on the curb in front of his house. We look nine or ten. His arm is around me, and my smile takes up half my face. "I made copies of that one if you want one."

"I do." My throat is tight as it hits me that despite lost years, we've managed to get here and do this together.

Rocky throws in her Popsicle stick with its scribbled joke. (*The past, present, and future all walked into a bar... It was tense.*) And, as promised, Benny offers a firecracker. I place the box in the hole and Sam buries it. A time capsule for the past.

"See you in the future," I tell it.

Sam drops off Benny and then Rocky, and when we reach our street, there are still a few straggling trick-or-treaters. My parents are at an event at the college, and my brother had to be home by nine, and me by eleven. Five years difference in age, two hours in curfew. Sam walks me to the end of the driveway, and I yank off my wig.

"I had fun tonight," he says, his voice quiet.

"Me too." I wish I knew how to prolong the night. I could ask him to hang out. We're friends now, but nerves hit hard when I imagine him in my room again, and home alone this time. The question is on the tip of my tongue when we hear the screech of tires and a scream. I spin around to see a car stopped, a mangled bike in the road in front of the headlights.

Sam is already running toward it.

Sam

I RUN DOWN the street with my heart in my throat, every sound swallowed by the roaring in my ears because the closer I get, the more certain I am that I know that bike. I remember riding alongside it. Always having to fix the chain back when it was Lou's. I reach it first.

Max. I reach Max first.

His face is ashen and frozen. He's bleeding and one of his arms looks wrong.

Lou screams when she reaches us and falls to her knees on his other side. "Max! Oh my god!" Her sobs turn Max paler.

"You're okay," I tell him, then Lou. "He's okay."

"Okay? He just got hit by a freaking car!" She turns to someone beyond us. "You hit my brother with your freaking car!"

"Lou, your phone. Call 911."

Max swallows a scream, and the hand on his good arm latches on to one of mine. His voice a whisper, he asks me, "Am I dead?" Arm. Face. Bloody scratches from falling so hard on the gravel. The driver is freaking out somewhere behind me, and Lou is talking to the operator on her phone, but I ignore everything except Max.

"Give me your coat," I tell Lou, and she whips it off. I hold it to the deepest scratch to stop the bleeding. "Remember how Lou never used to let you play in the treehouse?" I ask Max, shifting so I can still grip his hand firmly.

"What?" His teeth chatter.

"The treehouse," I say, my voice steady and calm. "Lou never let you follow us up there."

Comprehension comes into Max's eyes. "Yeah. I thought it was because y'all were kissing."

I laugh and shake my head. "Nope, it was because she was afraid you would fall and get hurt." I nod toward Lou. "She liked you all along, man."

I hear the sirens, and ice water hits my veins. I don't dare let go of Max's hand.

The ambulance flies down our street, stopping a few feet away. The fire truck stops on our other side. Our mostly dark street is now lit with flashing red lights. Just like the last time they came for Dad.

"Excuse me, son," one of the medics says to me.

"Dan!" Lou nearly cries, recognizing him.

"It's okay," Dan tells her, then Max. I stumble back as they work. A brace goes around Max's neck. They pick him up and settle him on the stretcher and into the ambulance. Lou grabs my hand, and suddenly I'm climbing in beside her in the back of the ambulance, even as panic strangles me.

The driver takes off, and my stomach lurches with a rush of nausea. I silently watch as Dan talks to Max and checks his vitals. Machines beep and my heart stutters with each sound. I think of Dad's terrible cough, his gasps for air. Even in the ICU at the end, I'd hoped. Maybe he would get better like before, and this time I would be better, too. A better son, a better brother. I wouldn't take a single moment for granted, and I'd ask him all the things I still wondered. I would collect as many of his memories as I could, so that when he did go, I would be ready. I would know how to grieve him.

"He's okay, right?" Lou asks Dan.

I grit my teeth and close my eyes.

"He's okay," Dan assures her.

"He'll be okay, Sam. He's a fighter. He's strong and he beat it before."

And then, *"I'm so sorry, Sam."*

I open my eyes and look at Dan, who smiles a little when he says, "Smart kids wear their helmets, and Max is brilliant, right, Max?"

"Right," Max says thickly.

I lean back and try to remember my breaths. Dan glances at me. "You did good."

"I had no idea what to do," I admit. Steady breaths through my nose to keep the nausea back. The ride is fast and loud as we race through town.

"You kept him still and calm, and Lou called us. A great night for smart kids, and let me tell you, we don't often see that on Halloween." Dan's tone is harried but friendly. He doesn't look much older than my dad would be.

Lou presses her hands to her face. "I need to call my parents." She grabs her phone, and though I can't hear her mother's side of the conversation, I remember what it is to get an urgent, panicked call like this. There's never enough time to prepare or to be reassured. There's only a desperate plea to get to the hospital as quickly as you can.

Lou squeezes my hand. "Hey." In her solemn look, I know she's worried about me. But I'm not the one on the stretcher.

"Dan, this is Sam Alvarez." She turns, introducing us. "He's my neighbor and friend."

"Nice to meet you, McFly," Dan says. "I'm a friend of the Patterson family. My husband works with their mom."

"Malcolm is an advisor at Port Coral Community College," Lou explains.

"I actually met him there, back when I was taking paramedic courses," Dan adds.

"Scandalous," Lou says on a laugh, and it feels like the

conversation is meant to distract me. And it's working. My breath comes steadier as the roiling nausea dissipates. The medical equipment and sounds are still unnerving, but Dan's competence as he tracks, talks, and heals is a steady beacon in a storm.

Everything moves quickly once we reach the hospital, where I lead Lou to the waiting room. I know the way well.

An hour later, my hands fall between my knees as my leg bounces in the familiar chair. Somehow, it's always this one.

I curl forward and wait for Lou, who went to see her brother. Her parents had arrived shortly thereafter and rushed to see him, too.

Waiting rooms are terrible places with awful, uncomfortable chairs. The long faces and sterile corners. It's clean and cold, and the emptiest place in the world when it becomes the unexpected fork in the road from where you have to get up and leave without your person.

Sometime later, a hand touches my back. Lou presses her face to my shoulder. Her breath catches. "Mom and Dad are with him. He broke his arm and three ribs and got gravel in some cuts on his face, but he's okay." The word comes out high and riddled with disbelief. Lou is barely holding it together. "Thank god my stupid, beautiful brother always wears a helmet." She smiles, but I see the effort she's putting forth to hold it. The night is finally catching up to her.

I wrap an arm around her, and she immediately buries her face in my neck. I make soothing sounds as she cries against me. "I know he's okay," she whispers, sounding so bewildered. "Why am I crying like this?"

"You went through so much fear so fast, and you can never process it in the moment. Now it's all hitting you in one big wave."

Another tremor of emotion racks through her, and I hold her through it.

She sits back and wipes her face. The quiet noise of the waiting room's TV reaches us, and I know we're not alone, but I can't look away from her. She exhales, and I press my forehead to hers and breathe in her warm scent. "Why do you always smell like coconut and roses?" I ask quietly.

"It's my leave-in conditioner." She sniffs. "And the rose-water mist I stole from my sister. I've already killed half the bottle," she explains, sounding rueful. "But I keep spritzing my face all the time."

Lou tips her face up as she leans closer and I realize she's going to kiss me. And this time, it won't be about anyone but us. I duck my head closer.

But over her shoulder, I spy her sister walk into the room.

"Elena," I choke out.

Lou jerks back from me. *"What?"*

I jump to my feet. "Your sister is here."

Lou whips around and spots Elena by the terrible coffee with her boyfriend, Nick. Mrs. Patterson flies into the room right behind them and immediately hugs me. "Thank you," she whimpers. She lets go and hugs Lou and pulls Elena into them. "My babies," she says, her voice strangled.

As they hug, I reach past them to shake Nick's hand. I remember him from school.

Mrs. Patterson sucks in a watery breath and looks at her daughters. "Your dad is with Max, but I need coffee."

"It's awful," I warn her, then try to clear the rough emotion still lodged in my throat.

She smiles softly and squeezes my arm before pouring two cups, one for Mr. Patterson.

Lou is now surrounded by her family, and my adrenaline is long gone. "I have to get home." She looks at me with her big brown eyes, and I wish I could say something more, but there'll be time. Because tonight, everyone lives.

At home, I tell Mom what happened and have a cup of tea with Abuela. And then I go upstairs, get out of my dirty clothes, and take a long, hot shower. Afterward, I get on my computer and scroll over to the community college's website. I find details about the paramedic and EMS program. When I'm still awake at three in the morning, it isn't because of anxiety or grief.

It's because of new ideas.

NOVEMBER

"SAM! GOOD TO see you, welcome to El Mercado," Mrs. Peña greets me at the entrance of the bodega after school. "Here's your apron, now follow me."

I hardly have a moment to put it on over my head before she takes off. I hurry after her, tying the strings in a knot behind my back.

"You know the store, but I give every new kid the tour so later, when you tell me, 'Oh, Mrs. Peña, I didn't know that,' I can say, '¡Mentira! It was in the tour!'"

"I would never."

"Well, then you're one step above Benny. Here are the registers, we've got two, but with you working stock, you probably won't be up here. That's my niece Paula—she's a flirt, so watch out."

Paula unwraps a lollipop and pops it into her mouth with a wink.

"You pay for that?" Mrs. Peña asks her.

Paula makes a face and digs into her apron pocket.

This past summer, I was the one to get Benny a job at the pool company, but now he's the one to hook me up since Emilio doesn't have extra work right now. I follow Benny's mom down aisles as she points out each section. When we reach the deli, she gestures to her husband behind the counter.

"Rafa, you know our new stock boy, Sam Alvarez."

He stops slicing the pork and wipes his hands on the towel over his shoulder. "Samuel?" he asks, and I nod. That was my dad. Mr. Peña offers me his hand over the display.

When he disappears into the kitchen, Mrs. Peña smiles at me like I've done something extraordinary. Even the tattooed guy with the dark beard who's unpacking pastries shakes his head with a small smile.

"What?" Mrs. Peña asks him.

"It took him six months before he shook my hand," he says. "And I bring the pastelitos."

Mrs. Peña laughs, a big, round sound that pulls a smile from me. There are trays of rice: white, yellow, and my favorite, arroz congrí. The smells of onions, garlic, and pepper are heavy in the air. "We started as a corner shop, now we have a ventanita and dinner service and are even sponsoring a festival, thanks to his girlfriend." She shoots her thumb over her shoulder toward the baker, whose smile is even bigger now. "But everyone still calls us a bodega."

"I think it's nice," I say. When her brows shoot up, I hurry to say, "You expanded, but still celebrate your roots." I shrug, embarrassed.

"One calls it a tienda, another calls it a bodega. You call it *nice*. You're a good kid, Sam. How'd you get to be friends with mine?" She laughs at her own joke and motions for me to continue following her.

"*¡Tía!* Phone!" Paula shouts from the front of the store.

"Ay carajo." She digs into the pocket of her apron and fishes out a phone without slowing her pace. "*¡No me grites!*" she shouts back before answering in a calmer tone. "Hi, this is Carmen—no, no, that's not what we agreed on. Since when?" She listens with a frown. "Go on back."

I nervously retie my apron.

"You, Sam," she says, and I start. She waves at the swinging double doors behind us. "Paula's brother—Junior—manages stock and will show you the ropes."

"Right, yes. Thank you! Again. I mean, for the job and opportunity and tour and—"

"Yes, yes, go, child." She shoos me away with a laugh before scowling quickly. "No, not you," she says to the person on the phone, and rushes off.

I enter the back room of El Mercado and find a table,

TV, bright throw rug, and comfortable chairs. Beyond it are a mountain of boxes. Benny's cousin, Junior, is stacking them on a dolly. "Hi, I'm Sam," I say, moving forward with my hand out.

He pushes the dolly into it. "Perfect. Get those plantains out before they turn yellow and everyone blames the lack of tostones on me." He slaps my shoulder. "Good to meet you, kid. You like hip-hop?"

"What?" I ask, trying to keep up.

"The plantains, man. Get them out, and then I'll play you my latest mix."

Four hours later, I'm finally sitting down with a plate of the food I've been drooling over all evening. Junior, true to his word, plays me his latest mix of lo-fi beats that he's about to post online.

"Does this one help you feel calm enough to study?" he asks, watching me closely.

Stocking at the bodega might not be *the* answer as far as work goes, but it feels like a pretty good one right now. They feed me, talk to me in easy, comfortable Spanglish, and don't make me feel small when I mess up or switch to English. And everyone seems very impressed about that earlier handshake with Mr. Peña.

"I heard my dad adopted you," Benny tells me later. "Welcome to the fam, muchacho."

His shoulders droop as he spies Junior. "I told you, the

last mix was better. All these dripping-water sounds you're adding are not relaxing."

Junior sucks his teeth with a hiss. "Dang, all right. Where you been?"

"Helping Lou," Benny says, and I perk up. "She was picking up a late dinner for her fam. Everyone is asking about her brother." He shakes his head, and we all grow quiet. It's been two days since the accident, and according to Lou's last text, Max is home with an entire family to hover over him. Junior crosses himself before returning to work.

Once he's out of earshot, I turn to Benny and lower my voice. "I'm thinking of going to the community college next year."

"Yeah? It's a good school." He tilts his chin toward Junior. "He goes there. What changed your mind? You want to get your two-year degree or something?"

"Or something" is all I'm ready to admit to yet. I want to talk to Lou about this idea first. She knows me and will be honest if she thinks I'm running on grief. But thinking about Lou stirs up other questions and doubts. I glance at Benny again. "I also need some advice."

Benny waves for me to continue. He has been a supportive sounding board this year, but talking about relationships is new for us. Tasha was right when she told Lou that I don't do them. Benny's not known for getting serious, either, but I'm desperate. "As you know, I've been hanging out with Lou again. And in that time...we kissed."

Benny's eyes widen and he leans closer. "Word?" He shakes his head, grinning. "Just 'friends' my ass. You should have said."

I check around to make sure no one else is close enough to hear. "The kiss is hard to explain. But then on Halloween night, after everything, it felt like she was about to kiss me again, but we were both running on adrenaline—and I think she might have been trying to thank me."

"Is that how people usually thank you?"

"And now I don't know if the ball is in my court." I drag my hands through my hair, then hold them there in frustration.

Benny looks confused by my turmoil. "Why don't you talk to her about it?"

"Because it's *Lou*," I say too loudly and then lower my voice. "I've messed up with her before, but we're finally hanging out again—and the last thing I want to do is ruin our friendship."

"Ask her to hang out in a way that has nothing to do with your list," he offers with a shrug. "See what happens then."

This stops me. The list brought us back together. If Lou hadn't found it and asked me for a ride to the beach that day, we would've gone a whole other year without speaking, and where would we be now?

Lou

BY FRIDAY, I'M exhausted from my sudden popularity. Or rather, Max's. Everyone at school has stopped to ask me about him after hearing what happened on Halloween. "He's halfway to his superhero origin story," I assure classmates who never speak to me. And Max is fine. He even got two weeks off from school. Lucky dog.

At lunch, I head to the table Rocky and I share. She isn't here yet, so I set out the containers of leftovers from the bodega. I have not only a beef empanada but also carne con papas with rice. Cubans know their food.

Sam drops down onto the bench beside me.

I hurry to swallow, without choking, the forkful of rice I'd just shoveled into my mouth. Sam and I have different classes, and come lunchtime, he has his long-standing group of band friends—and I have Rocky.

"How's Max?" he asks for the hundredth time in the past several days.

I take a sip of my drink. "Still good."

His gaze jumps from my face to my lunch. He seems nervous. Or maybe hungry. I push my food toward him, but he only smiles a little and shakes his head.

"I want to talk to you," he says, his voice low and serious. His eyes meet mine for a beat before his gaze turns back to the table.

The rice in my stomach tumbles into a sudden somersault, because I've been avoiding this conversation all week. I know exactly what he wants to talk about. I almost kissed him again, and he's here to tell me that practice kissing is one thing but waiting-room kissing is another. Sam knows how inexperienced I am. And I know he's not the having-a-girlfriend type, so now he wants to let me down gently before I get the wrong idea.

Rocky sits down on the bench across from us and slides a curious glance between Sam and me as she pops open the lid on her lunch. Sam leans closer to me in a bid for privacy. "Are you free this afternoon?" he asks.

Now that this awkward conversation is right in front of me, I'd rather get it over with than dwell on it all afternoon. But I also know my embarrassment will be easier to navigate if we're alone. "Sure," I tell him. He asks me to meet him by his truck in the parking lot after dismissal, then offers a quick but friendly nod to Rocky before returning to his own habitat.

"What was that about?" Rocky asks. She offers me her lunch and I do the same. The swap has become a lunchtime routine between us. She takes a cube of potato and piece of steak, and I grab one of her dumplings. We both chew happily before sliding our containers back to where each started.

"I tried to kiss him in a moment of weakness," I tell her.

Rocky's brows shoot up. "Really?" She grins. "So, it *is* a couple thing."

"Hardly," I admit. "My journey of becoming bolder almost got away from me in a moment of emotional vulnerability." I take a sip of my soda and set the can down like it's a stiff drink. "And now he will want to reestablish boundaries."

"Sounds fun."

I mime sticking my fork in my eye, and Rocky laughs.

Since we live less than a mile from school, I've taken to walking home this year with the majority of the freshmen. But after today's last bell, I head to the parking lot and find Sam waiting by his truck. He looks so tense, and regret slams into me. I made everything weird between us, and now he can barely look at me. When I reach his side,

159

the corner of his mouth flickers into the ghost of a smile before he opens the door for me. So polite. Kill me now.

I get inside and drag my clammy palms down my jeans. It's not until we're out of the parking lot that he says, "I have an appointment with the advisor at Port Coral Community."

"Wait. *What?*" I blurt out, confused as I realize we're not headed home but toward the college. "You're meeting Malcolm?"

"Yeah, and I'm hoping you'll come with me." His hand clutches the gearshift, and I'm racing to catch up. He doesn't want to talk about the almost kiss. He wants me to go with him to his meeting with Malcolm. This casts his nervous energy in an entirely different light.

"What's the meeting about?" I ask carefully.

He slides me a quick glance. "Remember how Dan mentioned taking paramedic classes the other night? I looked them up."

I'm too surprised to say anything. Sam had looked so pale and lost in the ambulance. Like it was the last place he wanted to be.

"Emergency Medical Services Technology," he goes on. "I could become an EMT. Or a paramedic, depending on how many classes I take."

I drop back in my seat. This is a lot of new information to get when I was expecting the conversation to be about something else entirely. This isn't about us but Sam's future.

I'm here for support because Sam is thinking about college again. I recalibrate as I reach for the aux cable. "You mind?"

He glances at it like he forgot it was there. "Go ahead."

I plug it into my phone. "What are we thinking... Chill vibes? Indie pop? Oh, this one is titled Sexy As Folk. Now that sounds like a really good, weird time."

I get the flash of a smile. His phone rings in the console, and I see that it's his mom. He doesn't answer. Mrs. Alvarez is a small woman who exudes strength, from her muscled shoulders, killer calves, and a steady fire banked in her eyes; something about her posture tells the world she may be sad, but she could definitely run a mile at the drop of a hat.

We get to the college, and Sam pulls into a visitor spot. I unbuckle my seat belt, but when I go to open my door, I notice he hasn't moved yet. I settle back into the seat.

"This is just to get information," I reassure him. "You're not signing up for anything. This is a sidequest. A fact-finding mission. This is not a point of no return on the main mission."

Sam tips his head back against the headrest as a rough laugh escapes him.

"And being an EMT could be really cool," I go on. "Remember whenever we used to play Spells & Order, you were always the healer?"

I watch his expression flit between surprise and awe. "I love the way you see the world," he says, turning to look at me with a grateful smile. "I'm so glad we're friends again."

Right. It's a much-needed reminder. Check out me being an awesome friend and not at all thinking about kissing him, or his hands and how to get them on me again.

"This can be another addition to the bucket list," I tell him, safely dragging my thoughts away from my confusing new feelings. "Sᴀᴍ ᴡɪʟʟ ɢᴏ ᴏɴ EMT sɪᴅᴇǫᴜᴇsᴛ. Even if it doesn't work out, it'll give you something to check off."

He glances away. "The list. Yeah." After he takes one more deep breath, we get out of the truck and set off to explore Port Coral Community College. The campus has recently been renovated, with updated buildings that showcase lots of glass and modern, curving lines. Food trucks are parked at the curb near the main entry. Students dot the grassy areas, many of them stretched out on blankets with books in their hands. But there are also younger kids and parked strollers and people who look older than what I would assume is the typical college age.

"What do you think?" Sam asks when we stop in front of one of the older buildings that's shaded by towering oaks covered with Spanish moss.

"I do love a good tree."

"The EMT classes are in there," he says. "I could be certified in one semester."

There's awe in his voice, and I wonder how much research Sam has put into this. I deeply relate to an idea grabbing hold of your entire self until the only way to deal with it is to throw yourself so far down the well of information that your brain becomes a series of open tabs. But this is Sam. And while this might be a sidequest, it's significant that he's standing here, considering an unexpected path.

He glances at his watch. It's still the calculator one from Halloween. "Time for my appointment."

"Not a point of no return," I remind him.

He exhales a slow breath. "Sidequest."

We walk into the administration building, and I go to take a seat in the waiting room—but Sam stops and looks at me with wide, panicked eyes. "You should come and say hi," he says. "Let Malcolm know we know each other."

The uneasiness is so unlike Sam that I simply follow him.

When we get to his office, Malcolm looks up from his desk and smiles. He is a tall Black man whose style I would describe as library chic, and his office smells like old books and expensive candles. Over his radio, I can hear the sounds of British commentators and a soccer match. Malcolm loves Arsenal. He says it's his tragic flaw.

"What are you doing here?" he asks me with a pleased smile. Malcolm is an important member of Team Get Lou into a Good College. After I helped the community college upgrade its *very* outdated website, he wrote one of my letters of recommendation and helped with my personal statement. "We've still got time to finalize your applications, but I'm dying of suspense over which schools ended up on the final draft of your list."

I hesitate, glancing between him and Sam. "Your appointment is actually with him," I say.

Sam and Malcolm shake hands and greet each other, friendly enough, but they both look at me—and I know I won't be able to escape until I answer his question and tell him—and Sam—about my schools. "Well, you know the big players: Georgia Tech, Vanderbilt, and Duke. The golden gooses. Or is it just *goose*? Anyway, then we've also got Miami, UCF, and Florida."

"I've never heard anyone be so blasé about the last three," Malcolm says.

"Yeah, sure, but they're not that far."

He laughs, but it's his college advisor laugh. The eternally patient one. "Florida is in the top ten of all public universities and consistently rising. UCF has an incredible computer science program at a fraction of the cost of comparable schools. Miami is as prestigious as your *geese* and has only a thirty-two percent acceptance rate."

I don't know how to explain what distance has to do with anything. How my idea of success is measured by how far I get from my starting point. But this is the first that Sam is hearing about all my college choices, and I don't even know how to talk to him about our kiss, let alone this. I point between them. "Not my appointment."

To Sam, I say, "I'll be outside. Be careful with that one." I nod toward Malcolm. "He's very good at his job."

Malcolm laughs as I race out of his office. I head down the walkway to a covered area with tables and take a seat. A few people are scattered around, and I try to visualize Sam in this space next year—and it terrifies me how easy it is to see him here. I've known Sam as only two people who've grown up together can, and I've watched him grow up from across the street, and I know that when he discovers something, he takes the time to get it right. Sam is patience and thoughtful consideration, and that's why I know this *isn't* a sidequest for him. On Halloween night, Sam figured out his road forward. Or at least part of it.

I check my phone. It's been a half hour. Too anxious to sit, I get up and pace. Seeing all the different students crisscrossing the campus makes me realize the *community* aspect of schools like this. And that despite all these months of trying to paint myself into someone else's idea of success, I still can't see my path as clearly as Sam can see his.

"Luisa?"

I spin around and see a beautiful woman wearing a fitted white button-up blouse, charcoal-gray slacks, and heels. She looks as academic and modern as the updated architecture around us. My mother, the professor.

"Hey, Mom."

"What are you doing here?" Mom asks, and I notice the two students with her. I offer them a quick wave.

"Waiting for Sam," I say. "He's meeting with Malcolm."

She looks surprised. "Is he applying to attend school here?"

I shrug. "Maybe. Jury's still out."

"You two have been hanging out a lot again."

I subtly jerk my head toward her students, reminding her we're not at home. But I can see the way her brain is working—drawing the line between Sam's reappearance in my life and his intention to stay in town.

In all our list making, she never once asked me if I wanted to stay in Port Coral.

Sam strolls up to us with a folder in his hands. "Hey, Mrs. Patterson."

"Hi, Sam." Mom's smile is distracted. To me she says, "I'll see you at home." She kisses my cheek, and I catch the scent of her sunscreen and the citrus perfume Dad buys her for her birthday every year. Something in my chest caves in a way that makes me feel like I'm ten, but not in an embarrassing way. A safe one, because this is my mom, and I trust her, but I also wish she didn't confuse me so much.

On the way back to the truck, I ask Sam how the meeting went.

"Really good," he says, tapping the folder against his hand. "I think I'm going to apply to go here."

"Hey!" I push him playfully and he laughs.

"And I'm going to the fire station tomorrow. It's an informal thing where Dan can show me around and explain their volunteer Fire Explorer Program to me. Since he did the EMS program here, he wants to show me the ropes."

"Is that part of the medic training?"

"It's a way to get some experience around the station, as far as training and equipment. Another fact-finding mission."

"Right," I say with a grin, but I already know. These are big first steps.

Before we get in the truck, Sam grabs my hand, pulling me to a stop. "Do you want to go to a party?"

The question is so sudden and unexpected, I laugh. "What party?" Is he asking me *out*? This whole day has been a nonstop roller-coaster ride.

"They're having a homecoming thing tomorrow night," he explains, still holding my hand. "I can pick you up after I get back from the station. It'll be fun to go together."

My brain gets stuck on *together* and is shouting *yes*. But my mouth can't form the word as I fight the outrageous smile that's lighting up my chest, and I fear my eyes are glowing. I'm going into the avatar state. *Be cool, Lou, be cool.*

As I try to gather myself to agree without blinding him, Sam rushes on. "It's on the list. Go to an actual party," he says, from memory.

"The list," I finally croak. *Right.* Sam isn't asking me on a date. We're finishing the list. I let go of his hand. "Sure," I say, barely keeping the sad trombone of disappointment out of my voice. "Let's go to a party, Sam."

Sam

ON SATURDAY MORNING, I lie in bed for a long moment and try to figure out why everything feels off. I stretch my arms over my head and let them fall above me on the bed. Scratch my left shin with my other foot. Roll over and check my phone. My alarm set for nine AM hasn't gone off yet. And for the first time in months I didn't wake up at three AM.

I fall back onto the bed and stare at the ceiling in shock that melts into stunned relief. *I'm getting better.*

Maybe I just have to get to the other side of all these firsts. Because then I'll have felt it all, and this loss will finally feel survivable.

I roll out of bed and reach for the outfit I set out last night like a nervous kid before his first day of school. But it's not hanging over my desk chair where I left it. Or anywhere else in my room.

"Sam!" Cora yells once before opening the door. She bursts into my room and gasps. "Super gross. You're in your *underwear*," she draws out in disgust.

I pull on a pair of shorts. "Which is why you're supposed to knock first, Cora. Where's Abuela?"

"¡Papito! Desayuno!" Abuela calls from downstairs.

"Breakfast is ready, Papito," Cora drawls, then flicks me in the stomach. "No shirt, no service. Papito or not."

I throw on a shirt and find Mom and Abuela in the kitchen. "Has anyone seen my dress pants?" I ask, not naming names or pointing fingers but worried they're in the dryer.

Mom raises her brows but says nothing as she takes a drink of her coffee.

"Sí!" Abuela calls out, then comes over to happily grab my face. "Estoy feliz de que vengas a la iglesia."

"What? Oh no, that's not—" I shake my head, her hands still on my cheeks. "I'm not going to church, Abuela."

She lowers her hands with a disappointed huff and directs a sharp look at Mom.

Mom's weary expression tells me she can't believe Dad left her without backup on this one. Aside from Dad going to Mass with Abuela, my family has never been all that religious. As the firstborn, I was baptized, in Abuela's church, but we were never regulars.

"I'm really busy this weekend," I point out.

"Too busy for God?" Abuela switches to English for Mom, sometimes for Cora, and whenever she's deeply disappointed in me, as the Cuban Son.

"I have to go to the fire station."

This appeases her a little. "Ay, sí. Un bombero."

Cora dumps a bunch of LEGOs on the table. "What's a bombero?"

"It means 'firefighter' in Spanish," I say, then glance at Mom, who's now wringing her hands. The other night after dinner, I admitted to her that I was thinking about applying to Port Coral Community College, and the idea brought a smile to her face. One that signaled relief, because she assumed I was back on course but just wanted to take things slowly.

The smile fell when I mentioned an EMT certificate.

The questions in her eyes were as loud as the sirens whenever another ambulance came to pick up Dad. I know how the choice looks. Spontaneous. Driven by grief. The boy whose dad died wants to be a medic now? The thing is, I *don't* know if that's what I want, but I know how I felt watching Dan react.

As Mom finishes her coffee, I can see the hundred questions she wants to ask me, but there is a chasm between us now, one that neither of us is sure how to get across.

"Dan's going to show me around and explain the Fire Explorer Program they have for students who are interested."

"Since when do you want to be a firefighter?" Cora asks, focused on whatever she's making.

"I'm just curious about the medic stuff. What are you building?" I ask her, trying to place the figure in her hands to distract her from this line of questioning.

"A guillotine," she says.

"What?"

She shrugs. "What?"

Mom falls back on the couch. "Leave your sister alone."

I wave my hand toward her. "A guillotine, Mom."

"It's not sharp, she's fine," Mom says, like it's a fight she already had and isn't going through again.

The dryer beeps and I sigh. "Has anyone seen my pants?"

"Is this a formal thing?" Mom asks. "What about your suit?"

I never want to wear that thing again.

Abuela disappears behind her curtains and then whips them open. My pants are currently on the ironing board in the middle of her room. "Un momento," she says, and gets back to it.

I try not to wonder when she grabbed them out of my room.

Mom gets up and sidles close. "She wants to talk to you about God, and I can barely talk to you about what you're doing."

The pressure in me gives at the sight of even a hint of vulnerability in Mom. "You can ask me anything."

She smiles. "How was your meeting with the advisor?"

"Informative," I tell her. "The college offers an EMT technical certificate, but there's also a whole emergency medical services associate of science degree that includes the paramedic stuff. That one takes longer, of course. Malcolm showed me a suggested course sequence, and I could start with the typical freshman courses before getting into the EMS ones." As I tell her about the possible first and second year, her smile turns sad, and guilt hits me.

Not that long ago, Mom was the one working toward her associate of science.

"The community college is great," she says, smiling. "And if you go there, you can pop into the coffee shop and see me on your breaks."

"I'm just doing some reconnaissance, Mom. For my own curiosity. Because really, this would be another bill, and that's the last thing we need right now."

Her shoulders fall. "Don't look at it like that, Sam. It's an opportunity with the possibility of a great career. Between the advisor and this paramedic, you're already networking and meeting responsible professionals. And that *bill* would be a whole lot cheaper than a university, right?" She tries for lightness, so I give her a smile and wish the world would give my mom a break.

The nerves hit halfway to the fire station. I glance at the passenger side and wish Lou were with me. She'd take over my radio and map her way around this new, big idea in a way that made it less scary. I try to conjure up the smell of rose water and coconuts.

Instead I reach the station and feel my breathing get too fast and shallow.

I grip my truck's steering wheel with clammy hands. I'm supposed to meet Dan in eight minutes. If Dad were here, he would tell me I am already late.

Desperate, I grab the aux cable and hook it into my phone. With shaking hands, I hit shuffle. At the first beat, my eyes fly open and a laugh tumbles out of me. A Ray Barretto song, and one of Dad's favorites. One of his Saturday afternoon and it's sunny, let's grill something outside songs. Gonna wash my car, come scrub the tires songs. Watch me spin your mom around the kitchen songs. It's a slow, languid beat until the congas get fired up. *"This is your part, Sam,"* he always said, air-drumming and then bursting with pride when I was able to keep up and stay on beat.

My hands loosen from their tight grip on the steering wheel to play along. My breath steadies and I relax. And when the song ends, I get out of the truck to go find Dan.

Inside the station, there are three bays, but only one truck is parked, making it feel eerily quieter than the bustle I expected. Coats with last names stitched to them hang from hooks on one wall. Farther inside, there's an exercise bike alongside a weight bench in one corner, opposite a wall filled with coiled hoses. I try to take everything else in, but the little boy in me is internally screaming, *Fire truck!* I finally spot Dan.

"Hey, Sam, good to see you," Dan greets me, then leads me farther into the building. We walk past a kitchen and communal living space with a TV and several recliners, and in the back, a long table. Several people sit around it, and they all look younger than me. They watch me openly and I recognize Jordan, the freshman on cymbals in marching band. He lifts his chin in greeting.

"Is he here to volunteer?" a girl asks. Her dark hair is slicked back in a tight ponytail.

"He's here to learn about the Fire Explorer Program," Dan tells her. He then says to me, "As you can see, it's designed to give teens a chance to see if they might be interested in a career in firefighting or EMS. We meet every Tuesday after school. There will be texts to study as well as practical exams. It's about responsibility, exposure, and experience."

"But he's so old," the girl says. I don't disagree. She looks about Max's age.

"You can't just call people old, Adriana," one of the other kids points out.

"What would I have to do?" I ask Dan. "If I did try to join."

174

"You need to attend three meetings before receiving an application, but since you're already eighteen, we shouldn't need your mom's permission."

I haven't needed my mom to sign a permission slip since last year. *What am I doing here?*

Dan introduces everyone around the table. "That's Jordan, Angel, Adriana, and Eli. Also, that big guy over there is Little Tim. He'll be your instructor if you join." Tim has to be almost seven feet tall. He stirs his coffee and doesn't argue with his nickname. As someone who goes by Papito most days, I find a commonality in this. "Tim, why don't you tell Sam a little bit more about the program?"

I pull out a chair and take a seat at the table.

Dan's phone rings. "I'll be in the office. Meet me there when you're done here, Sam." He looks to Little Tim. "Start him with something good."

"Will do," Tim agrees, and I start to feel nervous again as he looms over my side of the table. "Today we're doing a rescue simulation, and you all get to show off those knots you've been practicing."

"Are we using the dummy again?" Jordan asks.

Little Tim grins at me. "We've got a new volunteer."

Those knots all get tied on a rope that is wrapped around my torso and legs in different configurations as they practice getting someone out of some dire situation. And it takes a *lot* of tries. But after being tied up and dragged across the floor for almost an hour, I go to find Dan. When he sees me, he laughs.

"That shirt of yours was white when you got here." He shakes his head. "Someone needs to sweep the bay floor."

"Technically, I think I just did," I say, and he laughs again, and I can't help but grin. It was definitely a weird first day, but I have knots to practice and answers for what I might do in an emergency. That new, vital information is filed away with a sense of relief. I take the seat in front of him.

"You already talked to Malcolm, so you know that if you're truly interested in going my route, it's one semester for your EMT certification, but it could be three more years to become a paramedic."

"Yeah, but in that time, I could be working while earning my associate degree." I'm already using possessive words. *My degree.*

Instead of everything breaking, the pieces of my life are falling into place, and I almost don't even know what to do with the optimism. It's like my compass has finally found a way out of the fog.

Dan spins in his office chair one way, then the other a little, and it reminds me of Ms. Francis. But instead of pictures of Dobermans behind him, it's a wall of pictures of his husband and daughter. "And don't forget, you can apply to be a volunteer firefighter right after you graduate from high school. Spots are limited, but we'll be taking applications in the spring—and if you get a spot, that'll give you experience, training, and possible credits in the meantime until the EMT course starts next fall. We'll even pay for the certification." Dan must see my processing this information, because he smiles and claps his hands. "I got another one, Little Tim!"

Lou

TONIGHT'S PARTY IS taking place at some football player's house, which means that I am going to an honest-to-god house party. Unfortunately, I still don't have a car, so I told Sam I would meet him there; that way he doesn't have to drive all the way back home from the fire station to pick me up and then also go pick up Rocky, who I of course invited. All of this is why my very pregnant sister's boyfriend is driving us instead, with Elena along for the ride.

"Thanks for the ride, Nick," I tell him from the back seat of the Honda.

"No problem," he says, sounding chipper.

Elena groans in the front seat. "I need to pee again."

"Well hold it, because you can't pee at the party," I tell her.

She laughs. "Oh yes I can." My phone's GPS chirps out the next direction and Elena whistles, impressed. "A beach house? Hold up." She twists around in her seat. "Time for some big sister advice."

"Okay, fine," I concede. "You can pee when we get there."

Elena points between Rocky and me. "Stay together, don't drink anything you didn't pour yourself, and don't call your ex." Elena turns a flirtatious smile on Nick. "That's how we got back together, remember, babe?"

Nick puts a hand on her knee, and I gag.

"This is my first Port Coral party," Rocky says. She's wearing a short-sleeved burnt orange button-up tucked into slim jeans. She makes the simple outfit look like high fashion. "I promise to commit no grand larceny this time."

"Always wise." Nick laughs, probably thinking she's joking.

The street is busy up ahead, and Nick slows the car. The house is two stories with a detached two-car garage that is currently open, with a band playing inside.

"Oh my god, there's a band, babe!" Elena looks at Nick. "Maybe we can stay for a little while?"

I shoot a look at Nick, who shakes his head imperceptibly. Another point in his column.

Rocky and I hop out. Elena sticks her head out the window. "Sam is giving both of you a ride home, right?" I reassure her that he is, but Elena is transfixed on the band. "Whose party is this?"

"Sam said it's some homecoming thing for last year's seniors who are back—" I stop as I watch a hundred emotions fly over my sister's face.

"From their first semester at school." She sighs a little. "I'm definitely not peeing in there. Get me out of here, babe."

They go and we head down the driveway. I recognize social circles from school. Some of the crowd spills into the yard that leads down to the beach. It's noisy and wild and like being at school on my off hours, but without any of the proper adult supervision. I try to rein in my social anxiety as we move toward the garage.

"Don't forget to help me be cool," I tell Rocky. She's a bisexual girl from Miami who stole a car once. No one is cooler than Rocky.

"You're already cool, Lou." She sighs deeply, then glances over my ensemble of jeans and the striped blue sweater I pulled over my T-shirt because it's finally chilly enough for outerwear. "Just relax."

"Relax, sure." I sidle up even closer to her so no one else hears me. "This is my first party, and there's an actual band in that garage. I walked into a teen movie without knowing my lines."

Rocky pulls me aside and takes a deep breath, gesturing for me to copy her. She doesn't stop until I do. We then continue our journey, and when we reach the garage, I recognize the band from posters around town: The Electric. The only thing I know about them other than their name is that Benny's older sister, Ana Maria, is the drummer. The song they're currently playing is loud, but chill. I spy Benny, who slips away from a group of girls and looks delighted to see us.

"Are you everywhere in this town?" I ask him, relieved to find a friend so quickly. Maybe this won't be so bad.

"Luisa, I *am* this town." As if to prove his point, a Black guy with a skateboard yells, "Benny, get over here!" Benny waves at us in a *be back in a minute* gesture.

I pull out my phone to text Sam.

I'm here

"Sam said they have food, right?" Rocky asks as we stand separately from everyone else, but here, at least.

My phone buzzes.

I'm out back!

I look up at Rocky with concern. "He says he's out back. Am I supposed to go find him?"

"I would assume so."

"But he invited me, so he should come find me. I don't want to go traipsing around some stranger's house to look for him. Oh god, I hate this already."

The song ends, and feedback screams from the speakers as Ana Maria jumps forward, flips her wild mane of dark, curly hair back, and grabs the mic from the guitarist. "We'll be back in fifteen, but until then enjoy this mix." She points at someone in the audience. "Never say I didn't do anything for you, Junior."

The crowd shifts as people leave the garage and move toward the beach. I take a step closer to Rocky as the driveway gets busier. She puts a soothing hand on my arm and squeezes gently. "I bet I can still hotwire a car," she offers, and I laugh.

"Lou! Rocky!" Sam calls out as he comes around the corner with a huge smile on his face. He came to find me after all. He's in an untucked dress shirt with the sleeves rolled up to his elbows. He looks disheveled but happy. "You're here!"

"That's what I said," I joke as I slip my phone into my back pocket. "How was the fire station?" I've been dying to know all day.

Sam's eyes are bright, like he's been laughing for hours. It's a stark difference from yesterday at the college when he was so edgy with nerves. "They tied me up and dragged me around, practicing a rescue. It was amazing."

"Wow," I say. His shirt *is* a bit of a mess. "Big day."

He laughs. "We're all out back, come on." He grabs my hand and leads us through the crowd, and it hits me that I'm an idiot for not considering the fact that Sam inviting me to a party wouldn't be like Halloween, because this is *his* turf, and *his* people.

But there is no reason to be anxious about that. Because I'm super chill.

"Hey, you hear my song, college boy?" a guy calls out, and Sam laughs as he continues to lead me forward, past the inside joke and nickname and onto the very busy wooden deck. There are speakers that are playing the music from the garage. Down on the beach is a bonfire. Groups walk between both, plastic cups in hand.

"There's *alcohol*," I whisper in a hiss to Rocky, who says, "You don't have to drink it." She glances around, then glares at Sam. "I still don't see food."

"Inside," Sam tells her. "Big sandwich platter. I highly recommend it."

I pull my hand out of his and move to follow Rocky. Where she goes, I go.

"*Sam!*"

We all stop and turn toward the speakers from which Sam's name is shouted again.

"I think it's Tasha," says a boy I recognize from drumline. "She must have grabbed the mic." They all laugh like this is a thing Tasha is known to do. "Go get your girl, Sam."

His easy laugh turns into a startled wince. "What? No." He slides me a quick look. "Tasha is not my girl."

"Uh, yeah, she mentioned that." Because I was once silly enough to worry about *girlfriend privileges*.

"No more hookups in the band room?" the boy asks with another laugh, then turns to include Rocky and me on the joke. "They were once caught in the tuba shelf. Legendary."

While some part of me is happy to be in on an inside joke, the rest of me is ready for the ground to swallow me. Sam sends me a panicked look. "We're not together," he says, shaking his head. "We haven't—"

"No details, buddy," I squeak out, and then school my expression because I know we're not together, and I am *so* cool with this. But it must not be working, because Sam is worriedly frowning at me like I'm someone's little sister who snuck into the R-rated movie.

"*Sam!*" Tasha whispers, feedback hissing through the speakers. "There are drums in here!"

Ana Maria shoves past us with murder in her eyes, making a beeline for the stage.

"Hurry, before she kills Tasha," I tell him.

He grabs my hand again. "Come with me."

And find out what happened on the tuba shelf? No, thank you.

Before I can even shake my head, Rocky jumps forward and grabs my other hand. "We're going to get some food."

Sam looks at me, hesitating. Ana Maria's shout rings from the speakers followed by Tasha's yelp. Sam closes his eyes on a curse, then points at me. "I'll find you in a minute. Don't go far." He hurries to the garage, his friends right on his heels.

"Band kids," Rocky says ominously as we head inside. "You still cool?"

"Ice cold," I assure her as I squeeze up to the table of food. But I'm not. Anxiety crawls over my skin like ants as I grab a sandwich off a platter. This isn't a big deal. Sam's hanging out with his friends. He's hooked up with Tasha. I already know all this, but navigating the social cues of it is harder than I thought.

We take our food outside to the driveway, and as I eat my dry sandwich, I watch Sam in his element. His head falls back as he laughs at something with his whole entire body, and despite all my brand-new, leveled-up confidence, I'm right back in ninth grade, watching him from afar. This is the Sam he became without me.

The air is so much colder here by the beach, bracing and salty. The music is starting up again. I get the sandwich down and try to relax as I tell myself it'll only be another hour or two. I can survive that.

Except Rocky is now looking at her phone with a frown. "Bad news," she says. "My mom is on her way to pick me up."

"*What?*" I nearly shriek.

Rocky sighs. "She tracks the GPS on my phone and saw that I'm by the beach and not at your house like I told her." She curses, and I feel awful for getting her into even more trouble with her mom. "I'm still on party restriction."

"I'll go back with you," I tell her, but she's already shaking her head.

"Trust me, you don't want to be subjected to the lecture I'm about to get." She blows out a sharp exhale. "I'm breaking your sister's rule, though."

I wave that away and force a bright smile. Rocky is about to endure a parental guilt trip, and I don't want her to feel any worse. "I'm sorry you're only getting a sandwich out of this."

Her phone rings. "It was fun to dress up and get out for a night. Stick with Sam and you'll be fine. And don't forget, Benny's around here somewhere, too."

"Don't worry about me," I assure her.

"You got this," she says. "Ice cold, remember?" A car slows at the end of the driveway, and Rocky doesn't waste time hurrying to it. I wonder if I should wave at her mom, but I don't want her to remember my face and hate me.

Barely an hour into my first high school party, and I'm alone.

I glance at Sam. He stands tall and pushes back his wavy dark hair that's gotten too long, and I wonder if he realizes how people gravitate toward him. When you're telling a joke or hamming it up, it's Sam's laugh that everyone wants to hear. That's how you know you really got it right. Or how I always did. Ana Maria grabs the mic and shouts, "Top of the show!" and they all laugh. Another joke I don't get. I try to hold on to my smile.

Sam spots me and jogs over. "Hey," he says, standing close. "Where's Rocky?"

"She had to go."

"You okay?"

"Nervous—very, very dreadfully nervous I had been and am," I quote Poe with a cheerful smile to quash my growing disquiet.

He slips his hands into his pockets and offers me a boyish smile. "Now you have to hang out with me." And he sounds so happy about that, I can't help but melt a little. Whoever else he is with everyone else, he's still mine, too.

Someone takes over the music, and the song changes. Sam's head shoots up, his eyes shocked, and because I know Sam Alvarez and remember his dad's playlists blasting every weekend, I recognize the song "Tom Sawyer" by Rush and remember Sam idolizing Neil Peart. It's *the* song from our list.

His Mount Everest as a drummer.

"It's my song!" he nearly shouts. "From our list!"

Our list. The reason I'm here and with him again. "Can you play it now?" I ask, then can't help but laugh at his affronted glare.

"The time signatures are wild," he says, then open delight lights up his entire face. "But...I think I got it."

I shove him away. "Then go!"

They all chant Sam's name. Flustered, he hands me his phone out of his back pocket with a clumsy request for me to record him before running back to the garage. As soon as he slides behind the drum set, they restart the song. Sam spins one of the sticks before diving right into the song and smoothly playing along. By his animated smile, I know he's eating up the attention—and I'm rooted to the spot as I lift his phone and film Golden Boy Sam.

When the song ends, I cheer with everyone else as I move through the crowd toward him.

Just as Tasha leaps forward and kisses him.

SAM JERKS BACK from Tasha quickly and nervously laughs off the kiss even as their friends all hoot and holler. I swallow hard. It was faster than the one he gave her on Beach Day, this one a blink-and-you'd-miss-it, playful thing between friends. He's so easy with his kisses, but jealousy burns too hot and fast for me to reason with. It melts away all my pretend ice and reveals me for the emotional mess I am.

Sam searches the crowd for me, and the concern on his face steals away whatever bit of confidence I had left. Because Sam *knows* me again. He knows I'm so clumsily new to all this. He'll explain that they're just friends and I'll nod along, like the kid I am. But I'm even worse than that: I'm an exposed, insecure wreck that snuck into this party that is so beyond me and my stupid feelings. I disappear into the crowd, then hurry past the busy deck and bonfire onto the beach.

Benny jumps up from a chair. "Hey, you okay?"

Anger and vulnerability still have me by the throat as I grit my teeth at his look of concern. "Can you do me a favor and distract Sam long enough for me to make a call?" I'll tell my mom there's alcohol here and blame her for having to leave early. Foolproof.

Benny scratches his cheek and looks like he wants to say something but nods instead. "Sure thing, Lou."

Once he's gone, I pull out my phone with shaking hands. My emotions bubble up too fast, and I hate that, but also myself a little, too, for being so sensitive. Mom's face on the screen stops me, and I hesitate before dialing. The alcohol plan would really backfire on me if she kills me.

I scroll up to *Elena* and remember her wistful expression when she saw the band. I can't ask her to come back here. Ignoring my phone, I inhale a deep breath of cold sea air. It goes a long way in calming me down enough so I'm able to think past the jumble of angry, confused emotions.

After another minute, I mutter, "I can't run away."

"Sometimes you can," someone says. A girl is standing a few feet away. She's alone, too, her gaze also on the dark water. When she glances at me, I realize it's Liliana's daughter, the infamous Rosa Santos. She's huddled in a yellow cardigan, her hair and skirt both whipping around in the

190

sharp breeze. The Port Coral wunderkind grins at me. "I'm Rosa," she says.

"I know," I say, instead of offering my own name like a reasonable person. I cringe at myself and hurry to say, "Luisa. I'm Luisa."

"Luisa? You're Elena's sister?"

I nod. I should've expected this. *Elena's Sister* was my nickname my first three years of high school.

But instead of asking how Elena is doing, she says, "I just got into town, and my mom *cannot* stop talking about your app."

My bruised ego warms at the praise. "It's still deep in development," I say, and shrug. I should be home working on it rather than here, wasting time. "But it'll be ready to launch by Spring Fest."

"Spring Fest." A faraway look comes into Rosa's eyes, and she glances out at the water again. "I can't believe it's been a year. Or that I'm hanging out at the beach. At nighttime."

"Because you're cursed by the sea?" The old legend flies out of my mouth before I can stop to remember it might be rude to bring up, considering I don't know her all that well.

But she barks out a laugh, the sound swallowed by the waves. "I love coming home."

I glance over my shoulder and see a dark-haired boy walking across the sand toward us. My stomach drops, and I hurry to practice a smile for Sam, something easy and breezy and carefree. But then I see the beard and tattoos. Not Sam.

"What are you doing out here?" the boy asks Rosa. "It's freezing."

"Says the guy without a jacket," she teases in an aside to me, but her smile is as soft as his as he walks up close to her. He bends to kiss her, and I realize they're together and feel like I'm intruding even as I'm escaping.

I turn to leave, but Rosa stops me. "How's school? You graduate this year, right?"

I nod quickly as I hold back my flying curls. The guy is right—it's freezing out here. "Yep."

"Where are you applying?"

It's November, and deadlines are barreling toward me like a semi, and I'm standing in the middle of the road like a reckless squirrel. "Georgia Tech, Duke, Vanderbilt, Florida, Miami, and UCF."

"It's good to have different places you're interested in," she says. "I didn't get into my first choice."

"Really?" I'm shocked. Everything I've ever heard about Rosa Santos is how brilliant she was. She did dual enrollment between Port Coral High *and* Community College and graduated with not only her diploma but also an *associate degree*. Move aside, Level 2 Lou—we've got a Level 50 in the room.

"Yeah, all my hopes were pinned on the College of

Charleston because it has a great study abroad program, but I got into Florida instead, and it all worked out." She elbows her boyfriend, who smiles softly as he tucks her hair behind one ear. The gesture is intimate, and for some reason that I can't understand, my resolve cracks. I'm so tired of trying to be cooler and smarter than I am.

So I blurt out, "I hate school so much."

Rosa has big, honest eyes, and I want to emotionally throw up in front of someone who won't talk to me about any of it when tomorrow comes. Maybe this is what Elena means by sometimes we have to let ourselves be the drunk girl in the bathroom that we need in the world.

Rosa and her boyfriend share a look, and I'm positive I've made a mistake. Except he suddenly laughs. When he turns to me, he says, "I'm Alex Aquino. Also a big hater of school. Rosa's like a magnet for people like us."

I deflate with relief over the common ground. "I took the SAT *three* times and just got my last set of scores, and they're as bad as the first time." I laugh a little, on a roll now.

Alex scratches his beard. "I never even took them. I had an IEP and a few issues." He shrugs.

Finding an ally, I point at myself. "ADHD."

His eyes brighten, and I know he gets it when he says, "Dyslexia."

Rosa's smile is confused now. "If you hate school, why are you applying to places like Georgia Tech and Duke?"

I sigh deeply, and my shoulders fall as I try not to crumble. "I know I probably won't get into them, but I have to try. My mom's parents were undocumented immigrants, and now she's a freaking college professor." I say this like the miracle it is, the legacy I'll never be worthy of. "She worked too hard for me to slack off, so I just have to grit my teeth through it all. Which is fine because it's how I've always endured school."

"I did one semester of college," Alex says. "For my family, but also to prove to them that just because I hated school didn't mean I couldn't trust my own instincts. Now I bake for my family's restaurant and El Mercado, and help the local biologists with their big reef project."

Rosa smiles proudly.

"But that's the problem," I admit. "I don't even *know* what I want." I love my computer and my cat. Stories, video games, and sleeping in as much as I can. Computer science feels like a good enough focus for now, even if the thought of four more years of school haunts me.

We're all quiet for a moment until Rosa lets go of a long breath. "You know what you need?"

I nearly sag in relief. I have no idea, but Rosa Santos *has* to know.

"You need a bullet journal."

I choke, surprised, but Alex laughs and gently tells her, "That's not the answer to everything, Rosa."

"No?" Her surprise turns into chagrin. "Well, I definitely agree that family is complicated." Alex chuckles at this, and she elbows him again. "And also that it's hard to move away from other people's ideas of us, because it means figuring out who we are. Your mom's path was hers, but you have to figure out yours. You have to trust yourself."

I look at her for a long moment. "What would you have done last year if someone gave you the advice to just trust yourself?"

"Oh, I would have totally ignored it," she says honestly. "But I also had the bullet journal."

Benny heads toward us. "Well, look who I find together." He hugs Rosa and then comes over to me and throws an arm around my shoulder. "Your boy was looking for you, but then my sister challenged him to some kind of drum battle. It's all a lot of noise to me."

My carriage is suddenly turning back into a pumpkin, as all my earlier anxiety pulls me back down. I'm burned out and sinking into some depression hours. It's time to return to my cave. "I am ready to go home to my cat and my many deadlines."

"I could never say no to a deadline," Rosa murmurs. "Need a ride home?"

I hand Sam's phone to Benny. "Mind returning this to him? I got a really good video of him nailing that song."

"Yeah, no problem. I'll let him know the introverts have left the building."

I text Sam so he'll hear it from me, too, and check in with Rocky—who is still alive, though still very grounded—then turn off my phone. Rosa and Alex drive me home, and after what feels like a hundred years, I'm back in the haven of my room. Like always, Jupiter is happy to see me.

With a deep sigh, I let my body melt onto my bedroom floor. Jupiter takes my favorite position of distress as an invitation to climb on my chest and demand attention. The calming vibration of her purrs go a long way in soothing me.

"Whatcha doing?" Dad asks from the doorway, the concern in his voice obvious.

From my prone position on the floor, I say, "Having some me time."

"Cool," he says, but he sounds distracted. I glance over and see him texting. He looks up with an innocent smile. Before I can ask, my phone chimes. It's a text from Elena.

You okay?

I don't want to get into it, so I reply: **Yeah, I'm fine**

Then get off the floor, you're worrying Dad

"I'm fine, Dad!" I call out.
"I know, baby, you're perfect."
If only. I smile at him anyway.

Sam

AFTER ANA MARIA hands me my ass on her set as expected, I look for Lou. I can't find her anywhere, and since she has my phone, I can't text her, either.

I search the kitchen for her, then return to the beach for the third time. No one I ask has seen her until I find Benny, surrounded by the dance team by the bonfire. "Hey, muchacho," he says, and holds out my phone.

My stomach sinks. "Where is she?"

"Rosa and Alex took her home. She was all partied out."

She left. My head falls back as I let go of a frustrated curse. This is even worse than I feared. "She saw Tasha kiss me." I grab my phone to text her but see the last ones she sent.

headed home, see you later

also

master "Tom Sawyer" by Rush on drums ✓

This time I throw my head back and groan.

"Yeah, I wanted to ask you about that," Benny says. "I thought you were into Lou?"

I'd be heartened by his protective tone if I weren't so frustrated.

"I *am into Lou*," I blurt out, so loudly that others around the bonfire glance over in alarm. I lower my voice as Benny steps closer. "But it was a miscommunication."

He nods, appeased. "Good to hear, but also—yikes."

"Or a noncommunication? And it's not Tasha's fault that she didn't know things have changed for me." I utter another curse as I hurry to text Lou back. Maybe I can fix this tonight.

Hey, sorry about that kiss with Tasha

We're just old friends. And she came out of nowhere

Can I call you?

I'm fully aware that I'm panicking, because I know the last thing Lou will want right now is a phone call. I really wish there were a way to unsend a text.

"I have to be honest," Benny says. "She didn't seem mad or jealous. Just done with the night. I don't think this was really her scene."

I stop and look at Benny. He's right. Of course he's right. This was Lou's first party ever, and she was only here because of me and the list. I drag a hand through my hair. "I had a really good day and got caught up in it."

Benny's brows pull together. "You don't have to apologize for having a good day."

I shake my head, the burn of guilt rising in my chest. "I should have looked out for her more."

Benny laughs off my worry. "She was fine, dude. Just over it."

The problem is that I know that when Lou is over something, she's *over* it.

I wake up the next morning, my head pounding, throat scratchy, and I can feel the hot/cold ache of a fever. I ignore all that and instantly lunge for my phone, only letting out a breath when I see there's a response from Lou.

No need to be sorry, we're all old friends, haha

And I'm pretty busy today

She probably *is* busy. Finals are coming up, and so are

her application deadlines. But still, that little voice in my head worries that after letting me in, she's going to kick me right back out of the treehouse. Metaphorically.

I fall into a sneezing fit, and not two seconds later Abuela flies into my room with a very familiar blue tub of minty goo.

"I'm fine," I say as she sits on the edge of my bed. I am not fine, though.

Abuela touches my forehead. "¡Papito! Tienes fiebre!" She goes to work slathering it all over my chest. I get ready to flinch away, because for some godawful reason, she always tries to shove a pinky-sized amount up each nostril at the end.

I sit up to argue but fall into a coughing fit instead.

A look of alarm flashes in her eyes. None of us can deal with sickness anymore.

After plying me with more medicine, Abuela demands that I dress appropriately or else the chilly air will kill me. "El sereno," she warns. Under her watchful gaze, I put on socks and a sweater, then cover my head with a knit hat. I trudge downstairs, Abuela spraying Lysol in my wake.

"He's hungover!" Cora calls from her room.

Mom stops on her way to the kitchen, a cardboard box in her arms. "You're hungover?"

I roll my eyes. "I'm not."

"He was at a party," Cora informs us from the top of the stairs. She smirks. "You look like hot garbage."

"Thank you. Nice rainbow pajamas. They go great with your insufferable personality."

Her eyes light up. Another diss to add to her collection.

I follow Mom into the kitchen. All four of us are gathered there now as Mom drops the box on the table while I make a beeline for the coffee. "What kind of party was it?" Mom asks, and there's that anxious edge to her voice. The one that signals she's worried about all the time she's missing around the house because of work. Last week she almost forgot to pick up Cora at Girl Scouts and called me in a panic. She made it in time, and even though Cora didn't even realize it, Mom has been kind of a mess ever since.

"It was a homecoming thing by the beach. The Electric was playing." I take a swallow of coffee and appreciate the warmth even though I'm too congested to taste it.

"¿La playa?" Abuela shrieks. "¿Por la *noche*?"

"Uh-oh," Cora says, delighted that Abuela is turning her annoyance on me. "I bet he didn't have a sweater on, either."

"I wasn't on the beach at night, Abuela," I hedge. "I was mostly inside the house and garage."

But it doesn't matter. Abuela is on a tear now about all the dangers inherent in cold air. She disappears into her room, still complaining about it.

Cora tears a hunk of bread from the loaf Abuela bought this morning. "I still think he's hungover."

Mom smirks and steps closer to me. She studies my

eyes and then stands back. "Nah. Thanks to your dad, I can always tell."

Cora lights up like the sun. She loves when we loosen up enough to talk about Dad. "Why?"

"Well, before your dad started working as a restaurant manager, he was a bartender in Gainesville for a very long time—and I can sniff out a hangover from a mile away. Let that be a lesson or a warning to you both."

"That's where you guys met, right? At a bar?"

She laughs and rolls her eyes. "Yes, I met your father in a bar. The Tipsy Duck, great place."

Cora and I have heard their story a hundred times, but Mom slides a look between us, and maybe my desperation to hear something light, funny, and Dad-related is as obvious as Cora's, because even though Mom isn't the best storyteller, she gives in with a sigh.

"It was really more of a neighborhood pub for the professors." Caught in the memory, her gaze goes inward as her face softens. "There was an old jukebox and terrible trivia nights, but it was good and cheap and really welcoming. After a crappy loss, I went there with the rest of the soccer team. Your dad saw us and started grabbing pitchers, asking if we were celebrating. And when we told him no, we were commiserating, he grabbed more pitchers." Her laugh is so delighted, the memory so bright and golden, that for a moment, the shadows slink away. The kitchen is a bright place, the three of us smiling like loons. But as starved as we are, that joy leaves us exposed, as it sharpens too quickly into an ache over missing him.

I cough, and the curtains are jerked aside as Abuela appears from her room with her purse. She announces that she's going to El Mercado to get everything she needs to make chicken soup. When I cough again, she adds, "¡Y la botanica! Esta casa necesita una limpieza!"

The door closes behind her and I hoarsely grunt, "Our pious abuela, everyone."

"Devout or not, she's still from the island." Mom returns to the box.

"What's in there?" I ask.

She hesitates. "Donations," she says. "Julisa at work mentioned that this nonprofit needs some men's clothes for job interviews. Suits and shoes." She glances at me shyly. "Do you want to go through any of it?"

I clear my throat. "I'm good." I offer her a gentle smile. "Much to his dismay, I shot past Dad in height at sixteen."

We laugh, but the moment isn't light or free—and I wonder if new memories will ever feel as good as the old ones.

Mom goes to lift the box, but I step forward and grab it before she can. It's silly because she carried it in here, and I'm pretty sure my mom can bench more than me, but she lets me have this one. She relents with a little smile and says, "In my trunk, please."

In the garage, I'm faced with my mom's four-door sedan and Dad's car. A 1971 Plymouth Barracuda. It's well-loved but ridiculous as a family car, so it never really was one. Dad would drive it whenever he went to visit his parents in Miami or friends in Gainesville. And we'd drive it down to the beach, where Dad would play Tom Petty and Chucho Valdés way too loud—and I never felt cooler.

But it's been years. The cancer slowly stole pieces bit by bit until it took everything.

I drop the box in the trunk of Mom's car, then circle the Barracuda. In all the loss and desperation, I'm grateful Mom has never mentioned selling it. Even if neither of us can bear to try to crank it. The possibility of this car still sitting here, waiting for him, is like finding an unopened letter from him. And there are so many answers and last chances I want with my dad.

For years, it was the idea of remission that carried me. A future of healthy lungs and blood cells. But now I dream of getting another chance at his death. I'd take those last good days back and throw all that useless optimism away. That desperate hope that didn't let Dad just *be* in the end.

And I wish he hadn't waited to drive this car again. *"We'll take it to the beach this spring, when it's warm."*

Now it's November, and next month will be one whole year since he left us.

I lean against the car, too scared to open it and lose that last bit of him, even as my old wish flashes in my mind.

DRIVE THE BARRACUDA

I don't think this one will make it off the list, Lou.

Lou

I WOULD NEVER say I have a superpower, but *if* being able to intensely focus on something to the detriment of all the physical needs of a human person were one, I would be *that* Avenger.

Last night's roller coaster left me emotionally burned out. My batteries weren't so much empty as they were dead. Now the terrible morning sun and my very helpful meds are here to remind me how much work I've been avoiding by going on quests instead of meeting deadlines.

I need to be filling out my FAFSA form, not falling apart in front of strangers at parties.

Still, though, the bullet journal wasn't a bad idea.

LUISA'S TO-DO LIST

100 essays (an exaggeration, but not by much)

finish applications

watch more YouTube videos about coding

continue to wing it and not die

I need to start sending college applications next month and must have this app finished by my big presentation in March. That one still feels forever away until I actually remember—oh *yeah*, I also have finals to study for, an AP class to not fail, volunteering at the animal shelter, and now a crochet club.

RIP, Luisa Patterson, dead from multitasking.

I pick up where I left off with the app. Learning to design and code as a beginner is its own time-suck monster, but presenting this to everyone at the town meeting is a boss battle that I am *not* prepared for. To the surprise of no one, I hate public speaking. Mom wants to help me with that next. Can't wait.

I reach for the checklist I've made that breaks every digital task down into bite-size dopamine-fueled steps so I don't get overwhelmed. My "checklist" is designed as a sketched-out loading bar that I shade in as I go, because I've learned that by day three of any project, the sight of unticked boxes will make me lose my mind.

My inbox chimes with a new email. I click over to the tab. It's from a Samuel Alvarez.

My stomach drops. An email? How professionally distant.

It's just a link, which opens a folder of all the latest pictures he's taken for me. Wide panoramic shots of downtown Port Coral at sunrise, in the noonday sun of a cloudless day, and right at the golden hour before sunset. There are photos of all the shops along the boardwalk. Our harbor, saved from developers, still busy with boats and scientists.

My forehead drops to my desk as my heartbeat takes off wildly, the rhythm erratic.

Sam's deep, wondrous voice from last night whispers in my mind, *"The time signatures are wild."*

Without sitting up, I turn my head a little to look at Jupiter.

"It's just a crush," I confess in a whisper. A crush on my now-popular best friend from childhood. "And a little pining over your old BFF never killed anyone." But the thing is, if I let myself fall for Sam of the casual kisses, heart-stopping smile, and deep-rooted emotional connection?

No coming back from that one.

I sweep up from my desk and go to check the bucket list on my bulletin board. I grab a pen, and one finger slides down the faded sheet of paper updated with all our recent scribbles. I cross off the latest one.

LOU AND SAM'S TO-DO LIST
BEFORE WE GRADUATE:

~~GO TO BEACH DAY~~

~~help all the stray neighborhood cats~~

go to Disney World

~~join a club~~ (started one actually)

pull off the most epic prank of all time

~~win the town Halloween costume contest~~
(yay, Rocky the Ninja Mermaid!!)

~~apply to the same colleges~~

~~work on our Spanish~~

~~Lou will hold her breath longer than~~
~~Sam underwater *break into someone's pool~~

~~go to an actual party~~

~~get super good at kissing~~
*hang out on second base

kiss someone at midnight on New Year's Eve
(after getting super good at it)

~~be serenaded (à la 10 things I hate about you)~~

~~beat the viejitos at dominos~~ (not gonna happen)

~~bury a time capsule~~

write a letter to our future selves

~~drive Lou where she needs to go~~

SAM'S ADDITIONS:

MASTER "TOM SAWYER" BY RUSH ON DRUMS
(AND SOME CUBAN JAZZ FOR DAD)

DRIVE THE BARRACUDA

~~ALWAYS HOLD MY BREATH LONGER THAN~~
~~LOU UNDERWATER~~ (LOST ON A TECHNICALITY!)

GET A DOG (I'M ALLERGIC TO CATS,
YOU KNOW THIS)

~~SAM WILL GO ON EMT SIDEQUEST~~

I count what's left and realize we're running out of sidequests. But returning to the main storyline means racing toward graduation.

I tack the list back into place on the board and return to my desk. Later, Mom will remind me to eat, and Elena will probably text me about the show we're supposed to be watching together because I'm now three episodes behind on it. But in the meantime, I will disappear into work that might not be driven by passion or nostalgia but is still urgent enough to engage my superpower.

Luisa, assemble.

Lou

DECEMBER

THE CROCHET CLUB now has a total of four members who meet at the library. Me, Rocky, Mr. Restrepo of the viejitos, and Gladys from the bowling alley. The latter is here only because she's been told by her doctor to find a noncompetitive hobby. It might take a few more meetings, since she still hasn't stopped counting how many rows she's crocheted compared to the rest of us. Mr. Restrepo is making a scarf with aqua, navy blue, and orange yarn for his beloved Miami Dolphins, I'm attempting a festive holiday sweater for Jupiter, and Rocky has quit crocheting and opted instead for cross-stitching. She's aggressively working on a cactus that reads, *Hug me.*

"For my mom," she explains. "It's sweet, right?"

"Real sweet," I say, because who am I to judge other mothers and daughters?

Gladys chimes in, "A few more thorns couldn't hurt."

Rocky is leaving right after the meeting to spend the holiday break with her dad, who still lives in Miami. It's the first post-divorce. She figures it's easier for everyone if he picks her up from the library rather than the apartment where she lives with her mom.

"I'm now that kid whose parents have to find a meeting place to hand me off." She jerks the needle out of the pattern before stabbing it back through. "It's ridiculous. *They* are ridiculous."

Gladys harrumphs in agreement. "I keep saying. Marriage is for the birds."

The vibe is really contentious for a crochet club.

"I am not a bird," Mr. Restrepo says. He's one of the quieter viejitos, and his scarf is turning out beautifully.

"Me either," Rocky agrees with another stab of her needle.

"I'm more of a cat person," I say. "But there are definitely birdlike characters I can get on board with. Apollo in *Animal Crossing*, Garrus from *Mass Effect*, who is not technically a bird, but as a Turian—"

"Oh my god!" Gladys interrupts. "What are you going on about now?"

I bite my lip as I try to finish this sweater. Jupiter is going to hate it. "A video game."

"What kind of sewing circle is this?" she barks. "If I wanted this boring chatter, I'd have joined the book club. They at least serve wine."

"It's a *crochet* club, and we're underage, Gladys," I explain for the fifth time. "And this is a library."

"There's wine?" Mr. Restrepo wonders with a curious glance around us.

Gladys sits up and points between me and Rocky with her crochet needles. "You two are young. Your lives have gotta be more interesting than cats and video games."

"You'd be surprised," I tell her.

Rocky nudges my foot. "I don't have any exciting gossip because I'm eternally grounded until graduation, but our Lou here might need some romantic advice."

I shoot a glare at Rocky, who continues to stitch. It's been five weeks since Halloween and three since the party, but who's counting, right? There have been texts about nothing and hellos in hallways, but it was somehow easier to ignore Sam for four years than it has been to barely talk to him for these three weeks.

"You need advice?" Gladys asks me.

"From you?" Mr. Restrepo asks, doubtful.

Gladys scowls. "They don't call me No Gutter Gladys for nothing."

My hand jerks and I mess up my next slip stitch. "Can everyone focus on their scarves and sweaters, please?"

Even with only four members, this club is really getting away from me.

"She wants to find a reason to kiss her friend again," Rocky explains, and I gasp, but her smile is amused. She swings her needles between the two senior citizens like, *Who are they going to tell?* I know she's trying to tease me out of my bad mood. I've been a tragically morose thing for the past couple of weeks.

"There's nothing wrong with kissing your friends," Gladys goes on, and I only slightly die.

"Can we not?" I beg.

"Listen, I've learned a thing or two from life," No Gutter Gladys says as she abandons her scarf. "Friendship isn't always platonic, romance isn't always sexual, and you should always release the ball at the bottom of your downward swing."

Our crocheting and stitching stops.

With a worried look, Rocky asks, "The third's about bowling, right?"

When Rocky's dad arrives, I go outside with her. It's a short, friendly enough introduction as I help her get her bag into his car. And then we stand outside, both of us waving awkwardly in the wind like those dancing noodles outside car dealerships.

"I'll see you in January," I say thickly.

She rolls her eyes. "I'll be back before the new year, Lou."

I go in for a hug and she returns it, sighing against my hair. Maybe trying to be bolder in the name of the list didn't give me my old Sam back, but it can give me this.

She moves to the passenger door. "It's not over yet, okay?" she says, and I don't know if she's talking about Sam or the list. "Don't forget that you two still haven't pulled off a prank."

"Joke's on you," I say bitterly. "Life is one big prank."

She laughs. "You've been hanging out with Gladys too much."

Sam

IT'S THREE IN the morning on the first day of winter break, and I am awake, shivering, and drenched in a cold sweat, my heart beating so hard and fast I can feel it everywhere. I stare at the ceiling and listen to the quiet hum of the humidifier Abuela set up in my room after my cold. It still smells like the Vicks she shoved into it.

I was supposed to be getting better. I rub the center of my chest and try to reason with my racing thoughts, but I can only ever think about terrible things at this hour. When five minutes turns into twenty, I give up with a curse and get out of bed. I pull on a shirt and quietly go downstairs. The TV flickers in the dark, and I find Mom on the couch. She mutes it and whispers, "What are you doing up?"

"I could ask you the same thing." I drop down beside her.

"Couldn't sleep."

"Same," I return with a sigh.

She unmutes the episode of *Bake Off,* and I glance at the curtain down the hall. "Why not watch this in your room?"

She turns back to the TV. "Sometimes my bedroom gets too quiet."

We watch the technical bake, both of us murmuring over whether they had proofed the bread long enough. "Maybe you should start running again," I tell her. I'm still worried about her, but I know that my mom is happiest when she's active. "I'm going for one in the morning. If you want to come."

She makes a thoughtful noise.

"Marching band season ends soon, but I need to keep my mile short for the CPAT."

She slides me a look, familiar with the physical ability test. "You have to take that?"

"Not as an explorer," I return. "But I want to be able to keep up with the firefighters, even if I end up as a paramedic. Thanks to playing tenor, I'm not worried about carrying something heavy while running—but it's different when you're going up stairs. And that's one of the exercises at the competition in March."

"What competition?"

"It's between firefighter cadets and explorers from around the state. We'll run through a bunch of our training exercises. Dan and Tim have shown us videos of past events and are planning to set up a maze for us to practice."

"A maze?" Her voice is quiet but curious.

"Yeah, we'll run through it in our gear. There are only so many volunteer positions, and Dan said if I intend to secure one after graduation, the competition is a great way to impress the captain. There will even be a live burn."

"You'll already be in a fire?" She jerks up on the couch. "I thought you were learning about becoming a medic, not a firefighter."

"Most calls are medical, and firefighters have to be at least EMT certified."

"Yeah, but *fires*, Sam."

I try for a soft smile, hoping to ease her worry. "But imagine knowing what to do and being able to help someone on their worst day. I know it's not me going to a university and playing in some big school band like we planned. I'm sorry about that, Mom."

"Sorry?" She shakes her head quickly like I've misunderstood. "Sam, *you* wanted that. You talked about DCI since you were, like, ten. Your dad and I worked on building our savings to help you with your dreams, and it sucks so much that in the end that money was spent in a funeral home." She presses her lips together, biting back the emotion I can see welling up in her eyes. "I never wanted you to give up something you still want." Mom glances away. "Is this because of your dad? Because you're sad?" It's such a loaded question, but her voice is gentle, and I'm relieved for the chance to be honest with each other.

"Maybe," I admit, and she flinches. "But is that a bad thing? It's almost my last semester of high school, and I'm studying more than ever, but from an *Essentials of Firefighting* textbook. I'm practicing knots while in the break room at work and getting Junior to quiz me on questions while stocking. I want this," I admit, and my chest lightens.

It feels like a declaration.

When Lou reminded me how I always played as a healer in our games, it felt like a tiny gift. A reminder from that younger version of myself who dreamed and planned, and maybe he wouldn't be disappointed in me now. Because maybe these choices, while tangled in loss, are still plugged into some part of me that's always been there.

"You should come with me to the station," I tell Mom. "Let me show you around."

Mom looks utterly exhausted by all her worries, but when her mouth softens into a smile, the chasm between us doesn't feel so big.

The next day, Abuela prepares huge trays of rice, beans, and steaks for me to take for everyone working at the station. None of us know how to celebrate the upcoming holidays, but I can tell that Abuela is relieved to be able to cook like this for a huge group.

When Mom gets home from work, I drive her to the station. Her leg bounces with nervous energy beside me. When we get there, she helps me take all the food inside, and everyone cheers when we walk into the kitchen.

"Oh my god, that smells amazing!" Dan looks up with a big smile. Mom's still on edge, but the sight of his sweater that reads *I'm a Paramedic, of Course I'm on the Nice List* makes her smile.

"Dan, this is my mom, Josie Alvarez."

They shake hands, and Dan says, "You got a great kid here. I never have to ask him to do a thing, but I'll turn around and find him sweeping."

"Really?" She looks between us. "And here I thought he doesn't know how a broom works."

Everyone laughs at my expense, but I feel buoyant with relief. Because I'm eighteen now, Tim said I'll be able to go on a ride-along next month after I've spent eight weeks in the program. I explain this to Mom as I give her a tour. I'm showing her the lockers when Dan calls out, "Alvarez! Adriana here says you killed it in a turnout drill last week." Adriana has a gleeful look as she follows behind him, a plate of Abuela's food in her hands. By their different grins, I know Dan is giving me a chance to impress my mom, while Adriana is giving me a chance to fall on my ass in front of everyone.

"I did okay," I admit. The drill is all about getting into your bunker gear as fast as possible. I practiced for hours in my room with a pair of Dad's old rain boots, sweatpants, my only winter coat, and the gloves I use while landscaping. Cora caught me, and I gave her ten bucks to never say a word.

"Where's Little Tim?" Dan asks. "He out?"

"What?" Tim calls from the kitchen.

"I really wasn't that fast—"

"Come here!" Dan shouts, and Tim says, "Yup," and that's how Little Tim and I end up in front of the ladder truck with two sets of bunker gear in front of us, a timer in Dan's hands, and my mom standing among several firefighters and medics, all cheering and jeering, calling out advice and jokes.

"All right, everyone quiet!" Dan shouts. "You two, ready, set, *go!*"

I yank on the hood and kick off my shoes. Everyone is already calling out directions. I step into the boots—which are not like Dad's rain boots at all—and pull the pants up, then the suspenders up and over my shoulders. Zip the pants, secure the Velcro, and glance at Tim, who's already reaching for the jacket. It's a drill, for fun, but the bite of competitiveness is nipping at my heels. And Mom's here, too, bouncing on the balls of her feet in anticipation. I may not win against a veteran firefighter, but I want to get really close.

"Hurry up, Tim, the kid's catching on you!"

I sweep the coat on and punch my arms through the sleeves. Zip up to my chin and pull that Velcro over.

Everyone's screaming now. Even Mom and I want to laugh. I get the helmet on and pull the straps under my chin. I'm trying to get the gloves on when Tim throws his arms out. I don't stop until I'm done, too, ten whole seconds after him.

"Next we gotta see it with the actual packs," Mateo, a firefighter, calls to Little Tim.

"It's always the gloves!" Tim shouts back with a laugh.

Dan checks over both of us, looking for any exposed skin. Tim's good, of course. And as Dan looks me over, I'm dying of nerves again, but I get a quick smile and a slap on my shoulder.

Mom steps up to me with a huge grin. "Look at you!"

I think of her question about Dad last night. "I'm adapting, same as you, Mom."

Her eyes are bright as she pats my chest and the buckle at my chin. "This is good. And it's still you, too."

I take off my helmet, wrap an arm around her, and kiss the top of her head.

Sam

THE NEXT MORNING, I slip my running shoes on and head outside. I've got a couple of hours until my shift at the bodega, so I make my way to the boardwalk to run the stairs down to the beach. When I reach the square, I spot Lou outside the bodega, talking to Benny.

"Lou!" I shout without thinking. I call her name again, but she's too far away. The light changes and I run across the square. But she's gone by the time I reach the sidewalk. I rest my hands on my thighs and lean over to suck in air. I *really* need to work on my mile time.

"You know you're not scheduled to work until later, right?" Benny asks.

I look up, breathing hard. "Where'd she go?"

Benny points to the botanica, and I head to the

spiritual store with a different hitch in my chest. I've never been inside.

The bell over the door chimes a pleasant song, and it's nice and cool in the shop. Also empty. I glance around, almost afraid to look or go down any of the aisles. Something about the space unnerves me. The candles, saints, and perfumes feel like yet another piece of my language I'm not fluent in.

In the front of the shop, there's a built-in shelf with tall glass candles lit. I move closer. Beside them are pictures. I recognize the older woman—Mimi—who passed away last year and who is the shop's namesake, but I don't know the two men. There's also a bowl of candy, fresh flowers, glasses of water, and a familiar tub of night cream that Abuela uses. The space smells like incense, a citrus perfume, and something that reminds me of the sea.

Anyone who walks into this store will be greeted by the faces of this family's relatives who've passed. The idea is unsettling and stirs equal parts anxiety and curiosity in me. What must it be like to sit so easily with those you've lost? To invite them into your daily life every time you light candles or buy fresh flowers?

"Hi."

I spin around with my heart in my throat. It's the owner of the store, Liliana Santos. I step away from her altar, feeling guilty. "Sorry, I—"

Her smile is warm and easy as she glances between the

shelf and me. "No apologies needed." She tilts her chin toward the shelf. "My mom likes to introduce herself." She grins softly at her joke about her dead mother, her tone light, and I wonder how she can do it. Mimi Santos died not long after my dad. How can her daughter already be so casual about it?

"I was looking for Lou," I say.

The curtain in the back parts and Lou steps out. She stumbles to a stop when she sees me. "Hey," she says, sounding unsure. Liliana leaves us, a slight smile on her face.

She'd been right across the street or down the hall at school, but now it's almost as if September and October never happened. Like we're back to before. I've studied the bucket list, searched between the lines for any reason to hang out again, but every time I've texted her, her responses have all been about how busy she's been. I tug at my sweaty shirt, then drag a hand through my hair that needs a cut, and I wish I hadn't just been running.

"Hey," I say, and glance at the bag in her hand. "Shopping?"

"Yeah." She clears her throat and looks down like she already forgot what she bought. She smiles a little. "They're candles for luck. I'm sending my college applications soon." She blows out a sharp, nervous breath.

"That's right, wow. It's almost January." I can't stop nodding. "Which one is first?"

"Miami," she says, then her eyes widen, like she's surprised with herself and wants to snatch the confession back. "*Oh*, which one am I sending first? Not sure yet. I wish I could hit one big red button and get them all over with." Lou has a first choice, even if she's afraid to admit it out loud.

I smile and, without one single doubt, tell her, "You're going to do amazing."

She shifts the bag in her hand. "What's done is done. It'll be out of my hands soon enough." She tucks a curl of hair behind her ear, and I notice it's shorter.

"You cut your hair."

"Uh, yeah, you know what they say—stressed? Get bangs." She touches her neck, like she's searching for the missing length.

"It looks great. You look great," I say, moving closer, but it doesn't feel like enough. "It's very Korra in Book Four," I blurt out, because it is, but I'm also desperate to get us back to how we were before the party.

A shy look comes over her, but she seems pleased. by the comparison. "Thanks." A quiet song plays on the radio behind the counter as a sea breeze slips through the open window, and I can't stop looking at her. She glances around us in the silence. "Were you on a run?"

I glance down at my shirt regretfully. "I was headed to run the stairs but saw you talking to Benny."

"He was inviting me to his family's New Year's Eve

party." Her face falls at the mention of another party. "He assures me it will be more my speed, but I'm pretty partied out."

"Listen, I've wanted to tell you how sorry I am that homecoming was terrible."

"It's fine." Her voice goes all high with the lie. She glances away. "It was a party at the beach. Nothing terrible about that."

"Tasha and I haven't been together in a long time, and—"

Lou cuts me off. "Are you going to Benny's party?" she asks just before she closes her eyes on a curse. "Sorry. I didn't think—"

"It's okay." I hurry to stop her apology. The anniversary of Dad's death falls on New Year's, and that's something I have to learn to navigate.

"I should go," I say.

"Yeah, me too." She starts to leave.

"No, I meant Benny's party." I nervously rub the back of my neck, and my heart kicks hard as I decide to go for it. "For the kiss at midnight."

A nervous laugh explodes from her, and the bright sound and sight pull a smile from me. When I don't take it back, she says, "I bet Tasha's going."

I lower my hand. "I didn't kiss her, Lou."

She says, "It's *fine*" at the same time that I frustratingly declare, "I want to kiss *you*."

We both freeze. Lou's lips part in surprise. I move closer. A scream sounds from the back and we both jump away. Liliana rushes forward with her arm around Elena. I jump to Elena's other side.

"What happened?" Lou asks, trailing us.

Elena curses. "False labor, my ass. I'm going to murder my doctor."

"You're in *labor*?" Lou yelps. "You're not due yet!"

"Tell that to this baby!"

"I knew it," Lou says, breathless. "An impatient Sagittarius."

I stammer, "But I haven't studied this yet. I only know CPR and running vitals."

"I just need you to get her in my car," Liliana patiently reassures me, then races around the block as I help Elena outside. She hunches over and shouts as the next contraction hits. Everyone outside the bodega and around the square looks over at her.

"What's going on?" Mr. Gomez asks, then gasps when he sees the state Elena is in. "Ay, dios mío."

Liliana's car stops beside us, and I help Elena into the front seat. "You're going to do great," I tell her, because I have no idea what else to say.

"Oh, shut up, Sam," she says without heat, then lets out another cry. Lou jumps into the back, and Liliana is about to take off when she looks at me and says, "Will you close up the store for me? Benny's mom has a key!"

I agree, and they take off down the street. I find Mrs. Peña and then slip inside the empty botanica. I shut off the radio and turn off the lights. Elena left here as the person she's always been, but when she comes back it'll be as a mother. An ordinary day that ends with something as extraordinary as a new person. A bigger family. More stories and love. I remember Dad cradling my newborn sister, looking at her like he'd finally caught that shooting star. Candles flicker on the altar, and I nervously make my way closer. I don't know if I'm meant to blow them out or not. Does Liliana pray when she stands here? Or does she simply talk to her mother?

In the quiet of the store, I wonder what the difference is.

Lou

IT TAKES MY sister thirty-seven hours to bring her and Nick's daughter, Pearl, into this world, and me two seconds to fall deeply in love with her. We're all jammed into Elena's hospital room, where none of us can get enough of the baby, but it's finally my turn to hold my niece. Nick hands her to me, and she's wrapped up like the cutest little burrito.

"She's so tiny!" I say, worrying.

Elena laughs. "Tell that to my vagina." She slides a look at Dad. "Sorry, Dad."

He's barely listening because he's gone into bright sparkly eyes mode as he coos over his granddaughter. Mom is on the bed next to Elena, looking just as tired. She's been with Elena all thirty-seven of those hours.

❧

A couple of days later, my sister's tiny family comes over for Christmas Eve. With extra hands around, Elena passes out on the couch beside an equally haggard Nick, an old Christmas movie on TV. It's a mild party compared to our usual celebrations, but I'm not complaining as I take Pearl upstairs. I stop at Max's door. He's got both my parents locked in a very tense *Super Smash Bros.* battle. I continue down the hall to show Pearl my room. "That's a computer," I tell her. "Don't worry, I'll be sure to build you a decent setup. Also, that's Jupiter on my bed. You'll be chasing her soon enough, because she's going to live forever."

Candles from the botanica flicker on my desk as I sit down in my chair. I slowly spin in a circle before stopping in front of my computer, and with Pearl in my left arm, I hit Send on my first application. I glance down at Pearl's curious eyes and think maybe it's not as simple as two roads. Maybe life is a bunch of tangled timelines.

"Miami's not too far," I confess quietly. "I'd still get to see you all the time."

A terrible smell hits my very sensitive nose, and my head jerks back. "Are you serious?" I turn toward the doorway. "Elena!" I call out, because while I may be over-the moon in love as a brand-new Titi, I am *not* trying to change a diaper.

Dad flies into my room, his arms already open. "Someone's been busy!" he says to Pearl as he picks her up.

"No kidding," I say. "I just sent my first application."

He gasps as his gaze flies from the baby in his arms to my computer screen. "Really? Luisa, that's great! Holy crap, let's go tell your mom. She went out to her garden."

I smirk. "She beat y'all again?"

"She's an enigma." He smiles at me. "So proud of you."

"I may not get into any of them," I admit, and hope Elena's candles have protective abilities against saying fears out loud.

Dad shrugs. "It would be their loss." He makes believing in me look so easy. "Now let's go change this diaper."

I find Mom outside in her garden along the side of the house. The sun is better here. Broccoli, radishes, and turnips are in the beds, and her orange trees are bursting with blooms that smell delicately sweet. Mom looks over her space, happy in her rubber boots and ridiculous overalls, hair tied up on her head, and I don't understand how she can feel so different from Elena or how I can find so much comfort from her and still be so terribly afraid of disappointing her. The idea is unbearable.

Mom turns to me with a big grin, a spot of dirt on one cheek. "Hey, you! Come smell these orange blossoms."

"Trust me, I could smell them from inside." This obviously delights her. "I submitted my first application."

She spins toward me. "Which one?"

"Miami," I say, that dangerous baby bird of hope fluttering around in my chest.

Mom sets down her trowel and opens her arms. I step

into the waiting hug, and she rocks me a little, like the baby I am. "So proud of you."

Held by my mother in her garden, I inhale the orange blossoms and give myself the gift of letting myself feel the pride and possibility of this moment with my whole self. I wrote that essay and did all that work, and maybe it will be enough.

Surrounded by new life and growth, I glance over the safety of her shoulder, to Sam's dark house. No strung lights this year. Not a single holiday decoration. When we were kids, the Alvarezes had the best parties for Noche-buena. Old-school salsa music would blast all day as a whole pig roasted from the early hours in their backyard. Sam and I always snuck off with the best pieces of crispy skin and dared each other to eat the eye as our parents drank too much wine and told the silliest stories.

But tonight, his house is quiet and still.

Sam

DECEMBER 31

I'M STUCK IN a church pew, in that awful suit again, as a priest I don't know goes on and on about prayer, salvation, and the memory of my father. Abuela has finally gotten us to church because they offered a Mass for her deceased son on the anniversary of his death.

Anniversary. The word sticks in my throat.

I'm restless. I look over Mom's head to Port Coral. A few rows over, I spot Benny with his family. In front of them is Lou and hers. Even Elena and Nick are here, a car seat between them on the pew. Lou told me her name is Pearl, but I have yet to meet her. I spot the viejitos. Even Liliana Santos and her daughter, Rosa, are here. And Malcolm, Dan, and Little Tim from the station.

Beside me, Mom's leg begins to bounce.

"A reading from the Letter of Paul to the Romans..."

My gaze goes around the space and makes note of all the rituals. The holy water at the door. Lighting a tiny candle to remember. The smell of incense heavy in the air. Part of me understands the solace Abuela finds in this when I think of the altar in the botanica. But I never want to pray for something so desperately again, to break myself open and beg, only to be met with silence.

I watched my father die as I haunted the corner of the ICU. Every time he coded, it stole slivers of my shattered soul, and I bore witness each time the doctors brought him back by CPR, only for him to leave again. The howl that escaped me when he died was my last prayer. But still, I want to know where he went. That he's safe and healthy and remembers us.

I want to know if I still have a father.

Mom's hands tighten into fists in her lap. I reach over, but the moment my hand touches hers, she leaps to her feet like she's been burned. Without a second glance at any of us, she sweeps out of the church. The priest doesn't stop, but Abuela looks at me and offers a solemn jerk of her head, a signal to follow.

I hurry after Mom out the doors and into the morning sun. She paces the front sidewalk in a quick, jerky circle. She doesn't stop or pull herself together when she sees me. I slip my hands into my pockets and watch over her.

"I can't do it. I can't sit in a church and think about my dead husband right now."

I lean against the low wall. A breeze carries the smell of a nearby cookout. I inhale deeply.

"Your grandmother keeps asking me to go to their grief group. I went and listened to old widows reassure me that I'm still young and will move on. That I'll meet someone else. But I *hate* that." She points an accusing finger at the closed doors. "I hate that everyone in there wants me to pray and move on. Can I be sad? Or is that too much to ask?" She drops down to sit on the church steps. "Too much for them to bear?" she whispers, weary.

I move to sit beside her. The day is warmer than last year.

"Forever sucks," she says on a sigh, and lowers her head into her hands for a long moment. When she looks up, her gaze goes to the street in front of us. She huffs a bitter laugh. "In another life, your dad would drive up and ask me what the hell I'm doing in a church and get me out of here."

The answer hits me so suddenly, I jump to my feet. I chase the feeling like it's a butterfly as I race down the steps to the sidewalk. "Come on."

"We can't leave," she says, sounding confused but hopeful.

"We'll be back in time for them."

Mom catches up with me, and neither of us says a word

as we get back in her car. At home, I park behind my truck instead of the usual spot. I can feel her confusion, but I'm running on too much adrenaline and inexplicable certainty to explain. I open the garage door and grab Dad's keys from the hook.

"Sam—" Mom starts as I unlock the Barracuda.

I open the door and climb inside, where for the first time in a year, I speak to my dad.

"Come on, old man," I whisper as I slip the keys into the ignition. *Let this work,* I silently beg. The answer comes in the guttural roar of the engine coming alive. I grip the steering wheel and deflate with relief as my head falls back against the seat. Through the windshield, I see Mom's surprise turn into a bright smile. The radio kicks on, and she rushes to open the passenger door and jump inside. She turns up the volume.

"This is his driving playlist!" she yells over the music. "Tom Petty was a god in Gainesville. They played him every night at the bar." She runs her hands along the console with a faraway smile and murmurs, "Still smells like him in here."

I shift into drive and take us back to the church. We arrive as the service is wrapping up. I pull up outside the door, and at the sight of the old muscle car, the viejitos amble over to take a closer look.

Mr. Gomez whistles. "¡Qué chévere!"

I pass him and hurry to meet Lou on the steps. She

looks from the car back to me with awe. "You're driving the Barracuda," she murmurs with a smile, and I know she's thinking of our bucket list. "Where are you going?"

"I have no idea," I admit. Halfway down the stairs, Lou stops me with a hand on my arm. "Your dad was—" Her eyes shine as her voice breaks. "I just want you to know that he was the best."

I smile, my throat tight.

Abuela leaves the priest's side and makes her way down to the car, where Mom stands with an arm around Cora. The women of my family study one another for a long moment, but finally Abuela reaches for Mom's hand. Something gentle but unspoken passes between them.

So different, too tragically similar.

"Come on," I tell them, and move around to the driver's side. "Let's go for a ride."

They all climb in and I rev the engine—to the delight of the viejitos—and catch Lou's eye before pulling away from the curb. I wasn't lying; I have no idea where I'm going as I drive us out of town. I head north for the orange groves, down backroads that cut through the middle of our state. We lower our windows to enjoy the citrus-sweet air, and I'm thankful for the warmer winter weather as I drum against the steering wheel. Mom's short hair flies around her as she sings along with the playlist. Each song stirs another memory. Some she shares, some she keeps.

As the sun dips toward the horizon, the songs follow

suit, and the relaxed beat of the island finds us. Abuela grabs onto my seat from the back and cries, "¡Por fin!" Laughing, she insists Cora sway with her in the back seat. Somewhere between Tom Petty and Cuban ballads, I figure out where to go and ask Mom for directions. And then we drive another two hours before I pull into the parking lot of their old stomping grounds in Gainesville.

Mom laughs. "Your grandmother takes y'all to church, and I take you to a bar."

"Am I allowed in there?" Cora asks.

The door opens, and an older Black woman stops in the doorway of The Tipsy Duck at the sight of the car. Mom jumps out.

"Holy shit, Josie? Is that you?" the woman asks.

Mom laughs. "I didn't get *that* old, Tina."

"I'd know the sound of that car anywhere." Tina rushes forward, and Mom meets her halfway for a big hug. Tina lets her go and looks at us. "Your kids! I haven't seen them in forever. Oh my god, he looks just like Samuel." She searches around us. "Where the hell is he?"

In Port Coral, everyone knows. And it sucks that the people closest to loss, over and over, become the bearers of that heartbreaking news. Mom shakes her head, her bottom lip trembling. Tina's hand flies to her mouth before she grabs Mom and pulls her into a hard hug. They stay that way for a long moment.

"Damn it all," Tina murmurs against Mom's hair.

When they break apart, Tina looks at us. "Come inside and let's toast your dad."

Between the two of them, we have a hundred new stories about Dad.

I don't have an altar and hadn't found him in prayer, but today I heard his wild laugh in the growl of an old car and traced my finger across a map to the place my story began.

And I find an old set of congas that have been collecting dust by the dart board in the bar. When Mom sees what I've dragged over to the bar, she laughs at Tina. "I can't believe you still have those!"

"What else was I supposed to do with them?" Tina lowers her hands to her hips. "Samuel couldn't play them for shit but told me to hold on to them for his kid." She tilts her chin toward me. "I hope you got room in that trunk."

"Are you serious?" I ask, thrilled.

"They were already yours," she says, then slides a look toward Cora. "Unless you're the drummer?"

Cora shakes her head. "Nope. But do you have a dog I can have?"

Tina looks thoughtful. Mom and I both say no.

The Tipsy Duck is definitely more of a pub than the college bar I'd first imagined. The holiday crowd looks older, mostly grad students, professors, and their families.

And they haven't minded that Tina let us have control of the jukebox. Abuela's on her third rum cocktail as she dances with a philosophy professor, and I play along on the congas.

CUBAN JAZZ FOR DAD

"I can't believe we might finish the list," I say to myself, wondrous.

Mom glances up from her drink. "What list?"

"And who's *we*?" Cora asks. She's on her second basket of fries and the handful of cherries she's plucked from the bar.

"It's nothing, it's just—"

Tina lowers her elbows onto the bar and her chin into one hand. "He's got that same look in his eyes that Samuel had when he met this one." She points her thumb at Mom, who grins happily.

I keep playing. "Lou and I have been finishing an old bucket list we made years ago. Learning to play jazz like this for Dad was on there."

Mom's eyes shine. "I love that," she says. "What else is on it?"

Because she's smiling and happy, I tell them about Halloween, the time capsule, and working on my Spanish. "Technically, all that's really left is a theme park, prank, and—" My timing falters and I stop because my face feels hot.

Tina whoops in laughter. "Oh, that one must be good."

I hesitate and glance at the clock. It's eight PM. "A kiss at midnight on New Year's Eve."

Cora makes a face. "Gross."

Mom sends Tina a concerned glance. "It's a four-hour drive back to Port Coral."

Tina responds with a look of disbelief. "In *that* car?"

"Mom, no," I say, because she's having a good time and we planned on staying with Tina tonight. But it's also four hours exactly until midnight, and this could be the perfect opportunity to show Lou how I feel about her. In a big, romantic, unmistakable way.

Mom jumps to her feet and shoots back the rest of her beer. She leans over the bar and kisses Tina on the cheek, then spins back to me with a serious look. "Grab those congas. You're driving." To Abuela she calls, "¡Vamos!"

Back in the car, Cora excitedly shakes my seat. "Go fast, Papito!"

As we race home, I open the car up on the interstate and imagine Dad making this drive with Mom, a new car seat like Pearl's in the back. As Mom cries softly beside me, I wonder if she regrets any of it. Would she do it all over again, knowing how it would end? The little kid in me, made from the love they shared, wants to believe she would. That all this means something good or even great in the end.

She reaches for my hand and squeezes it. "Don't be afraid to miss him," she says. "It's an act of love."

243

This is the life that's left. Year one, step one: Grief doesn't disappear. In my desperate bid to survive by avoiding it, I might have missed out on this. A messy, marvel of a day that feels like breaking the surface after so long and finally taking that first full breath.

Maybe this is what an anniversary can be now. A simple reminder to breathe.

Lou

I'M AT THE kitchen table when the clock strikes nine. The party in Times Square rages from the TV in the living room, where Max is currently hanging out with a huge bowl of popcorn. My parents sit beside me as they offer to make me yet another cup of chocolate caliente con queso.

I'm on my third mug. "I've had enough cheese, Mom."

"Whoever first thought to dunk some melty cheese in hot chocolate is a genius." Dad clinks his mug against hers.

There are taquitos in the freezer and a new *Spells & Order* expansion pack. My night's going to be a Luisa Patterson classic. Except that I have a funny text from Benny, reminding me that I'm invited to his party.

"We can drive you and Rocky to Benny's party," Dad offers.

"Rocky can't go," I explain. "She's still grounded."

Mom sips her hot chocolate. "*You* could still go. There will be other friends there, and Dad can pick you up after midnight."

"Why do you want me to go so bad?" I'd mentioned the invite to them in some bid to prove I'm not a total loser, but it makes no sense for my parents to be so into the idea of me going to a party. "There might be booze."

Mom's smirk is amused. "I want you to go because you've worked really hard this year. You sent your last application in yesterday and deserve a break."

"Wow, can you repeat that?"

Mom rolls her eyes. "Also, I trust the Peña family and know you'll be safe there. But mostly because of how forlorn you look whenever you watch the party on TV."

I mulishly glance over at it again. "They make it look more fun than it is."

"Perhaps, but it's still okay to want to go out sometimes."

I get up and am halfway up the stairs when there's a knock. "I got it, I got it!" I shout, and race back down. I whip open the door to find Elena on the front porch.

"Hey, you," she says before sailing past me. The disappointment hits hard when I see Sam's dark house behind her. When I turn back inside, I realize Elena is all dressed up. Flowy skirt, cute top, her hair in an intricately messy updo. "Where are you going?" I ask her.

"With you. The Patterson sisters are partying on New Year's Eve," she announces happily, and lifts her hand for a high five.

I high-five her, still confused. "What? How did you—?" My gaze shoots to my sheepish parents. "Are you serious? You called my sister? How pathetic do you think I am?"

"Excuse me?" Elena demands.

"And you had a baby like two weeks ago!"

"Your point? Pearl has another parent, and I pumped plenty."

Mom holds out two small sandwich bags of green grapes. "Don't forget to eat all twelve at midnight. Are you wearing new underwear?" Mom, for being such a pragmatist, is very serious about New Year's traditions and rituals, and right at the top is eating twelve grapes within the first minute of the new year. For luck. Try not to choke.

I take my grapes as Elena dances in place.

Mom, suddenly serious, says to her, "Remember yourself."

"Oh, I plan to." Elena turns her moves on me.

So many cars line the street outside Benny's house that it takes us almost two blocks to find a place to park. Even that far away, we're greeted by the bass of a popular reggaeton song and the scent of roasting meat. Every window of the Peña house is lit. We don't even bother knocking before going inside to find a living room full of kids bouncing on couches as a video game flashes on the TV.

"This is my stop," I say, but Elena pulls me farther into the house.

We follow the sounds of wild laughter into the kitchen, where we find grown folks talking over one another, everyone laughing as they all try to tell the same story. Mrs. Peña spots Elena and me and directs us to the back porch. It's like moving through generations of the Peña family, but outside, we finally find our people. "This is like the Goldilocks of parties," I say.

There's a smoking grill on the deck beside us, and Mr. Peña reigns over it. I know whatever comes off that grill will be life changing, and I consider staying up here to get first dibs. But Elena isn't done as she pushes me down the steps and deeper into the party. Lights are strung between the trees, illuminating the backyard. Wireless speakers sit on the patio table, where a very animated and aggressive card game is in progress. On the other side of the yard, Ivan, a funny Dominican boy I recognize from calculus, sweeps a girl into a dance as a classic merengue song starts, and their friends cheer them on.

Elena is beside me, but her expression grows sad as the wind leaves her sails. "I should have stayed inside," she says with a touch of weariness. "I'm already a hundred years older than everyone out here."

From the moment she cornered me in her bedroom

to tell me she was pregnant, my sister has been defiantly confident, daring anyone to tell her the odds. Mom did, of course, but if Elena ever flinched, she never let us see it.

But here, in her party dress, she flinches.

"Hey, none of that," I tell her. "Your whole life changed, and you made it work. You got a job, adapted, found an apartment—all while dealing with Mom." I try for an easy laugh as my sister turns a watery smile on me. "Everyone out there has their own insecurities, but they're here and ready to dance, same as you. Plus, your boobs look ridiculous in that top."

"Right? Almost as big as yours." She grins cheekily, then wraps one arm around me and pulls me close for a quick squeeze. She whispers, "Love you," and I say it back with a happy knot in my chest.

Elena shows me that being bold can take so many shapes.

And then magic-via-playlist happens as another old-school song kicks off, and the Colombian in me cannot stay chill when the flute starts. Elena spins to me, and we both scream in happy recognition. I grab her hand and tug her to the middle of the makeshift dance floor, and we're already swirling our hips like Mom taught us.

Off to the side, Benny calls out, "We got some Colombianas, y'all!"

I wouldn't go so far as to call my sister my friend (how embarrassing), but it's as we dance together that I realize we have finally found each other outside the family nest.

But soon enough, Elena is checking her phone and chewing on her lip. I stop dancing and glance over her shoulder, and I see she's looking at a picture of Pearl wearing a onesie with the numerals for the new year written in glitter. Elena notices me and shrugs, then says, "I feel like I can smell her through the phone."

I grin at the blatant yearning. "Go spend your first New Year's Eve together."

"No!" she argues. "I don't want you to spend tonight at home."

"I won't," I assure her. "I'll stay here."

She frowns at me. "Well, I'm not going to *leave* you here."

I return the same look. "I'm at the Peña house. There's like fifteen sets of parents inside."

"Still, though," she says, but she's hesitating now.

An arm comes around my shoulder, and it's Benny. He says with a big smile, "She's got *me*. We'll take good care of her."

Elena glances between us, and her relief is so obvious that I almost laugh. My sister is *such* a mom now. "Okay, but text me as soon as you're home." She pulls me into a tight hug and kisses my cheek. "Happy New Year, Lou."

"Don't forget your grapes!"

My sister waves goodbye to a few others but is already on her phone with a happy grin as she races back to her car.

I look up at Benny. "Thanks for that."

"Of course," he says, and leads me toward the food. "I'm glad you came."

"Me too. I'm having a great time," I tell him honestly.

He hands me a can of Jupiña and introduces me to so many cousins it's hard to keep track, but I'm not overwhelmed. I don't know if it's the party or me and this whole year, but as the hour creeps toward midnight, I'm laughing at stories and helping Mrs. Peña fill up buckets of water for others to throw out onto the street at midnight. Slips of paper are passed around for all to write their wishes for the year ahead. There are also suitcases that adults will drag around the block, to signal their dreams of travel. The circus of rituals and traditions makes me realize that growing up doesn't mean we have to stop playing along, because a new year can be its own spark of magic.

Kind of like finding an old bucket list.

"Here we go!" Benny changes the music for the countdown. "Ten! Nine! Eight!"

I grab my grapes and smile big as I watch others grab theirs, along with their suitcases, buckets, and wishes. The anticipation builds, and instead of grappling with anxiety, I'm bursting with excitement.

"Seven! Six! Five!"

Everyone shouts along and I'm almost giddy.

"Four! Three! Two!"

Sam suddenly appears on the back porch. My heart stops as I watch him frantically search the backyard until his eyes land on me.

"One! *Happy New Year!*"

He tries disentangling himself from everyone hugging and hollering on the porch. Someone is already shooting off bottle rockets. I shove grapes into my mouth as I watch Sam give up trying to get down the steps and instead vault over the railing. He's wearing the red scarf I made him. Halfway to me, he calls out, over all the noise around us, "I'm not late!"

I hurriedly pop another grape into my mouth.

"A kiss at midnight," he explains, because, oh my *god*, he was serious about that.

I swallow the last grape as he reaches me, the minute almost gone, so I tell him, "Hurry."

His lips meet mine in a dizzying rush, and I don't hesitate to kiss him back as the first seconds of a new year slip past us in a glittering shower of fireworks.

When I pull back to look at him, it's like the rest of the party has disappeared. This is the moment. The big movie moment, born right from our list. The one where we get it right. Cue the music and more fireworks.

"It was my turn to kiss you," he explains again, still holding me.

I nod and watch his gaze return to my mouth. This close to him, I'm over all the games. I want it to finally be for real.

"¡Papito!" someone yells, and Sam slowly releases me as the rest of the party surrounds us. Benny has *so* many cousins, and one of them gives a riotous laugh as he shakes Sam. "Y'all see my man run over here to kiss her at midnight like this is some romantic movie. Bro! That was dope."

And it was. I press my hands against my lips and try to settle my racing heart.

"Leave him alone, Junior," Benny says, breaking through the crowd and all who are crowing over the grand gesture.

Sam looks frustrated but offers me a shy smile, and I try my best to return it. Another checked-off wish. A way to start the year with a bit of extra luck. No different than eating all those grapes.

Benny shoos everyone away, then looks between Sam and me with a conspirator's smile. "That kiss on the list?" he asks.

I nod and he laughs. "You two are something else. Kissing at midnight? What little romantics." He gives me a teasing look. "Though since I'm a part of the list now, technically I could have kissed you."

"No," I say without heat. I fix my bangs with a gusty exhale. Sam looks a bit shell-shocked and lost for words. He's still wearing his suit. "Where'd you end up going?" I ask him, then gasp when he tells me. "You drove all the way to *Gainesville*?"

"And back," he admits, and I know he must be wrecked

with exhaustion. Despite the emotional roller coaster of a day, he still made it back in time for me. He's such a good friend, but I'm so outmatched. Because I can't be cool when it comes to him. He takes up so much space in my heart, and I both regret and am wholly thankful there aren't any more kissing quests. I can't handle them.

"As for the rest of the list, I have an idea," Benny says.

Sam drags his hands down his face and takes a deep breath. He sounds weary when he says, "Junior doesn't have a Disney ticket hookup."

"No, about the prank," Benny explains. "But we need Rocky."

"She's grounded," I tell him.

"I have a plan about that, too."

Sam

JANUARY

WHEN I GET to the station the following Tuesday, there's a maze set up. The explorers hang around it, all of us laughing like we're kids who got a new playground. Plywood is squared off into three big sections, and I lean over the side of the structure and study the intended obstacles. They don't seem too bad.

"This is a single part of what you'll actually go through," Tim explains to us. "And there will be more challenges in the competition, but I figure you yahoos needed some practice." He stands over the opening in the first section. "You'll get down on the ground and crawl in here with your air packs on."

We've practiced with the air packs but haven't been tested on them yet.

"And your masks will be blacked out."

I glance up quickly.

"Wait, what?" Jordan asks.

"It's to mimic the smoke," Tim points out. "Can't always see where you're going inside a burning building."

"But Angel is afraid of the dark!" Adriana teases the other explorer.

My heart pounds as I study the passage between sections, to make a note and maybe memorize how I'd move from one to the next without being able to see.

"Jordan, Sam, come here. Let's do a daily check." Tim calls us over and goes to grab a set of air packs. He holds one up. "Now, as we all remember, this is a SCBA. What does that stand for, Angel?"

"Scuba!" he jokes before his smile falls under Tim's glare. "Self-contained breathing apparatus."

"Very good," Tim says. "What are the three components to this SCBA, Adriana?"

Her playful look also disappears. As much as Adriana likes to joke around, she takes what we're doing here seriously. "A high-pressure tank, a regulator, and a face mask."

That new trap door in my mind opens and drops me back to the ICU. The ventilator. The mechanical hush and clicks of the machine breathing for him.

A cold sweat crawls up my neck, but I do my best to shake it off.

Tim hands one of the packs to Jordan and the other to me. We inspect the cylinders, checking their psi and making sure there's no damage or dents, like Tim taught us.

"Good, now reattach the bottle," Tim coaches. "Finger tight."

We move onto the frame, checking over the padding, straps, buckles, and hoses. The different alarms. My head is in the present, and I'm good until Tim gives us the blacked-out masks.

"Decide which of you goes first while I explain the obstacles to my other knucklehead," he says to Jordan and me.

Jordan grins. "Age before beauty."

I slip on my mask. My heart punches my ribs harder as everything disappears, and I'm left alone with the sound of my own forced breathing. *Hush. Click.* There's a sour taste in my mouth and a sharp ache in the center of my chest.

I rip off all the gear. The pack's alarm rings.

"You all right?" Jordan asks as Tim eyes me with concern.

The fear hit me too fast, and now nausea swims up my throat. "Yeah," I say thickly. "I just need some water." I move toward the kitchen but detour into the bathroom. I collapse against the sink and throw cold water on my face before taking steady breaths as I grip the counter.

When I look up, I see a mess in the mirror. I drag a steadying hand down my face, and as the frantic spike of fear levels off, I also know that it's yet another wave that I've survived.

And that's just what progress has to look like for me.

I leave the bathroom as the alarms and lights go off, and over the system, we're informed of an MVC.

"Motor vehicle collision," Tim tells me, and then gives me a quick look-over as he decides something. "Okay, you're in the engine with me."

My first ride-along. Anticipation catches hold of me.

The intersection is called out, and I pass Dan as he jumps into the ambulance with Nia, an EMT. I climb inside the engine. Tim hands me a headset.

The others put on their gear. They're calm and steady. I gaze out the window.

"As part of our training, we learn a lot about other people's trauma," Tim says, and even though he's gazing out the window, too, I know he's talking to me. "But also our own. What we see and have to do as the first ones to arrive at an emergency takes a toll, and that's not weakness. As first responders we have to take care of ourselves, too. There's no shame in that, right, Mateo?"

"No, sir. To thrive, we must survive," Mateo returns.

Tim smiles. "I like that." He looks at me. "Write that one down, kid."

I nod, tucking the words away for the next time I face that mess in the mirror who's trying his best.

We arrive at the scene, and Tim tosses me a yellow high-vis vest to throw on over my explorer uniform. "Hang back, and we'll let you know if we need you to grab anything." We're at an exit right off the interstate, where the two cars got into a minor collision. The day is gray, with a bite in the air.

"Sam, come here!" Dan calls me toward the ambulance parked up ahead. A young boy is sitting inside with his grandmother. Neither has any obvious injuries, and her posture is relaxed. "You're going to run vitals," Dan tells me. He hands me the blood pressure cuff, and I slide the boy's arm through it as gently as I can.

"He's very handsome," the older woman tells Dan.

"Don't fluster him," Dan says easily. "He's new but working to become a paramedic."

The accident isn't critical, so I ignore them to focus on the kid. "What's your name?" I ask him.

"Felix," he says.

"I have a daughter," the woman says to me. "And a son."

Dan laughs. "He's only eighteen."

"Well, my kids are thirty and single!" She sighs like it's the worst thing she's ever heard, while sitting in the back of an ambulance.

It's so different from every single experience I've ever

had around ambulances. The chaos and sirens barreling down the road toward my house, or past me on the street, leaving me wondering whose whole life is in the back of them. This could've been terrible, someone's worst day, but instead it will be an ordinary one.

Every day, I am learning to be grateful for each of those.

Back at the station, they put a sticker on the calendar for me. "Baby's first ride-a-long!" Adriana crows. I can never let her meet Cora; Port Coral would never survive.

Around eight PM, I get a text from Lou.

Rocky's ready.

Fortunately, it's plenty dark and cloudy out, and we should have enough time. I double-check the toolbox in the back of my truck, then drive to the apartment complex Lou directed me to. I check my reflection one more time and then hop out. I go to the door and knock.

A woman answers and I smile. "Hi, I'm the firefighter you spoke with on the phone." I'm neither the firefighter nor the person she spoke with on the phone, but I hope Benny and I don't sound too different.

"Nice to meet you," she says while shaking my hand, a mildly distrustful tone in her voice.

"We're grateful your daughter is interested in volunteering for our spaghetti dinner."

"She has a lot of community hours to get through." She turns and shouts, "Veronica!" over her shoulder, then looks at me again. "She'll be back before ten." It's not a question.

"Of course."

"Ten," she says again, and I know if this woman even scents that I'm lying she will kill me.

Rocky passes her mother with a look of disinterest. "Let's go, Fireman."

Her mother watches us walk all the way to my truck. Once we're inside, I say to Rocky, "She's terrifying."

Rocky says nothing. Unlike others, she doesn't seem bothered by the silence in my truck, but I still offer the aux cable. She scrolls around for a moment before landing on an indie rock song I don't know.

"So, you and Lou are close," I say in an attempt at friendly conversation. We haven't really hung out since that disastrous house party and Halloween.

She slides me an imperceptible look. "As are you two."

My heart kicks, and my next desperate question is out before I can stop it. "Does she talk about me?"

"You must think little of me if you think I'd ever tell you."

I stop at a red light and study the stoic girl beside me with new understanding. A slow smile turns into a huge one, because I'm so glad that this person is Lou's. "You're right."

Her lower lip quirks. "Of course I am."

We reach the town square, but I park down a side street, beside Benny's car. Lou's inside with her laptop, looking like your everyday super hot hacker.

"You got everything?" Lou asks me.

I open the toolbox and she smiles, obviously pleased.

Benny rubs his hands together. "Time to steal a turtle again."

Lou

ADDING A TREASURE hunt component to my beta baby tourism app is easier than I expect. I have to create new interactions, but instead of starting from scratch, it's like getting to copy and paste something I already made.

The shortcut is a total thrill.

I'm simply taking the map and navigation tools I've built so far and using them to play a quick game of *Find the Turtle*. I'm not wasting time but instead getting a practice run before Spring Fest and the big presentation. And if anyone asks, it was Benny's idea.

Sam pops his head through the open window, startling me. He leans on the door and glances down at my laptop. "Hacking it up?"

"It's not hacking when it's already *my* app," I argue,

then glance to where Rocky is moving through the shadows toward the lit-up statue.

Sam watches her, too. "Let's see if stealing a car translates in any way to stealing a statue."

"Screw statues, man," Benny says before following after Rocky to be her lookout. It's a cold January night, so the square is mostly a ghost town. But best of all, the nosy viejitos are all home. The lights around the statue blink off, leaving the space pitch-dark.

So far so good.

Sam hunches down to lean farther through the window in a bid to look at my screen. It's been a couple of days since New Year's, and I hate that I'm counting. Like Halloween and that awful party. I'm tracking every kiss, yearning to find any reason to add another.

Friendship is confusing when you really want to make out with your best friend.

Sam's eyes shift to mine before slipping down to my mouth, and I think maybe I can be easy and playful, too. *He isn't the boyfriend type.* And maybe I'm not, either.

"I ran my first call today," he says, his eyes on mine again.

I wonder by his rough voice if it was difficult. "How was it?"

He leans closer on his elbows and lowers his voice. "I freaked out a little before. Dead-dad stuff, but I got myself together."

"Hey, that's great," I say sincerely.

He nods once, and his laugh comes as a low rumble. "And then it was a totally ordinary call." He says this like it was a wondrous thing.

The car shakes, and Benny's hands are spread across the hood where he was bouncing it. "Time for phase two."

Rocky stands in front of the car, and in her arms is the infamous Golden Turtle. It's a golden turtle shell the size of a football, and Rocky's holding it like it might explode at any moment. The lights around the square are back on. She did it.

I jump out of the car and press my laptop to Sam's chest. "Don't let anything happen to either my computer or Rocky." She cannot get in any more trouble for something as silly as this.

She hands me the turtle, which is heavier than I thought.

"No curfews will be broken on my watch," Sam promises as he walks past us, then looks at Benny. "Don't let anything happen to *her*," he says, pointing to me.

Benny sighs dramatically. "Everyone will make sure nothing happens to anyone."

We watch the truck leave, and then I tape the piece of paper with the printed QR code to where the turtle used to be. Benny and I head toward the botanica. The night is quiet and cold, and after a minute of walking, Benny turns to me. "Can I ask you a question?"

"I hate when someone leads with that. Ask the question, don't torture me with it."

He laughs, his hands in his pockets. "What's up with you and Alvarez?"

My steps slow. Is Benny about to give me a heads-up about Sam? Unlikely, but I have no idea how to answer the question. "What do you mean?"

"I've never seen the guy so twisted up over someone."

Hope slips through my fear like a stubborn little weed, even though I know it might not be true. Not like I want it to be. And it's not just what Tasha said to me on Beach Day or witnessing their kiss at the party. It's because in four years, I've never seen Sam in a serious relationship. The obvious kind with handholding in hallways that everyone knows about.

And I'd have known, because even in all these years of not talking, I have always looked for him. At the start of every school year, I searched each new classroom for him: disappointed when he wasn't there, an anticipation I refused to name when he was.

A breeze blows past us as the night grows colder, my thoughts spinning away with memories.

"I don't think Sam is the type to get twisted up over anyone," I tell Benny finally.

His chuckle is quiet. "You don't see it, do you?"

"I never trust what I see," I tell him honestly. "I've read too much fanfiction."

Outside the botanica, Liliana Santos is using pastel-colored chalk paint on her big store window to paint a map that looks almost exactly like the one I showed her for the app.

"Wow, it looks incredible!" I tell her.

"Who knew you were so good at graffiti, huh?" Benny asks Liliana, who laughs.

I stand back and take a picture of her window with this bright, colorful map of downtown Port Coral. On the spot by the square where the Golden Turtle once stood, there is now a golden question mark.

"This picture will be blasted out to the junior class on Monday morning as the first clue," I explain. "Hopefully, everyone being stuck at school will give it a chance to spread before dismissal."

"Forgive my person-of-a-certain-age question, but how will it work exactly?" Liliana asks.

I point at the question mark. "If they go to that spot on the map, where the turtle used to be, they'll find a piece of paper with a code. Take a picture of it with your phone, and you'll get a link to download the current beta version of the app. From there it gives you prompts that are tied to your location and work as clues for the treasure hunt. *I* know how the game should be played at Spring Fest, but it can be hard to figure out how others will use the map and the app, so this will help me see and correct user-entered data." I stop and cross my fingers.

Benny whistles and gestures like it all went over his head.

"But all the clues should domino from one to the next until someone gets to this golden boy." I tap my knuckles against the turtle. "And a major bonus for me is that this will allow me to check for as many bugs as I can before Spring Fest."

"Genius," Liliana says, and I start to dismiss the awe in her voice, but Liliana isn't hearing it. "Another family of witches in Port Coral."

A surprised laugh tumbles out of me. "Maybe Elena, but not Mom, and definitely not me."

"Spells come in all sorts of forms. Prayers, poems, even codes." She goes inside and leaves me gaping after her, feeling a curious sense of power and confidence.

Benny sighs. "I know. The woo-woo is strong with that whole family."

He walks me to the animal shelter, which I have a key to. The second-to-last clue will take participants to the bodega, where they will be directed to "buy" a small can of cat food that is already paid for. The can will have the last hint, which leads them to the shelter. By donating it, whoever is first will get the turtle in return. But even the participants who don't win will have the chance to celebrate all the fun they just had by dropping off those food donations at a shelter where they can also meet some cute cats (and dogs) in desperate need of foster or forever homes. A win-win for everyone.

Benny peeks into the cat crates and greets my favorite tuxedo kitten with a small scratch. He turns back to me and says, "And here I thought we were pulling off a prank."

"A little chaotic good never hurt anyone," I return with a happy shrug.

Sam

FIRST DAY BACK to school after break, and I'm already back in Ms. Francis's office. Thankfully, I actually have positive stuff to talk about this time, instead of letting us sit in strained silence.

I tell her about my first ride-along. "I know the call wasn't intense, but it was also really great to see how ordinary the work can be, too," I say. "It's not always running into emergency rooms."

She smiles as she leans back in her chair. "And the big competition in front of all the firefighters is in two months, right? Are you nervous?"

I try not to think about the maze. "Excited mostly," I say. "Running keeps my nerves in check."

She leans forward and studies me. "Your four years

in marching band should be a big help." When I nod, her smile slips. "But you're going to perform at the concert before Spring Fest with the other seniors, right?"

"Don't think so," I tell her. "The concert is the same day as the competition."

"You miss it yet?"

"Drums?" I ask, and she nods. "I mean, not yet. But I know I will." My hand taps against my knee. "I sold my personal drum set a couple of months ago, but maybe I can save up for another in a couple of years, just for fun."

She makes a sad sound of commiseration. "It's hard to grow up so fast."

My hand stops. "It's not faster than any other senior."

"True, but you've had to make a lot of new decisions about your future quickly. Choices about work and finances and your family. It's a lot of responsibility."

Guilt rises like a scheduled tide. "I'm trying to become a volunteer, when there's no money in that, and I'm applying to community college, when my mom still can't go back to finish her own degree." I lean back in my seat with a shrug. Quieter, my voice rough, I add, "None of that sounds very responsible."

"You'll still be working, right?"

"Full-time between the bodega and Tío Emilio's."

"And the classes you're signing up for will be *much* more affordable at a community college, and don't forget about any support you're able to get if and when you become a volunteer." She doesn't wait for me to respond. "And you're planning on continuing to live with your family, another hand on deck in the absence of your father."

And with that, we're back to Dad again. I fold my hands over my chest and let my gaze turn to the window. It's not that I don't want to talk about Dad. Most days it's a relief to find some way to talk about him, and Ms. Francis is one of the few people I know who doesn't flinch over bringing him up. She doesn't forget that I'm sad, but she also doesn't act like I'm made of glass.

But when she—or anyone else—draws a connection between whatever I'm doing now and the grief I'm learning to live with, the deeper meaning they've applied to my motivations feels dismissive. Losing Dad was unthinkable, then it was gut-wrenchingly sad, and now it's meant to be poignant.

Yes! I want to shout. *Of course* I'll be nineteen and living at home with my mom, sister, and grandmother. I don't have the money to move out and try to be independent because we're adjusting, and this is how we survive. It's math, not poetry.

"Did you hear the big news about the Golden Turtle?" she suddenly asks.

Lou would be proud of my poker face.

"Seems like someone yanked it from the town square and hid it again."

"How do you know?" I ask, wondering if the picture is already being shared.

"Well, there's always a map whenever the turtle is hidden, and word is there's one on the window at Mimi's, downtown," she says. "And I heard through the grapevine that its usual spot in the square is empty except for a mysterious piece of paper."

"Mysterious?"

"The viejitos don't know what a QR code is, apparently." She laughs, sounding delighted. "Whoever did it is brilliant. I can't wait to see how it plays out."

The setup was Benny's idea, and he was smart enough to ask Lou, because it would never have been possible without her and Rocky. Brilliant, beautiful, bold Luisa Patterson.

The bell rings, and Ms. Francis lets me go with a friendly wave. The hallway is packed, but at the end, by her locker, I spot Lou. She stares at her phone with a preoccupied scowl as she chews on a thumbnail. I glance up at the clock on the wall and know she's worried about her app and whether it will all work.

"Hey," I say when I reach her side. "I was thinking about skipping next period."

"Scandalous," she says, and puts away her phone to exchange one textbook for another. She sighs wearily at the thick book. "I swear calculus is going to kill me. Take me back to geometry, because I'm already dead tired of trying to conceptualize imaginary numbers."

"You should come with me."

She looks up with a confused frown as she hesitates with the calculus book in hand. "Where?"

"Downtown," I say. "We can get something to eat and then find a spot to watch your treasure hunt happen."

A smile flutters at the corners of her lips, and I wish I could lean in closer. Brush a loose curl behind her ear. Kiss her after making sure no one else is looking. Oh, how I wish, and I want.

She shoves the book back into the locker and slams the door shut. Delight dances in her eyes when she says, "I've never skipped."

"We'll add it to the list," I offer.

"I do love to check off something I've already done."

I do a sweep of the hallway, then step away from the lockers and gesture for her to follow.

We have two hours to kill until school lets out, so I park by the square and we walk down the boardwalk. I buy us ice-cream cones, despite the cold afternoon, and we take them down to the harbor, where we find a spot that overlooks the beach.

Halfway down her cake-batter cone, she laughs like

she's realized something. "This is where we sat when we spied on those high schoolers. That first Beach Day before we made the list."

I glance down at the water, then again at the girl beside me. "You're right."

She takes another lick of ice cream, and I try not to watch. "You ever think that some things are meant to be?" She cuts me a quick glance. "Not in a fate way, but in an unfinished one."

"Maybe," I say, but I don't want to think that Lou and I are simply about finishing something. But in a couple of weeks, she's going to start hearing back from all those colleges, and Brilliant Lou is going to leave Port Coral. And me.

I lose interest in the rest of my ice cream. Lou glances over and says, "I told you not to get mint chocolate. Tastes like toothpaste."

We head back to the square and lie in the grass until finally we see a handful of people from school gather in front of the window at Mimi's. Lou and I jerk up to sitting and watch as they run toward the golden turtle's former spot. They all grab their phones when they see what's inside.

"They know what a QR code is," I mutter thankfully, then glance at Lou, who's transfixed. She nervously chews on a thumbnail as she watches them download the app.

With her other hand, she checks something on her phone. I gently move her hand away from her mouth, and she grips my arm.

"Come on, come on," she whispers under her breath as more people gather in front of the map on the botanica's window.

The first group cheers as the hunters run off to find the next clue. Lou playfully punches me. "It worked." She laughs, the sound deliriously happy. She turns her bright, open smile on me. "It worked!"

"Of course it did," I say, never once doubting it. Together, we watch groups race to download the app before running off to the next clue. Lou points out each stop as they run across town from the ice-cream shop to the florist to the bookstore. West to the old fire station's mural of the boy on the sailboat. Down to the marina and then back again to another corner of the square, a tiny little Port Coral adventure, until we finally see the first group race into the bodega, cheering and shouting, before running back out a moment later.

"They're headed toward the animal shelter," she says, wondrous.

"You should keep doing this," I tell her sincerely.

"Doing what? Trick people into helping animals?"

"Yes, but also *this*." I circle my hand in front of us at the laughing groups, racing around town like they're on the best quest ever. "You should develop games. More apps like this."

She barks a laugh. "That would mean I finally gave in and refused to grow up." Her thumb returns to her mouth, but before I can remind her of her attempt to stop chewing her nails, she confesses, "I once drew up an idea for an augmented reality, location-based RPG. Not one based off any of the big properties, but like a cute indie slice-of-life sort of game."

"You should do that, Lou!" I tell her earnestly. "Why didn't you work on it?"

She falls back in the grass. "It's just a game, Sam. It's not real. Not like training to become a firefighter. Or computer programming, or teaching. *That's* real."

I hate that she always stops to compare herself to others. "You're brilliant, Lou. Games are real. Creating things that make people happy is important."

She looks at me for a long moment before saying, "This was just Benny's idea for a silly prank. And I happened to have the toys to play along."

We watch the first group run toward the square, all of the participants screaming with joy, the turtle held up high over their heads victoriously. Others cheer and jeer their classmates and friends, but it looks like everyone continues playing the entire hunt anyway. I turn to watch Lou's happy face, full of so much joy and longing, like

she wants to jump into the game, too. Playful Lou. Peter
Pan Lou.

Let's stay here and never grow up, Lou.

Please don't leave.

I fall back beside her, my selfish heart heavy with the
wish that we had more time.

LOU AND SAM'S TO-DO LIST
BEFORE WE GRADUATE:

~~GO TO BEACH DAY~~

~~help all the stray neighborhood cats~~

go to Disney World

~~join a club~~ (started one actually)

~~pull off the most epic prank of all time~~

~~win the town Halloween costume contest~~
(yay, Rocky the Ninja Mermaid!!)

~~apply to the same colleges~~

~~work on our Spanish~~

~~Lou will hold her breath longer than Sam underwater~~ *break into someone's pool~~

~~go to an actual party~~

~~get super good at kissing~~
*hang out on second base

~~kiss someone at midnight on New Year's Eve~~
~~(after getting super good at it)~~

~~be serenaded (à la 10 things I hate about you)~~

~~beat the viejitos at dominos~~ (not gonna happen)

~~bury a time capsule~~

write a letter to our future selves

~~drive Lou where she needs to go~~

~~skip school together~~

SAM'S ADDITIONS:

~~MASTER "TOM SAWYER" BY RUSH ON DRUMS~~
~~(AND SOME CUBAN JAZZ FOR DAD)~~

~~DRIVE THE BARRACUDA~~

~~ALWAYS HOLD MY BREATH LONGER THAN~~
~~LOU UNDERWATER~~ (LOST ON A TECHNICALITY!)

GET A DOG (I'M ALLERGIC TO CATS, YOU
KNOW THIS)

~~SAM WILL GO ON EMT SIDEQUEST~~

MARCH

THE DECISION FROM Miami will be posted tonight by five PM.

By three, my parents are hovering. "Don't you two have work?" I ask.

Dad gasps and looks at his watch. "Oh my god, she's right, babe."

Mom points at herself with the spoon she's been using to stir her tea. "Spring break."

Dad clutches his chest and exhales with relief. Someone give my parents an award.

I slam closed the book I've been too anxious to read. "You guys are so dramatic." I hurry upstairs to pace in peace. An hour later, I head back to the kitchen for a drink, but halfway down the stairs, I see that Elena, Nick, and Pearl have come over.

Suspicious, I glance at my sister. "What are you doing here on a Tuesday?"

"Can I not visit my own family?" she shoots back way too defensively.

I look at Mom, who offers a blasé shrug from the table. "They're visiting, Lou. Not everything is about you."

"Right." I slowly take the last few steps down and stop in front of my sister's boyfriend. "Hi, Nick."

He swallows, looking nervous. "Hi, Lou. Good to see you."

"Leave him alone," Elena says, with Pearl in her lap.

I cross my arms and tilt my head. In my best interrogation voice, I ask, "Why are you *really* here, Nick?"

His alarmed gaze darts past me. "To see you."

"Don't look at them, Nick, look at me."

"Luisa," Mom warns.

"I mean," he stops and clears his throat before trying again. "We're here to see all of you." He is definitely starting to sweat.

"Is that a gift bag on the couch?" I lean to the left so he can't see past me to the others, who are probably trying to coach him. "Why is there a gift bag on the couch, Nick?"

"It's for Pearl," he says.

"Pearl?" I ask.

My three-month-old niece shrieks.

The door swings open and Sam barrels inside. Winded, he reports, "I got my camera! We're good."

My entire family groans. Nick is triumphant as he spins to Elena and says, "It wasn't me! I didn't break!"

Elena kisses him. "You did good, baby."

Sam doesn't look bothered in the least as he holds up the camera to start documenting the day like he does everything else lately. "Aren't you supposed to be at the station?" I ask him.

"Spring break," he explains. He stops in front of me, smiling behind the camera. "Big day."

I blow out a nervous breath. I think about Miami's acceptance rate, and my SAT scores and mediocre grades, and I try not to be invested, but seeing everyone gathered around like it's a party makes that tiny little secret voice in my head whisper, *Maybe.*

Maybe I *am* as smart and creative as my family and Sam think I am.

Maybe I'll be accepted.

Maybe these next four years won't be as hard as the last ones, because I'll have finally tricked my brain into doing this the right way.

Despite all the ways I try to steel myself against being embarrassed, excitement creeps into my pessimistic despair as Mom asks me to set up my laptop on the table.

"Mom, no, this isn't some vlog," I complain without heat before racing up the stairs to get it. I think of all the videos I've watched of families cheering around their newly minted college students and run faster. In my room, one of my study playlists quietly sings out from my desktop, and I stop only to light those candles again. Next time I'm up here, all this might be behind me. I kiss the list for luck, grab my laptop, and get back to the party.

We order a bunch of pizza and crowd into the kitchen. Seated at the kitchen table when five o'clock hits, I flip open my laptop, and my family creeps in closer to stand around me. Sam backs up and picks up the camera again. He offers me a quick wink and big smile.

Click. Click. Scroll. Click.

There it is. The link to check the school's portal.

Mom shakes my shoulders. "We're so proud of you, whatever happens," she whispers. Dad drops a kiss on my head.

I nod and click the button. I swallow, feeling faint.

My eyes blur and I read words that don't make sense at first. And then I read them again, and my stomach swims with pizza and anguish as I realize, *Oh, here it is.*

The rejection I expected.

A hand lands on my shoulder. From somewhere far off, I hear myself squeak, "It's fine. I'm fine." I glance up and meet Sam's worried gaze. The camera comes down, and I hop up out of the chair that squeaks against the floor in my rush to get as far away from my laptop and the smell of pizza as I can.

"Luisa—" Mom starts, but I wave a hand to stop her.

"It's just one school," I say before she can. "There are others, I know, I'm *fiiiiiine*," I say, dragging the word out as I take the stairs two at a time back to my room. I shut the door and slam my hand across the light switch, throwing the room into welcoming darkness. I blow out the candles that didn't work. I don't even glance at the list. Instead I disappear beneath the neon glow of the lighting around my computer. Safe in my cave, I sink down to the floor.

It would be more satisfying if I could cry about it, find some kind of release after months of buildup. But it's such a hollow feeling for that negative voice in my head to be proven right all along, the little witch.

"Lou!" Mom calls and tries to open the door. I've committed an actual crime because, for the very first time in my entire life, I've locked my door. I wait to hear her knock again, for her to wiggle the knob and demand entry. She is my mother, and I'll have to answer it.

But silence follows instead of her voice. I throw one arm over my suddenly burning eyes.

A few moments later, my window creaks open. I shoot up and watch Sam climb inside. He says nothing as he moves to lie down beside me.

"We shouldn't have put you on the spot," he finally says.

I laugh darkly. "I wanted it, too. I love those videos of kids getting into school and their families losing it around them. I wanted tangible proof of all that pride."

"But this is just one, Lou."

But it was *the* one. Because even as I waved my hands like a magician and distracted everyone with impressive faraway places that proved Lazy Lou was smart enough to get into those schools, too, I held Miami close like a secret baby bird that was almost ready to fly.

"What if the rest are the same?" I ask, my gaze on the ceiling. "What if they all say no? What's plan B?" I turn my head to look at Sam's profile, and my gaze goes past him to my bulletin board, where the corner of our list sticks out.

"I hear Port Coral Community isn't too bad," he says, his voice low. "You can get your two-year there and then transfer anywhere you want." He turns to look at me. "There are more roads."

"But not quests," I return, and by the way his chest rises and falls on a deep sigh, I know he's also thinking of our nearly finished list. "Maybe we can say phooey to all this college business and run away to Disney World," I say, my voice low, just between us. "We'll live like kings. No, better yet, ducks! You see those videos of the ducks there? We can swim in lakes, hang out at water parks."

Sam smiles. "Live off fallen ice-cream cones and the fries that tourists throw us." He turns to me. "There are more quests, Lou. We still haven't written our letters to our future selves." He props himself up on one elbow and leans closer, and my heart flies into my throat because he's going to kiss me, and I arch toward him, ready to kiss him back. But instead he pulls his phone out of his pocket. "Let's write them now."

My hand flies to my chest, and I exhale sharply as I come down from that sudden rush. "What?" I ask, my voice rough.

"Our letters to our future selves," he says again as he scrolls around on his phone. "We'll look past this *one* rejection, and all our combined anxiety, to imagine where we'll be once all this senior year uncertainty is over." He shows me his phone and it's opened to his email. A blank message is already addressed to me.

"Why are you sending it to me?"

"Because, like I said months ago, we can hold the letters for each other." Sam leans back against my desk as he begins typing. "And then we can send them to each other in five years. It'll be like finding the list again, but on purpose this time."

Sam not only trusts me to hold this message for him, but he believes we'll still be friends in another five years, despite all the unknowns between now and then. The show of faith is enough to make me sit up and grab my phone. I open my personal email and start a new message to Future Me. Minutes pass as we sit on the floor of my dark bedroom, lit only by the rainbow neon illuminating my desk.

When I finish, I look up and find Sam watching me. His head is tilted back, and a smile plays on his lips as he taps his screen. My inbox chimes with a new message.

Sam

THIS WEEKEND IS not only Spring Fest, but Friday is the day of Lou's big app presentation and my Fire Explorer competition. I'm preparing by running the stairs at the beach, wearing a backpack loaded with a sandbag. Lou helped me find a workout online that helps prepare candidates for the CPAT. She did that even though she's been busy dealing with the bugs the treasure hunt revealed in her app.

But today, she needed air. So she sits cross-legged on the sand and times me with her phone.

"I like when you mention the GPS stuff," I tell her after she finishes running through her presentation again. My legs are dying, but the stair climb is a huge part of the test.

She makes a note, then glances up and looks at my legs for a beat. She shakes her head quickly before focusing on her stopwatch again. She shoots me a thumbs-up, letting me know I'm good on time. She returns to sifting for seashells through the sand around her legs.

Lou has been quiet ever since last week's rejection. I can see her mind spinning, and I'm doing my best to keep her spirits up. But I don't know if it's better to be positive about all the applications she still has out or to distract her from them.

"I'm going to do one more lap," I tell her. We plan to pick up dinner from the diner afterward.

"Have fun," she says, but she stills when she glances at her phone's stopwatch, and I worry I'm moving slower than I thought. I pick up my pace, but when I get back down to the beach and look at Lou for my thumbs-up or thumbs-down, she's staring off into the distance.

"Lou?"

She snaps back from wherever she was and looks at me. "Oh no, I'm sorry. I think I accidentally stopped it." Her eyes are tearing up.

"Hey, it's okay," I quickly assure her. "No big deal."

She jumps to her feet and wipes the sand from her shorts. "I've got to get home."

"Wait, what happened?"

She won't look at me. "I need to go. I have so much to do." The words are thick.

"Lou," I say seriously.

She spins back toward me, and her eyes are lit with anger. "*What*, Sam?"

It's such a flipped switch. I drop the heavy backpack that falls off my shoulders like a boulder and step closer. "Hey, it's okay."

"I know it's okay," she grits out. "It's just *one* more, right?"

And suddenly I understand. "Which school was it?"

Anger sparks off her as she presses her lips together. There's a storm brewing around her. She lifts her phone and dares, "Guess." There's so much fire in her shadowed eyes, and when I don't play along, she finally gasps, "Georgia Tech," like it's winded her.

"I'm sorry—"

She cuts me off. "Remember on Beach Day when Tasha asked me what schools I was applying to? And I told her Tech and she was so impressed? I should have known then. What in the world was I doing applying to a school like that?" Her laugh is bitter and crackles with emotion. "But here I am, crying *again*, when I don't even know if I wanted to move to Atlanta, but I had to pick schools that were far, but not *too* far." She holds a finger and thumb up to signal the distance. I know she's trying to make fun of herself even as the emotions choke her. I swallow hard, feeling useless.

"They were places that sounded impressive. But also popular like Marvel?" She slams a hand over her eyes. "I am *ridiculous*. A ridiculous crybaby."

"You're not. You're amazing." I can see it's the last thing she wants to hear, but I desperately want to know how to help her. "What do *you* want, Lou?"

She lowers her hand and waves at the stairs and backpack at my feet. "I want *this*. You found your answer and now you're glowing. I want to feel like that about my future." She exhales, and I'm sucker punched with a new guilt. Because while my answers are becoming clear, Lou is drowning in rejection.

A drive of panic hits me at the sight of her doubt, and I'm frantic for another relic from our past. A quest or game. I'm scrambling for a flashlight to fight off this new wave of darkness. "Let's go to Disney World!"

Lou pulls back, surprised. "*What?*"

"It's still on the list," I explain.

"Yeah, but we don't have any tickets and it's a school night."

"You're right." I shake my head quickly and drag a hand through my hair. "We can go to the animal shelter. I should get a dog for Cora! That's the other one still on the list."

"Sam, you can't just go adopt a dog right now," she points out, sounding impatient. She rubs her brow like she's holding off a headache. "I should go home." She heads past me up the stairs, and I follow behind her.

"You said that you're not sure if you even wanted to go to Atlanta," I say, my tone more urgent now. I'm determined to reassure her before she can fall beneath the wave of depression I know too well. We reach the boardwalk. "So much of your motivation was because of Elena and—"

As she spins around, flames sparking in her eyes, I realize it's the absolute worst thing I could have said. I know that look.

She wants to kick me.

"We all do that, Sam!" she argues. "Your whole year was about your family and grief, but suddenly I'm some flaky leaf in the wind for pushing myself because of *my* family?"

I flinch at the hot rush of frustration. "I never said 'flaky,' and we're not talking about my grief, Lou. For *once* we're not talking about that."

The sky rumbles with thunder, and her voice is low and unguarded when she steps close and says, "You're right that Elena is the one who kicked off this parade for me, but I wouldn't be doing this if it didn't *also* matter to me. That's how it's always been with me. I'm stubborn and run away with exciting ideas, and then a barrier derails me, and I fall apart for a minute, but I'm *trying*." She growls, frustrated. "Disney World, Sam? Right now? *Really*? Like

I'm some kid you have to appease with a lollipop after a crap day?"

A wave slams against the boardwalk like her anger called it forth.

I have no idea how to fix this. Or how to be who she needs right now even as I'm desperate to make her feel better. "I offered because it's the only thing left on the list."

"Right, the list. Of *course*, it had to be about the list! Everything we've done this year together has been because of 'middle school shit.'"

"Once!" I shout, surprised to find myself blisteringly frustrated. "I said that *once!*"

"I can't believe you brought up adopting a dog to me under false pretenses."

"Because we don't talk." At her look of disbelief, I hurry on. "About the future beyond these next weeks or *us*. You're dealing with all of these rejections, and I have no idea how to talk to you about it, because I'm so afraid of messing up in some unknown way and you not talking to me ever again."

Her expression shifts from anger into something so open and honest it disarms me. "You don't know how to talk to me because I'm sad. And you want me to make you feel better about that."

"What?" I ask, not understanding. Except my heart is racing, hard and heavy, because I do understand. I know all too well what she's about to say and I hate it.

"I'm getting all these rejections while everything is falling into place for you, and you feel guilty."

My breath leaves me as panic unspools. The ache in her voice slips past my ribs and untangles all the knots I've carefully tied to keep myself together.

"I *know* that I can make new plans!" she shouts to the boardwalk and everyone within hearing distance. "But I get to be depressed about this for one stupid minute before I have to bottle up all my messy feelings for someone else's comfort."

I can't speak because I'm painfully reminded of Mom falling apart outside the church.

Lou's face twists beneath my silence. The wind has picked up, and she pushes her dark hair back just as her phone chimes. She checks it, and her next words are a string of curses in Spanish as she turns away from me and marches down the boardwalk, the ends of her hair wild in the sea breeze.

"Lou, wait!"

"And you know what else?" she calls over her shoulder. "You don't get to climb through my window this time just because *you're* sad!"

"Lou, come on!"

"*¡Vete pa' carajo!*" she shouts over her shoulder before disappearing into the botanica. The door slams behind her, the bells clattering in an ominous shriek.

"Lou!" I call again, but when I reach the door to Mimi's,

it's Elena standing on the other side of the glass. She flips the sign to CLOSED.

"The parting shot was lethal," Mr. Gomez murmurs from the viejitos' spot in front of the bodega.

"I know." I close my eyes on a heavy sigh and mutter, "We've been working on my Spanish."

Lou

I HAVE BEEN hurled into this store like a brick by emotions that now swirl through me like a tornado. I know it's not just Sam. It's all these rejections and how deeply they cut despite how strong I want to be. How carefree. I pace as Elena and Liliana stay behind the counter. "Lazy Lou. *Sensitive* Lou," I spit the last adjective like a curse.

"Legendary Lou," Liliana offers.

"I've been rejected by *every* school so far," I announce, and it's so ridiculous that I can't help but laugh. "I am allowed to be mad! Or sad! Or disastrously disappointed."

"Of course you are," Elena assures me.

I look toward the window, my heart still racing. "And maybe also a little bit in love," I say more quietly, like a question I already know the answer to. "Because I really want to go finish this fight."

Liliana smiles a little as she leans over the counter. "As the last person to yell like that about love by the harbor, I definitely think you should."

I nod decisively before flying back outside. Sam is pacing the sidewalk in front of the shop, and there's a lit spark in his eyes when he sees me walking toward him that matches the one I feel sizzling beneath my skin. No longer a golden boy but a realer one. His hair is a disheveled mess from his own hands. I'd kiss him if I weren't so frustrated.

"You never give me a chance to explain," he says.

I hate public shows of anything, and yet here we are, fighting in the middle of downtown Port Coral. There are faces in windows, outside the bodega, and around the square. I'm torn between embarrassment over my outburst and everything I still want to say to him.

"I've leveled up this year, but I'm still a mess," I tell him. "And I'm starting to realize that you are, too."

His eyes go wide with surprise. But before he can say a word, the sky splits and releases a heavy, instant rain. The kind that immediately drenches us. The vieijtos jump up and scatter as Sam grabs my hand and we run. I don't even think about not following him. Across the square, beneath the flickering lamps. We reach his truck and we're both soaked. Sam opens my door first, then dashes around to the driver's side. Once he's inside, he turns on the heater.

He searches around. "I don't have any towels."

"It's fine," I say, my teeth chattering. "Just take me home."

He says nothing as he jerks the car into reverse and drives us out of the marina parking lot. He hands me the aux cable, but I don't take it. At a red light, he plugs it into his phone instead and scrolls around.

A Janelle Monáe song plays. And I want to laugh. *Look at us now, Janelle.* My hair is a frizzy, wet mess, and I wore a white shirt today that is probably now totally see-through.

We get home and he parks in his driveway. After a long moment of strained silence, he says, "I'll go get an umbrella."

"No, it's fine." I reach to open the door, but Sam dives across the seat and puts his hand on the handle—not on me, like I wished. My head is all over the place. "Give me one minute," he begs. "Don't walk out of here and stop talking to me. I can't do that again, Lou."

His honesty disarms me. I'm an exposed, vulnerable mess who's terrified of changing things between us. But I'm also a total wreck over the rumpled, desperate Sam in the wet clothes who's looking at me like I'm the one with all the power.

It's intoxicating. I dive across the console.

He welcomes me immediately, helping me navigate my way over the stick shift as I bury my hands in his hair. We each let out a sigh of relief the moment our lips touch. The truck is too warm and probably running out of oxygen, but stopping to breathe means thinking and I want no part of that. I want to shut my brain off and disappear in the safety and heat of him. I deepen the kiss in search of reassurance because I'm *burning*.

My phone rings. I ignore it as I bite his bottom lip like he taught me, but when the phone continues to ring, I tear my mouth from Sam's and see Elena's face on my screen. Sam's lips fall to my neck. Instinct tells me to answer my phone or else she's going to call Mom. I grab it and hit the green icon.

"Hey, you make it home?" Elena asks, worried. "The rain is super intense."

"Yeah," I choke out. Sam's mouth falls to my collarbone. "Almost."

"Okay, good. I told Mom you were on your way."

I close my eyes, pained. "Thanks."

"Wait, unless you two are deep into the post-fight makeup. Because I've been there and—"

I hang up. I'm in Sam's lap, and I can see the porch light turn on across the street. Sam's head falls back against the seat like he knows: The moment is broken.

All that's left is the ringing of our words and the utter exhaustion that seeps into my bones after such a storm of intense emotions.

I press my forehead to his, fear of failure tearing me in half. "I also got rejected by Florida today. Out on the boardwalk." His mouth falls open in surprise, and I slide my thumb across his parted lips. "My dad's alma mater."

He whispers my name, pained.

"It's very true that I wanted to do this for a lot of people and for a lot of reasons, but in the end, it's just me. Trying to accomplish the impossible." I lean over and push open the door on the driver's side, then hop out of his lap and the truck.

I cross the street to home, and I'm a bedraggled mess when I step inside. Mom, Dad, and Max are in the middle of a game of Rummikub in the living room. There's a movie playing on the TV. My hair is surely a soggy mess, and I haven't been brave enough to look down and check if my shirt is actually transparent now. They all gape at me, but Mom is the fastest. She jumps to her feet and tells them, *"Out!"*

Dad and Max scramble to standing. "What about the popcorn?" Max asks.

"Get it, get it," Dad hisses, and they grab the bowl and disappear upstairs.

"Tell me," Mom says, and opens her arms.

I walk right into her arms. My clothes are still wet. I'm crying again and I *hate* it. "Florida said no."

Mom's arms tighten. She holds me and maybe the world doesn't stop, but in my mother's arms, it feels like it does. "There will be so many noes."

I choke out a laugh. "Not helping."

"But you and your joy are bigger than all of them."

Lou

I'M SITTING ON a huge bag of cat food at the shelter when my fourth and fifth rejections find me. Duke and Vanderbilt let me down gently.

And yet again, I'm not even waitlisted.

They're all coming furiously fast now. Despite Mom's reassuring words last night, I am consumed by a history of sacrifice and so many celebrated ideas of what my success is meant to look like that by not being exceptional, I am falling short for everyone, including me.

I have one school left. UCF. Orlando. I try not to think about Sam offering to take me to Disney World, because I need time to catch my breath.

And then I get up and focus on collecting everything our newest volunteer at the shelter will need.

"Thank you," the woman says. "My daughter did your treasure hunt and hasn't stopped talking about this pregnant cat she saw."

Cande, a junior, smiles. "My friends found the turtle! It was awesome."

"Really? Well, we're so grateful for your help fostering this mama and her future litter," I tell them before they leave. "And don't hesitate to reach out if you have any questions."

"Thank you!" the woman says, and they happily carry the crate and supplies to their car.

"You okay?" Rocky asks me once they're gone. "You're usually dancing by this point when we get a new volunteer."

I steel myself to say it out loud. She already knows about Vanderbilt. "Duke also said no."

"To hell with Duke and the other one," she says immediately. She's gotten into a few of the schools she's applied to but is still waiting to hear from UCF, just like I am.

"What do you mean?" I'm surprised enough to laugh. "Duke is like an Ivy of the South, and Durham is very cool. They have *seasons*. Big trees that change colors and old bookstores."

"Yeah, but did you *want* to go there?"

This is the question everyone keeps asking. "At this point, I want to go live under a bridge and curse anyone who comes near it."

"Troll witch, I like it," she says. "There's stability in that line of work."

I imagine how I'll tell Mom. I text her to let her know I'm headed to the botanica. Inside, the air is warm and smells like incense and dryer sheets for some reason. As Elena finishes up with a customer, I collapse in the window seat.

"What's the matter?" she asks when she finds me draped there, one arm thrown over my eyes.

"I don't want to talk about it," I say, weary and forlorn.

"Which one?"

"What do you mean, *which one?*"

"Which one do you not want to talk about?" she asks. "Miami or Georgia Tech?"

"Obviously, I don't want to talk about either of those, Elena."

Or my three latest rejections.

A lighter flickers, and the sweet scent of burning herbs hits the air. My sister stands over me with a smoking bundle. When I give her a sardonic look, she explains, "Your energy is real dark, Lou." She continues to swirl the smoke around us. After another minute or two, she says, "I saw Sam running around the square the other day. He's looking...real fit."

Sam is running and working out all the time, focused on his upcoming competition. I peek at Elena sideways, and admit, "When he takes his shirt off, I want to die."

My sister nearly drops the lit bundle. "Jesus, Lou! Are you two . . . you know?"

"We're not, but—" I exhale slowly and wonder how to explain how I feel about Sam, especially after last night. "I love that I can read his smiles. And how good he smells. He's safe and exciting, and it's like my head finally speaks the same language as my heart whenever I'm with him."

Everything's different with Sam. I can care about him as much as I want to. Because even as the world tells me no over and over again, I get to keep the memory of Sam, on a warm, spring afternoon, both of us sprawled back on the grass as he tells me I'm brilliant.

The sweet smoke stills. My big sister smiles down at me. "That's beautiful, Lou. You should tell him that."

I shrug and bite my lip. "I think we messed it all up again."

Elena shakes her head like she's already a hundred years older than me. "You have to believe that the trust you just so poetically described goes both ways."

The bell over the door chimes, and Mom walks into the shop. In one arm she carries her usual pile of papers to grade, and in the other the baby carrier with Pearl. Elena jumps over to grab her daughter as Mom looks at me. "Ready to go home?"

"I was actually hoping to run through my presentation one more time in front of both of you," I say, then reluctantly sit up and grab the pile of notecards from my bag.

Elena turns the sign to CLOSED, and then my mother, sister, and niece settle on the window seat and wait for me to begin another practice run before my presentation.

"What's up, Spring Fest?" I call out in a big, cheery voice.

Mom stalls me. "Well, it won't be Spring Fest yet," she says.

Elena rolls her eyes. "Don't interrupt her over silly details, Mom."

"It's not *silly*," she argues. "This is how she's preparing—she wants notes."

"Not two seconds in."

"But it's—"

"Duke and Vanderbilt rejected me today," I blurt out, both to waylay the passive-aggressive fight that's clearly brewing and because I can't hold it in a moment longer. Because it *sucks*. Everyone kept asking what I wanted, and it's as they all reject me that I realize, I want *this*. I want to go to college like I once wanted to go to Beach Day and to run away to a theme park and win a Halloween costume contest. I want college years and late nights and new stories and the chance to meet other nervous, anxious freshmen who might become new friends for life. I want to build new treehouses. And it's starting to hit me that I might not get any of that.

They both still. "What?" Mom asks.

My laugh tastes bitter in my mouth. In a choked

whisper, I admit, "I wanted to give you a good story, Ma. The bedazzled graduation cap, the big scholarship, a viral video of all of us crying and screaming when I got into a fancy college."

"Ay, Luisa." Mom's chin trembles with swallowed emotion.

I pop one fist on my hip and paste on a fake smile, because I can't bear to see her cry. My nerves have strangled me, but I'm trying my best to be light about it so this doesn't swallow me whole. "The old girl tried her best, but the odds aren't great. I've only got one school in play. I know UCF isn't as fancy as an *Ivy* or *Princeton*—"

"Don't do that," Elena jumps in. "You do not need to go to an Ivy or some ridiculously expensive school to prove anything to anyone, Lou. They're institutions stacked with inequities that thrive off a broken system." She turns a stony look on Mom. "Higher education is great and important, and it has a lot of value, but we can't let it define *our* value."

Mom nods. "You're right."

A laugh of disbelief tumbles out of Elena as she gapes at Mom.

"Oh, don't look at me like that," Mom says. "I'm a teacher, dealing with garbage from up top and trying to sort through it for kids even more marginalized than either you or me." She sighs deeply, and it's like a mountain falls off her shoulders as she melts back against the window seat. "When I applied to college, I had to figure it all out on my own. I couldn't get aid because of my parents' status, and every piece of paper I signed felt like a trap and a taunt. Here was the only way to climb their proverbial ladder." Mom shakes her head. "I swore it would be easier for all of you. *I* would make it easier. I'd bend the world to meet you halfway if I could get my hands on it."

Elena looks overwhelmed, like this is the last conversation she expected to have tonight. "Our lives are easier and still complicated in different ways. I didn't go to Princeton and had a baby at nineteen," she says. "But I am so *tired* of being made to feel small about my life."

"I do that?" Mom asks in a small voice.

"The whole world does," Elena says, sounding winded but resolute. "And I needed you to make me feel strong, but your fear for me always gets in the way." With a patient look, Elena reaches for Mom's hand. "But you were right there when Pearl was born, assuring me I could do it even when I was screaming that I couldn't. And you're there every single time I need you, even when you're driving me nuts. And I *love* my life, Mom. Even when it feels like I have to defend it from everyone else's definition of self-worth or success."

Mom sits up. "Those nebulous ideas of success are bullshit."

"Whoa!" both Elena and I say. It's not rare to hear mom curse, but it's still fun to tease her when she does.

"They are," she insists. "Those supposed markers are poisoned by racist systems that have dismantled our communities and sense of identity."

Elena's abrupt laugh is loud. "Okay, Professor Mom."

Mom glances down at Pearl with a soft smile. "And in the midst of that mess, you're building a beautiful life." She looks at me and says, "What I want most for all of you is the chance to make your own choices."

"I made these choices, Mom." I lift my chin. "They're just not choosing me back."

Mom leans forward and is quiet for a long moment. "Some doors aren't ours to open, but every single one of those rejections and struggles are steps to something more. Something that is *yours* and deserving of you." There isn't a drop of pity or softness in her voice. She isn't trying to soothe or coddle. She's dead serious, and I'm overwhelmed by what I see in her eyes.

Certainty. About me.

"Even if the last college rejects you, you can do two years at Port Coral Community and then transfer to a university. And there are so many paths that follow your interests. Computer science, digital production, arts, sciences, even game design."

I stare at her, unblinking, feeling both seen and forever confused by my mother. It'll probably always feel like that between us. I can't help but laugh.

"And when you walk through that door," she says, "you'll make sure others can follow."

I sober quickly and nod, my heart in my throat.

Mom sits up straight, and that familiar teacher light sparks in her eyes. "Now start the presentation from the top."

"Are you serious?" I choke out.

"Always."

Sam

THE CONCRETE HISSES from the heat released with the rain. Once I'm out of my neighborhood, I finally stop thinking. *Breath in, breath out.* Because this is all I can do with the competition only a day away. I run past the bright ranch-style houses closer to downtown. The small yards are manicured, many of them studded with fruit trees. The sweet smell of lemons is strong in the air as I pass a yellow house.

When I hit the town square, I continue all the way around the wide sidewalks for several laps. The sun slowly sets as I pass warmly lit windows. I can smell the ocean beyond the boardwalk, the rain steaming off the street, and the dinner rush outside the diner and bodega. Spring Fest is coming, and all the flowering trees around the square

are in bloom. I remember Dad telling me how much Mom loved them when they first moved here.

The bright rush of memory is sudden and disrupts my footing. When Mom and I were in the midst of our grief, the world wanted us to make them feel better. And here I've been doing the same thing to Lou: As she dealt with one rejection after another, I wanted her to tell me she was strong enough to handle it.

Make me feel better about this awful thing you're experiencing. I don't know how else to help.

I stop as my body's screams catch up to me.

Herbs and wildflowers are growing around a nearby bench. I sit and lower my elbows to my knees and hang my head as I try to catch my breath. As the orange horizon dips into darkness, the lampposts around me all light up at once.

Someone sits down beside me, and I have to steel myself against the sudden, desperate wish that it's Dad. Maybe he's here to tell me about the trees and Mom. To listen and give me advice in his voice that I miss so much. But when I glance over, I see that it's Liliana Santos from the botanica. She isn't looking at me, but instead at the twig in her hand.

"I used to be a runner," she says.

I say nothing, still catching my breath.

"Not literally." She laughs. "God, I hate running."

I don't understand the joke or why she's sitting here,

making it. I wonder what Lou said when she ran inside her store.

"This is my mom's bench."

I sit up quickly like I've disgraced another altar and notice the plaque behind me.

Dedicated to Milagro Santos
Our Mimi and Healer of Port Coral

Liliana smiles. "My mom with all her potions and soup, all served from a laundry room window. I can hardly bear to close it because maybe I'll hear a knock, and it'll be her."

Emotion chokes me. This is worse than nostalgia. This is admitting to all the secret, impossible wishes of hearing or finding our parents even after everything. The bond *has* to be that strong, right? I keep my head down.

She goes on, "One of the things someone said to me after she died that stuck the most was that healing isn't linear."

I swallow hard. I want to jump up and leave. Run home, slam the door closed, and lock it tight. But I'm frozen, a desperate child.

"Sometimes it's soft. Sentimental. You're humbled by the power of having loved someone who loved you back that much." She runs a thumb across the leaf.

I let myself imagine telling Dad about volunteering

at the station. Would he be proud? Surprised? Every new answer points me in a new direction with one hand, and stabs me with the other, because Dad isn't here to see any of it.

"But then it becomes so angry and endless," she continues. "Everything gone, and everything that will never be again chokes you. Wave after wave, and there's nothing to do but cry until you can breathe again." She shakes her head a little. "So endless and impossibly fast."

I can't speak. My throat is tight, and I grit my teeth as my hands tangle into knots.

"Say their names. Talk to and about them. Relish the softer moments, the songs that stir a good memory and ease that angry, broken thing in your chest a little." She lifts the leaf to her nose. She still has yet to even look at me, and that somehow makes this vulnerable moment possible. "The memories are the gift."

"Liliana? You ready?"

I look up and see a man waiting a few feet away. I recognize him as Benny's carpenter friend who works out of the old fire station. Liliana smiles at him and gets to her feet. "See you around, kid." They leave together.

The leaf is left behind in her place. I pick it up and realize it's a sprig of rosemary.

On my run back home, I detour down the boardwalk—and it's just me, the ocean, and my Dad's favorite songs in my earbuds, and as the night softens around me, I remember our rides on Saturdays and my eyes burn, but my breaths pump through my lungs and blood in big waves, with bracing, living gusts of air, and I'm grateful.

Back at home, I shower. Afterward in my room, I see Lou's bedroom light is on. I plug my camera into my laptop and hit Play on the last clip.

It's Lou getting her first rejection.

I skip further back. I watch Lou from a couple of weeks ago on-screen, walking ahead of me down the boardwalk. She stops at the bookshop window to show me the black cat sleeping inside. Her smile is bright and open as she drops to her haunches and presses her face to the window. I watch myself lean in to see past my own reflection in the glass when Lou leaps to her feet, bumping into me. The camera jostles as I drop it. Still aimed up at us, it catches her shocked face as she races to apologize. I laugh to soothe her worry before bothering with the camera.

The memories are the gift.

Liliana's words repeat like a song in my mind as I open the old editing program and begin to upload all my new files.

Lou

IT'S FINALLY FRIDAY. The day circled on my calendar in a demanding shade of red. My presentation and Sam's competition. I step away from my bulletin board and watch him leave his house. He's wearing his Fire Explorer uniform. His last name is stitched over his heart.

"He's going to be a paramedic?"

I startle at Max suddenly standing beside me. He's watching Sam, too.

"Looks like it," I say.

"He got to me so fast that day," Max admits with wonder. He still doesn't like to talk about the accident.

"He runs a lot." It's a little ridiculous.

Max considers this. "I'm glad he was there."

I smile at my brother. "Me too."

"You should talk to him."

My smile disappears. "What do you know about it?" I ask without heat.

"I know you guys are friends, and friends talk." He's out of the sling, but he still favors his injured arm. "Whatever else you are, you were that first." We continue to watch as Sam loads gear into the back of his truck.

He's right, and I hurry to jerk up the window and stick my head out. "Good luck!" I shout into the warm, spring air.

Sam stops and glances over. Even from here, I can see his surprised smile. He nods at Max, then says to me, "You too, Lou." He sounds relieved to say it. Two kids who can never seem to get it right, but I know we really want to.

I kick my genius brother out of my room and get dressed for my presentation.

I pace outside of the library meeting room where Port Coral's monthly town meeting takes place. I'm silently practicing my speech when Mayor Simon opens the door. "Luisa? We're ready for you."

The nerves hit in one huge rush. Weak knees, clammy skin, short of breath. My mind makes note of each sensation as I walk to the front of the room and set my laptop down on the empty table. "I just have to set up my stuff."

The room is full of local business owners. Mrs. Peña

from the bodega is sitting beside Liliana from the botanica. Clara from the bookshop. Ms. Francis, the florist, librarians. But there are others here, too. Malcolm, along with both my parents. Even Rocky has snuck into the back row.

I blow out a shaky breath and plug my laptop into the ancient projector.

The four viejitos are up front beside the mayor. They don't even own a business, but they're all sitting with their phones out, probably streaming this to their blog as we speak.

"Está bien," Mr. Restrepo says. "No hay apuro."

Mr. Gomez checks his watch. "Sí, no rush, Luisa, pero lunch is in an hour."

I am way too nervous to eat, but the prospect of a pile of yucca fries with my favorite cilantro garlic dipping sauce is the carrot at the end of this stressful morning. I set up the screen mirroring between my phone and laptop, and imagine the relief of getting this over with. *Full breath in, steady breath out.* Like Sam taught me. I glance up at the crowd and immediately find my mother.

She smiles. One more breath and I begin.

"So, as you can see, the app can offer self-guided tours with this interactive map." I click on it, and this is the part that everyone loves because it's their town and businesses up there. "This will help with guiding tourists from one point to another during the festival and can be coordinated with any signage that's put up for the event to direct traffic around the square and remind users of events down the boardwalk. Like the regatta in the harbor."

"Which we plan to win again," Jonas, from the marina, jokes from the back. The tattooed guy next to him smiles.

"Oh wow, the boat people won the boat race. What a shocking plot twist," grumbles No Gutter Gladys.

Mayor Simon sits forward. "And what about the town's website? Will that work with the app or is it separate?"

"From the festival page they'll be able to find the link to download the app, but the page will also be really mobile friendly, so if they don't want to download it onto their phones, they can still have access to the schedule and map."

"And what about our coupons to get people into the stores?" Mrs. Peña asks.

This is where I went a bit off script in my design. "When I first started incorporating your coupons, the app started to feel a little…" *Boring*, I want to say but don't. "Like a flyer or a spam email."

The energy in the room changes as people shift in their seats.

"There are no coupons?" Gladys demands. "How else are we supposed to get all those people off the square and into the bowling alley?"

Mr. Gomez sucks his teeth, the sound of disappointment. "Everyone loves coupons, Luisa."

"I promise there are coupons; I simply wanted to find a way to include them in a more interactive, user-friendly way that matches our super cute map." I point them to it in a bid to get them back on my side. "Instead of stuffing the coupons in an email or having them appear in obnoxious pop-ups in the app, I thought it would be cooler to make them part of the user experience so they can earn those discounts like rewards in a mobile game."

Saying the word *game* makes the energy in the room change again. Everyone studies the map reluctantly, reconsidering their enthusiasm. It's no longer a valuable asset to their festival or businesses. It's a *game*.

I quickly tap the icon for the bodega so they can see what I mean but realize they have to get out there and see it. "Okay, everyone grab your phones, you're going to help me test the app right now." I already had most of their email addresses for the closed test, so I open the developer console and send out the link. I talk them through downloading it then announce, "Come on, class, it's time for a field trip."

I march out of the room as everyone scrambles to follow me out of the library and into the bright sunshine. My hands automatically go to the top of my head for my sunglasses, and I realize not only was I wearing them this whole time, but they're my ridiculous heart-shaped ones. The leaders of this town trusted me to deliver this project, and instead I'm leading them outside to play a game.

The sizzling smell of the lunch hour at the bodega hits me, and I mentally chant *yucca fries* to myself. When we reach the bodega's window, I turn to witness the chaos I've left in my wake. Several people are ordering coffee.

"Okay, if you turned on your GPS—"

Mr. Saavedra interrupts, "I don't trust GPS."

I ignore that. "If you've turned on your GPS, when you open the map, you should see your icon outside the bodega. Is everyone with me so far?"

There are grumbles and assents, and more people are getting distracted by the scent of coffee. I open the Admin Tool on my phone and send out a notification. Everyone glances down as their phones buzz.

"Hey, a coupon!" Mr. Gomez happily announces. "It says free coffee!"

Mrs. Peña jumps in. "That's not valid! That's just an example."

"That was triggered by your GPS location," I explain, trying to pitch my voice above all the noise. "But it'll be more than that because when you get that free coffee in the special festival cups I ordered, you can scan a QR code that will make a riddle pop up on your phone that, if answered correctly, will lead you to the ice-cream shop, where you'll get a free cone of chocolate—"

"I like rocky road," Gladys argues.

"—which will come with a bookmark that takes you down to the bookstore and everyplace else along the boardwalk. The tour becomes a self-guided treasure hunt that gets people into every single shop in a way that doesn't simply feel like you're just handing over your email for ten percent off your next purchase. It's more interactive than that."

Some of the business owners glance around the square looking curious, while others I've already lost to the nearby lunch. The realization that I might have got it all wrong hits me. I tried to put my big girl pants on and do something in a professional manner, and instead I made a childish mess of it.

Think of it as a game. I am ridiculous.

"Can we try it out?" Mayor Simon asks. "Do the other businesses have their QR codes?"

I nod quickly. "Yes, they do."

Mayor Simon smiles. "Sounds great. We'll stop for lunch here and meet back in a half hour. That work for you?"

"Yes, that works," I agree like a total professional who happens to be wearing bright red heart-shaped sunglasses.

"See you then," he says. "Can't wait."

Mom and Malcolm are looking at me with bright eyes and geeked-out grins, and a very potent bubble of joy strangles me. My phone in my hand, still in the admin panel, buzzes with a new email.

I click over. It's from UCF. The last school. My stomach immediately turns.

I walk right up to Mom, who's now standing with Malcolm and Elena outside the botanica. Rocky coos at Pearl as Dad bounces the baby in his arms.

"UCF released their decision," I announce, and everyone stops to look at me.

It's a long, tense moment before Elena bursts out, *"And?"*

My hands are a puddle of sweat. "And I haven't checked it yet."

"Are you kidding me?" she nearly shouts.

"Check it when you're ready," Mom says gently. "There's no rush."

Elena laughs. "Oh, *now* you're patient? I swear, being the oldest daughter is a trip."

I turn to Rocky, who tells me, "You got this." Malcolm nods in agreement. Dad drops a kiss on my head. "No matter what happens, you're the best."

"Thanks, Dad," I say, then playfully (seriously) announce, "I am prepared to cry."

Everyone stills as I click on the link to the school portal.

Dear Luisa,

Here it is. Deep breath in. Steady one out.

Congratulations!

It's a new word.

My eyes skip all over the screen—jumping ahead, afraid

I'll find fine print or terms and conditions, something that says it's all a joke. The paragraphs blur, and my pulse pounds in my ears.

My voice thick, I say, "I got in."

"*What?*" Mom, Rocky, and Elena scream at once.

"I got in," I say again, louder. "UCF! I got in!"

"Oh my god!" Mom hugs me, then gasps. "Where is the camera?" she demands as Dad spins in a circle. Pearl shrieks in delight, copying everyone around her.

As my family loses its collective mind, my parents and siblings and Rocky scrambling with their phones and cameras—Mom trying to figure out how to set up a livestream to Colombia—I smile at Pearl, who looks amused by the rush of activity. Rocky shakes my shoulders, singing about how we're both going to be in Orlando, and I'm dizzy with relief.

I did it.

Luisa Freaking Patterson got into her last school, and she couldn't be happier.

Sam

I DRIVE A half hour away to Nova Creek, where an old, abandoned citrus-packing plant has been repurposed into a training facility for local fire departments. Battalion chiefs are out and about, watching us, and I need to impress them if I want a real chance at becoming a volunteer—or getting any sort of funding for the EMT program.

"You ready to suit up?" Little Tim says as he strolls up to me. Jordan, Adriana, and I are the only ones from our station participating today.

I lift my heavy gear bag in reply, not really trusting myself to speak.

We're surrounded by all the different simulated exercises we'll have to make our way through, including a live burn, victim rescue, vehicle extrication, and the dreaded maze. The day is already too warm, and smoke is heavy in the air from the burn.

Jordan stops at my side and asks, "You good?" He's already dressed in his bunker gear.

"I'm ready to do this," Adriana says before I can answer. She's chewing gum, smacking it loudly as she talks, turning to me. "Is your girlfriend here?"

"What?" I ask, distracted.

"Your girl. The one I saw you with at school. Curly hair, big—" She cups her hands out in front of her chest but quickly lowers them, taking in my dark look. She hitches her thumb toward the small audience of mostly spouses of cadets and the parents of explorers who have gathered to watch us. Mom's bringing Abuela and Cora, but I haven't seen them yet.

I shake my head, then ask, "Do you have any more gum?" Maybe she's onto something and it'll help soothe my nerves.

Around the wad in her mouth, she says, "Sorry, nah. I'm chewing it all."

"Sounds like it."

A group from another station cheers as one of their own heads inside the maze.

Adriana's nervous exhales continue to war with her chewing.

The competition is a way to get the explorers and cadets

some hands-on experience. The live burn is controlled, but I bet that fire doesn't know it's only a test.

Cheers erupt as the cadet makes it out. She rips off her mask and is embraced by her team.

"Hey," Adriana says, smacking Jordan's and my shoulders. "Soon that will be us. A couple of old pros."

I look sideways at the two freshmen but don't disagree. Because maybe she's right, and in ten years we'll all be old friends who work in the same station. Time is weird like that.

I think of Lou and wish she were here. The crackle of her laugh, a quick, sure smile that lights her whole face. I spent all day yesterday planning out what I want to say to her. The words she deserves from me. I owe her honesty and space. No matter how much I'll always need her, I want her to see me as someone who has her back no matter what.

The minutes pass too quickly as the other group finishes up. Every one of them has made it out of the building looking relieved but exhausted. Tim waves for us to head over.

"You got this, son!"

Jordan and I stop and turn toward the fence. An older Black man waves at him, pride shining in his eyes.

"Thanks, Dad!" Jordan calls back.

I try to imagine my own Dad out there, too, but it doesn't help. Instead I just feel sick.

"Sam!"

I turn and spot Mom in the crowd. Abuela and Cora are beside her, and I have no idea where they got them, but all three are wearing shirts with my name on it.

"You got this!" Mom calls.

Abuela sticks two fingers in her mouth and blows a sharp whistle.

I can't help but laugh as I wave at them. My stomach swims with nerves, but the ground steadies beneath my feet.

Once we reach Tim's side, he points at me. "You first, Alvarez."

I bite back a sigh, because when your last name starts with *A*, you get used to going first. I pull on the rest of my gear, and Tim gives me a once-over to make sure there's no exposed skin. As he goes to grab the blacked-out mask, I focus on what I might find inside the maze. Trap doors, entanglements, a lot of confined space. At every turn, I'll be monitored. Judged, and graded. I have to be careful to follow the hose.

"All right, Sam, you're up."

I pull the mask over my eyes, and everyone else disappears. My breaths sound louder. Mechanical. Wrong. I remember the oxygen alarm and begging Dad to keep his mask on when the delirium hit.

Because he was dying.

Don't.

From far away, Tim tells me to start. I drop to my

knees, grab the hose, and crawl forward into the tunnel. My shoulder knocks into one side of the wall, and I lose my hold on the hose. I'm not even out of this first part, and panic is already erasing everything I've learned over these past three months.

Full breath in, steady breath out.

I pull myself out of the tunnel only to get tangled in the ropes. With one hand on the hose, I keep the other out in front of me, searching for my way through. If only I could hear something other than the forced sound of my own breathing. The darkness, uncertainty, and harsh gasps between me and a machine are all that I'm aware of.

Was Dad scared at the end? Or relieved?

Stop thinking about Dad.

I slip the pack off my back to squeeze into a tighter space. I push it ahead of me before turning onto my back and pulling my way into the gap. I feel my muscles pull. Cramped and cornered. I'm desperate to rip this mask off.

I don't need to see. I need to breathe. I need this thing off my face, to know that my lungs are mine and that they work and that when I get out of here, Dad will be alive, whole, and waiting for me outside.

Stop thinking about him!

Calling a Mayday is an option, but I don't only need to finish, I *want* to. Because maybe Dad isn't outside, but if he could've been, he would've been cheering the loudest.

I stumble when my hand hits empty space. The drop is

ahead. I pull my pack back on before dropping down into the square, shoulders first, holding the edge as I ease the rest of my body down. The controlled fall brings back a sense of certainty.

I meet the next drop with surer movements, steadier breaths.

Full breath in, steady breath out.

Me, back down, hose in hand as I crawl through the next obstacle. Tight corner. The dreaded trap door that mimics a floor collapse. My mind quiets, and my body takes over like in drumline. Create the beat. Follow the hose. Whatever this is, I'm in sync with it.

And then, a whistle blows and I can hear all the voices. It's the end. I did it.

I tear off my mask and am met with bright sunshine, fresh air, and the cheer of my team. Jordan, Adriana, and Tim surround me. In the distance, I hear my family shouting my name. The relief builds and builds until it, too, surrounds me. I take in a greedy breath of it.

"You killed it!" Jordan says.

Tim smiles. "Great job, kid."

Beyond them I note the other instructors. Dan steps away from them and offers me a big smile. "You impressed old man Hanson over there," he tells me under his breath and jerks his chin toward the chief. "Two and a half minutes. Not bad at all."

"Wow, really?" I get out after a hungry breath. The day

is suddenly brighter, everything turned a little louder. The sound of my heartbeat is something I could follow anywhere.

"Yeah, wow." He laughs. "Maybe you're good at this."

I can't help it: A grin breaks out across my face. After everything, I stumbled onto something right. This isn't a second choice, or an accident. In spite of everything—or maybe because of it—I've figured out the next step.

I watch Jordan and Adriana as they go through the maze and cheer them on. And by the time we get to the live burn, we're all running on so much adrenaline but also careful instruction. Little Tim's steady voice is in my head as I face a very real fire, but at every single point I know what to do.

The confidence is exhilarating. I'm terrified and capable and so blissfully alive.

As we head to the vehicle extraction, my phone buzzes. I fish it out of my pocket to mute it but almost drop it when I see it's Lou.

I hit Answer, but the call doesn't go through. I curse backwoods Florida's reception.

"Come on, come on," I mutter, and hit Redial as I walk farther away, hoping for a signal. I don't want to miss the chance to fix things between us.

"Hello?" Her voice battles static. I hold my phone tighter to my face, like I can physically get close enough to hear her.

"Hey, it's me!" I say, moving farther away. "I missed your call."

"...what?"

"Your call! I missed your call!" I wince. *Obviously, Sam.*

"...because...they...so we're going!" She says, sounding even farther away, but my adrenaline picks up at the sound of excitement in her voice.

"Wait, where are we going?" I ask.

"...downtown...fest...can you...?"

The call clicks off. I try to send a text, but the big red X shows up each time. I curse under my breath and hurry back to the others, who are waiting on me to start the vehicle extrication.

"You good?" Jordan asks me.

I nod quickly. I need to stay focused. "Time to save some dummies."

"Fine," Jordan says. "But you do the CPR."

We break a record for how fast we cut the roof off, even though Adriana trips over the dummy. She immediately jumps to her feet, holds it up, and screams, *"We're okay!"*

The day ends with a handshake from the chief. Little Tim notices and slides me a thumbs-up. I head to the fence, where my family is bursting with joy. I hop over it and throw my arms around all three. "We're so proud of you," Mom tells me, and I know that she means Dad, too. Because her love is big enough and we've got one another. My family, shattered by grief, but still alive with joy.

When we finally get home, I run across the street. Halfway down the driveway, Max sticks his head out of his bedroom window.

"She's not here," he calls. "She's out celebrating."

"Celebrating what?"

"No spoilers," he says, sounding so much like Lou. "But she's at the Spring Fest kickoff."

The concert. Too many thoughts hit me at once. Lou. Happy. Celebrating.

And a realization that the list isn't done because there's something we didn't get right the first time. Something I crossed off prematurely.

I hurry home to take a shower and change.

"Where you headed now?" Mom asks me as I save the video and upload it. "I figured we could do dinner out. Celebrate our fire guy."

"God, never call me that," I respond with a laugh. "And I'd love to get dinner tomorrow, but I have to go to the concert tonight." I face the mirror to double-check my shirt and jeans.

Mom stands behind me, watching my reflection.

"What?" I ask, curious about the look in her eyes.

Smiling, she says, "Life, kid. You'll get it soon enough."

I drop a kiss on her head. "I've got to get downtown." But as I head downstairs, she calls after me, "Fair warning, traffic will be a mess by the square with the festival starting tomorrow."

I switch directions and head to the garage. I'm waylaid in the kitchen by Abuela with a plate of food. "No time," I say on my way out, to her horror.

In the garage, I push up the sliding doors, touch Dad's car for luck, and not a minute later, I speed down the driveway. My well-loved ten-speed keeps up with me as I race downtown. As I ride my bike through my neighborhood, I feel like I'm seven again. Swearing to Dad that I'll practice enough to earn my expensive drum set. I'm ten and daring him to a race before jumping on his back when he gets ahead and starts to win. I'm twelve, getting my heart broken by Lou for the first time, but he assures me I still have so much time to get it right.

The booths are closed down around the square, but the stage is busy tonight. Spring Fest once saved our town's harbor, and everyone will be showing it off for tourists tomorrow, but tonight is for us.

Behind the stage, I find Ana Maria Peña. I drop my bike and rush over to her.

She stops twirling her sticks when she spots me. "Oh, so, you decided you *aren't* too cool to hang out with the band kids one last time, huh?" Some of the other graduating seniors are preparing for this last show together, and I already feel nostalgic over the sound of them warming up their instruments. Hearing it bolsters my plan, and I'm grateful to see Tasha and her trumpet.

With my heart in my hands, I ask for a favor.

ROCKY, BENNY, AND I hang out in front of the stage, waiting to watch The Electric, the headliner for tonight's concert. We've already listened to the elementary school chorus sing a rendition of "Heaven Is a Place on Earth" and Gladys try out her stand-up routine (which might have been great for those who knew anything about bowling). A showcase of the different groups of graduating seniors from band is next.

"Is Sam playing with any of them?" Benny asks me.

"I don't think so," I say. "He had his competition today. And he was still there when I called him earlier."

"Did he say anything else?"

"I'm not totally sure," I admit in a small voice. "And I think he might've hung up on me."

Rocky and Benny both suck in a sharp breath in sympathy. She looks at Benny and says, "Not great." He concurs with a deep frown.

"What does that mean?" I cross my arms to stop myself from checking my phone again.

"We're invested now," Rocky says.

"In what?" I ask, confused.

"You and Sam!" Benny blurts out, and my mouth falls open in shock. "*Everyone* can see it but you two!"

Feeling trapped by my very exposed feelings, I scoff and cross my arms against my chest.

Benny chuckles. "It is exhausting being the insightful friend."

I uncross my arms and ask in a small voice, "Am I that obvious?"

"You both are," Rocky says wearily. "Always staring when the other isn't looking. The tension has been ridiculous. Just kiss again already." She sees something on my burning face and barks a laugh. To Benny she says, "You owe me ten bucks."

I press my hands to my face. "This is what I get for starting a group text," I complain.

Rocky jerks one thumb at Benny. "He's been rooting for you and Sam to get together since Halloween. He's going to be devastated if you guys don't work out."

"My ship will sail," Benny says absently. His phone rings, and he checks it, then looks toward the stage. "I'll be right back."

My phone rings a moment later, and a wave of relief washes over me when I see it's a text from Sam.

Walk over to that quiet bench

Confused, I look around. The crowd around the stage has grown, but I spot a wooden bench off to the side. Benny returns to us and hands me a pair of headphones.

"What is this?" I ask, confused.

"I'm just ensuring my ship makes it to harbor," he explains.

I shake the headphones, utterly perplexed, but before Benny can further clarify, I get another text from Sam.

Trust me?

I go to the bench in question, but there's nothing obvious on or around it, so I bend to look beneath it, but there are only wildflowers. Suspicious, I sit down and wait for something to happen. My heart is pounding with both expectation and stomach-twisting nerves. My phone dings again, but this time he's sent me a link. My hands shake as I slip on the headphones.

I click and the link sends me to our old YouTube channel. The most recent upload is from only an hour ago. I click it.

It's me, years ago. I've got braces and hair I haven't learned to properly condition yet, and I'm leading Sam through the woods to the mysterious tree behind our middle school.

"We should bury the time capsule here," I tell him.

"What are we going to put in it?" he asks from behind the camera.

I look at him like that's obvious. "Stuff that will remind us of each other and this moment in time. And then we'll dig it back up when we're old."

"What if we forget? Or we stop being friends?"

On-screen, I look at Sam and the video starts to flicker, and I worry something's wrong, until I see it's me again but in my costume on Halloween, standing in front of the tree. I'm still looking at Sam, but with a huge smile. On-screen, it's like I just time traveled.

"We made it," I tell him, looking like a mad scientist.

And then it's a flood of new clips of us as a soft instrumental hip-hop song that samples something old and romantic plays in the background. I watch as we lose playing dominos against the viejitos. Sam plays his drums at the party. Riding in his truck after we jumped in the pool. Sam showing off my scarf at school. Me sitting at the kitchen table surrounded by my family and then writing a letter to my future self. Lying back in the grass while the town plays my game. The last clip is us in middle school again, two kids racing off on our bikes together, bound for another adventure.

The video ends, and I'm at a loss for words. This feeling of hope isn't a baby bird, or too many butterflies. It's just me and my sensitive, sometimes too big to carry heart, but it's gotten me this far—and right now it's pointing me to Sam like the arrow on a compass.

I start to text him back in all caps. But the band onstage starts to play a song.

I yank the headphones out. Shocked and not totally sure what's happening is *actually* happening, I slowly get to my feet and move closer to the stage. The trumpet, that slow drumbeat. My dream movie moment.

I know this song. Just like I know Sam Alvarez.

Ana Maria slowly strolls to the front of the stage as she sings, slow and charismatic. A low flirtatious purr to her voice.

"You're just too good to be true..."

Ana Maria is not behind her drums because *Sam* is. And he's playing them with all the confidence and joy he always has around music. The crowd is going wild at the sight of them, all cheering for their hometown stars, and the seniors playing one last time together—but I'm frozen to the spot.

Because I know what's happening. They're playing "Can't Take My Eyes Off You."

~~be serenaded~~

Sam leans into the drums, and I can't look away as my heart explodes into pieces that must shimmer like stars.

There's wild applause as the rest of the band gets into

the act, and the song hits its stride, an emotional crescendo that crashes over us like a wave. The whole square cheers. Whistles and shouts pierce the air. The band kids look delighted. Ana Maria looks electric. Sam sweeps the crowd, and his bright smile turns huge when he finds me.

Sensitive Lou. Deliriously Happy Lou. I turn the dial in my heart all the way to eleven and let myself experience this grand gesture with my whole self as I fall in love with a drummer.

The song ends, but the moment is ripe with magic.

"Thank you to the seniors! Oye, viejitos, tell me y'all got that? Finally, something people actually want to see." Ana Maria laughs at their complaints, then waves them off. "All right, all right. Now get off my drums, Alvarez."

The audience sends up another burst of cheers, and Sam bows shortly, then returns Ana Maria's purple drumsticks. As he steps off the stage, Ana Maria faces the crowd again, and as if she were in a metal band greeting yet another city on her world tour, she screeches, *"Spring Fest!"*

I watch Sam cross the square on his way to me. His smile is soft, his steps sure. I move through the busy crowd to meet him halfway. We still have so much to tell each other. New obstacles and conversations. Miles and a million ways for all this to go wrong again.

I raise my hands to mime crossing this one off our imaginary list, then crumpling it before tossing the list over my shoulder. When he reaches me, he immediately goes to pick me up, and I wrap my arms and legs tightly around him.

Somewhere beyond us, Rocky and Benny let out a triumphant cheer.

I fold into Sam and he presses his face into my neck, inhaling deeply before sighing, and his sigh is filled with so much relief, I sink beneath the same wave of rightness.

His mouth gently travels up my face. "Hoy fue un gran día," he whispers against my cheek.

"Love that for you," I say, and sigh happily. "Tell me all about it."

We were friends first.

And we're not done yet.

LOU AND SAM'S TO-DO LIST
BEFORE WE GRADUATE:

~~GO TO BEACH DAY~~

~~help all the stray neighborhood cats~~

go to Disney World

~~join a club~~ (started one actually)

~~pull off the most epic prank of all time~~

~~win the town Halloween costume contest~~
(yay, Rocky the Ninja Mermaid!!)

~~apply to the same colleges~~

~~work on our Spanish~~

~~Lou will hold her breath longer than
Sam underwater~~   ~~*break into someone's pool~~

~~go to an actual party~~

~~get super good at kissing~~
~~*hang out on second base~~

~~kiss someone at midnight on New Year's Eve~~
(after getting super good at it)

~~be serenaded (à la 10 things I hate about you)~~

~~beat the viejitos at dominos~~ (not gonna happen)

~~bury a time capsule~~

~~write a letter to our future selves~~

~~drive Lou where she needs to go~~

~~skip school together~~

SAM'S ADDITIONS:

~~MASTER "TOM SAWYER" BY RUSH ON DRUMS~~
~~(AND SOME CUBAN JAZZ FOR DAD)~~

~~DRIVE THE BARRACUDA~~

~~ALWAYS HOLD MY BREATH LONGER THAN~~
~~LOU UNDERWATER~~ (LOST ON A TECHNICALITY!)

GET A DOG (I'M ALLERGIC TO CATS,
YOU KNOW THIS)

~~SAM WILL GO ON EMT SIDEQUEST~~

Sam

JUNE

I'M BACK IN that awful suit.

"Should've burned it," I murmur to myself with a smirk before stopping in front of my bedroom window. I tug the sleeves into place and slip the tie around my neck. As I loop it into a proper knot, I watch a car stop in Lou's driveway. Elena and her boyfriend get out, both dressed up. Baby Pearl is there, too, in a tiny dress covered with frills.

I go across the hall and, with a great flourish, loudly knock on my sister's bedroom door. "Cora! Time to wake up!

An answering growl puts a pep in my step as I slip my hands in my pockets and head downstairs. I stop beside the new shelf we made. A picture of Dad, sunflowers, a fresh cup of coffee, art by Cora, and a lit candle.

I don't get another chance at goodbye, but I can tell him good morning every day. I kiss my fingers before touching the corner of the picture.

In the kitchen, I find Abuela and Mom. They're drinking coffee together and laughing about something. Abuela is in her favorite blue dress, and Mom wears fitted slacks and a dress shirt with the sleeves rolled up, showing off the new tattoo on her forearm. It's a Tom Petty lyric. Abuela doesn't approve but still insistently reminds her to keep the skin moisturized.

"So handsome," Mom says as Abuela shoves a piece of buttered toast in my hand.

"¿Café?" she asks.

I check the time and shake my head. "We have to get there early."

"Go," Mom says, and steps close to kiss my cheek. "We'll see you there."

I step outside just as Lou's front door opens. She yells something over her shoulder before spotting me. She flashes her Cheshire cat grin at me and then dramatically gasps as she points from her graduation gown, to the one draped over my shoulder. "Look at us! I think we're headed to the same place!" she calls.

I toss and catch my keys. "Need a ride?"

"Okay, but no small talk," she says, crossing the street.

Once she's standing in front of me, she tips her smiling face up to mine, eyes shining. "Hey, you finally got a haircut."

I bend to kiss her and, against my lips, she whispers, "Graduation, can you believe?"

"Can *you* believe?" I click the garage door open without looking away from her. Lou's confused smile turns into hyper delight. "We're taking your Dad's car?"

"There's no aux cable, but I figure it'll do."

Lou screams and runs past me to climb in the car.

I drive with the radio on low and windows open to the warm, almost summer air. Lou hops up a little to curl her legs beneath her in the seat, her legs hidden by the big black gown.

We drive past the town square, decorated with signs congratulating the graduating class. The bodega is closed today since the whole Peña crowd will be in attendance to shout and cheer the moment Benny's name is called, even though our principal asked families not to get too loud. The Peñas laughed really hard when they heard that.

My family will be smaller, but I know everyone at the bodega will yell for me, too. Plus, some of the firefighters are planning to attend. According to Little Tim, they have good news to tell me after the ceremony.

We make it inside the town civic center, where we're all separated alphabetically for the last time. Rocky stands closer to me, laughing at our last names. "An Alvarez and a Chen walk into a bar...," she starts before we're sent down different rows. Then she shouts after me, "If you hurt her, I'll kill you!" It's a threat I know she'll follow up on since she's going to the same college as Lou.

"Hey, that's my girlfriend you're talking about!" I shoot back.

She rolls her eyes. "We *know*, you tell everyone."

I throw her a proud smile and two thumbs-up.

When it's my turn, my full name is called. I step onto the stage, with my father's name, and receive my diploma. There are cheers and applause, and my chest squeezes with tenderness even as my heart aches for the one person I don't hear.

It's a shadow, an eternally empty spot.

One I'll live with because it's an act of love to miss him. But I know he'd be proud. Wildly and loudly proud of all of us. I'll carry that like I will our shared name.

I tap the diploma against my heart.

Later, they finally get to Lou's row. "Luisa Patterson!"

I follow the sound of the riotous cheers and spot her family in the audience. They're all losing it, and I can't help but laugh as I cheer along with them.

Next is Benny, and every single Peña in the auditorium shouts at the top of their Cuban lungs. And there are a *lot* of them. The room and floor shake when he stops in the middle of the stage and tips his cap to them. There's no other way to send off Port Coral's beloved son.

We're offered more thoughtful words about the future,

but I'm bouncing in my seat, ready to get to mine. The moment we're released, I jump up to find Lou. Her grin is wild when she leaps right into my arms.

She kisses me for a moment that melts into more. I'm long gone when she pulls back and thoughtfully says, "The most surprising twist of all is that I'm nostalgic about all of this." She slips out of my arms with a mildly shocked expression. "I already miss high school." She shakes her head. "I can't believe it ended up being such a great year."

"There'll be more," I assure her with another quick kiss.

"I know," she says. "Plus, we've still got a whole perfect summer ahead of us."

"You and me?" I press my hopeful smile against her knuckles in a kiss before taking her hand and tapping it twice against my collarbone in a promise. "We have an always."

She laughs. "Who knew *you* were the romantic all along?"

"Party at my house!" Benny shouts, using his fake diploma as a megaphone, and I grab Lou's hand as we follow him outside into a bright, sunny Port Coral afternoon toward everything that happens next.

Dear Future Lou,

    I really hope we get into college and that it isn't as scary as you feared, but even if it was, I still bet you collected some decent memories that we can look back on through a cool retro filter.

    And I hope you're enjoying the moment. The one you're in right this second. Maybe it's finally that perfect summer you hoped for with Sam. Because the past is the future, but also the present? Or something like that.

    Tell Jupiter I said hi and that she's perfect.

yours from somewhere in time,

Past Lou

Dear Future Sam,

Hey.

Don't be afraid to get older
and find new favorite songs.
And if you make a mistake,
take that next breath and keep
going. Grief is going to take
new shapes, but so will you.

And do your best to remember
everything. Even this part.
Because even though you have
no idea what's going to happen
next, and there's so much that
sucks right now, Lou is sitting
across from you, writing her
letter, and she's smiling again.

Give her a kiss for me.

always,
Sam Alvarez

LOU AND SAM'S (UPDATED!) TO-DO LIST

LOU WILL DEVELOP HER VIDEO GAME

SAM WILL GET SCUBA CERTIFIED
(thus _super_ hold his breath longer than Lou underwater)

ONE CONVERSATION A WEEK ONLY IN SPANISH

get even better at kissing and other stuff

summer-break trip to visit Lou's abuelos in
Medellín

winter road trip to see snow

finally go to Disney World!!
(NO MATTER WHAT HE SAYS, JUNIOR DOES NOT
HAVE A HOOKUP)

Heath Ledger movie marathon

choose our matching Halloween costumes by
August

GET A DOG
(Moose! for Cora!)

ACKNOWLEDGMENTS

After I wrote and published *Don't Date Rosa Santos*, I dreamed of the chance to go back to Port Coral but promised myself the next story wouldn't be about grief. I would write something funny, light, and romantic. But as I gently untangled this story, grief kicked the door in and laughed at me. Loss is a strange thing. We all have experienced or will experience it, and yet most of the time, it feels like no one knows how to talk about it.

So, this is me talking about it. The year after. Mine and Sam's. Maybe yours. All the ways it shadows and breaks us. Paints, reshapes, and nudges us clumsily forward.

To my agent, Laura Crockett. Your emails are organized poetry and confidently help this messy knot of a person keep doing this author thing. I was lucky to have you in the quiet years, but I'm eternally grateful to have you in the chaotic ones. Thank you, Brent, for loving Rosa and helping her see the world, and Uwe for your stubborn faith in dreams I didn't even think possible. I'm so grateful that in the roller coaster of publishing, I have the unstoppable Team Triada on my side.

I have two very special Hannahs to thank. Thank you to Hannah Hill for saying yes again. You have a really great habit of changing my life just when I need it most. And thank you to my editor, Hannah Milton. You stepped into this world and not only helped me lead Sam and Lou through their (and my) wild year, but you let me make so many *Mass Effect* references. N7 all day. Thank you to Karina Granda for designing and Erick Davila for illustrating the carefree Latinx summertime cover of my *dreams*.

Returning to my make-believe town was such a thrill thanks in part to a community of readers who have my whole entire heart. Thank you to every single one of you who loved the Santos women and made it possible for me to come home again. To Adriana and Cande for bringing so much joy and yellow into my life. You have the networking power of the viejitos and utterly changed my debut year. To Rocky for letting me borrow your name and shouting about my book so much that at several signings—in different states—I heard, "Rocky told me about this book!"

To Carmen (@tomesandtextiles) for the breathtaking pictures and incredible support. And to the entire Latinx Squad who embraced my first book and have shown me so much love and creativity. A sincere thanks to Gabi for everything from the incredible Port Coral shirts to the book in Decatur and the piece of my beloved Milo that now sits on my altar. To Las Musas and my community of Latinx folks in publishing who've passed the ladder back and are always lighting candles and making space. Alexis Castellanos for your friendship and that killer website. Thank you to Maika and Maritza Moulite for helping me launch my debut and making every event that much better. Thank you, Zoraida Córdova and Shelly Romero, for believing in me and my words enough to give me the chance to get weird and go back to my middle school diary. Cristina Russell for creating a home base in Miami and every single bookseller and librarian who put *Rosa* in a reader's hands. I hope you love Sam and Lou, too. To Tehlor Kay Mejia for being a safe place to fall apart and my witchy Gemini twin. And a huge thank-you to one of *Our Way Back to Always*'s earliest readers, Kristina Forest. I sent you an awful first draft, and you not only read all of it, but reminded me of my potential and that I better fix that kissing scene. And on that note, a heartfelt thanks to my favorite romance authors. Having you on my shelf saves me time and time again.

To my circle. When all my stories are about family, they always end up about us. In Sam, I snuck in pieces of my brother. My fellow Miami kid who ran off into those Georgia woods with me and created worlds and silly games even as we lost too much of our Spanish. To my sister, best friend, and *my* Elena. You are fierce loyalty, unconditional love, and our sunflower who always points us back to the sun. Anyone who has you in their corner is the luckiest, and I am forever at the very front of yours. And to my mother. You started building all of this as a teenager, you bold, steadfast, bighearted Virgo. Missing him is an act of love, and *your* love has always been the gift. And to Dad. In another timeline, you'd be reading this one, too. Or maybe you are? Here's to alternate dimensions and all those galaxies you told us about. This was my chance to give you back the Barracuda, and old man, I took it. I miss you every single day.

Also, a heartfelt thank-you to Gainesville, UF, Valencia (community) College, and Tom Petty.

To my babies who aren't babies anymore. Being your mom is the greatest. You never let me forget how fast this whole life thing is really going and inspire me to stop and save all the memories I can. I just hope I'm leaving you enough bread crumbs. Is it obvious that I've been with a drummer since high school? Here's to Craig, still pointing out signs and tapping on everything. Hey, who's better than us? You make writing love stories easy.

And to you. Whether you're returning to Port Coral or finding it for the first time. You picked up this book now, but somewhere in time, an anxious, sensitive, teenage bookworm is deliriously screaming her head off, because you just made her whole entire bucket list.

Craig Hanson

Nina Moreno

is a YA writer whose prose is somewhere between Southern fiction and a telenovela. She graduated from the University of Florida and writes about Latinas chasing their dreams, falling in love, and navigating life in the hyphen. She lives by a swamp outside Orlando, where she enjoys listening to carefully curated playlists, hunting through thrift stores, drinking too much Cuban coffee, and walking into the sea every chance she gets. She is the author of *Don't Date Rosa Santos* and *Our Way Back to Always*.